"You didn't listen to me!"

The voice she heard was that of her informant, shrieking into the wind. "Where are you?" she called into the rainy night. "Please, don't leave."

"You're in danger, Teddy. Don't you understand? You could be killed."

The ghostly figure of a tall man separated from the shadows surrounding an ancient oak tree. He was moving away from her.

From another direction, she heard the loud roar of a motorcycle engine starting up. She whipped around, turning toward the sound. Disoriented, she peered through the trees that seemed to close in upon her. "Who is it? Who's there?"

"Run, Teddy." Her informant's voice carried faintly on the wind. "Run while you can."

Dear Reader,

When his U.S. postage stamp was issued on January 8, 1993, Elvis Presley officially became one of America's national heroes. His charisma, his talent and his legendary sex appeal, combined with the hint of danger evoked by black leather and motorcycles, seemed to set the perfect tone for a Harlequin Intrigue novel.

My mind started whirring with ideas, and I couldn't have been more pleased when Harlequin gave me the go-ahead for my first Elvis Intrigue, #237 *Heartbreak Hotel*, which was published in August, 1993. Because of all your positive response, I am doubly pleased to bring you my latest book, *Are You Lonesome Tonight?*

While researching for *Are You Lonesome Tonight?*, I found information about Elvis sightings impossible to avoid. There were movie references, newspaper articles and magazine stories. I had so much fun writing this book that I can only hope you will have just as much fun reading it!

For me, *Are You Lonesome Tonight?* was an opportunity to take a nostalgic trip down memory lane . . . and to create Vince Harding, a man I hope every woman will fall in love with!

Sincerely,

Cassie Miles

ARE YOU LONESOME TONIGHT?

Cassie Miles

Harlequin Books

TORONTO • NEW YORK • LONDON
AMSTERDAM • PARIS • SYDNEY • HAMBURG
STOCKHOLM • ATHENS • TOKYO • MILAN
MADRID • WARSAW • BUDAPEST • AUCKLAND

To Julianne Moore, an incredible editor who has the good taste to believe in Elvis

ISBN 0-373-22269-6

ARE YOU LONESOME TONIGHT?

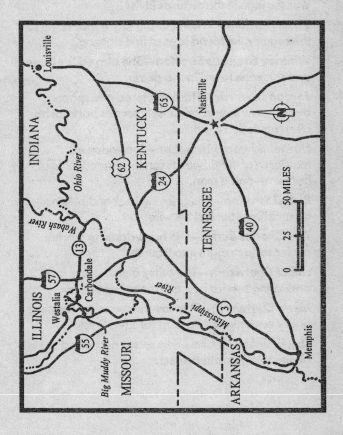

CAST OF CHARACTERS

Teddy Edwards—Her photographs didn't lie. But was the man in the pictures Elvis?

Vince Harding—When this big-city editor came to the country, he found love at first sighting.

Whitney Edwards Stratton—She played the tease, and someone loved her to death.

Jordan Edwards—The embittered newspaper owner knew everybody else's secrets but kept his own reputation spotless.

Harriet Edwards Timmons—The widowed matriarch of the Edwards family wanted a life of her own—and a man.

Russel Stratton—The grieving husband attained his ambitions but lost his wife.

Tom Charles Burke—The hard-drinking Harley owner rode straight into trouble.

Lilibet Chatworth—The sultry owner of an answering service had questionable motives.

Merle Chatworth—The has-been country-western singer once played backup for Elvis Presley.

Sheriff Jake Graham—His secret past affected his ability to serve and protect.

Prologue

The downward trend for the top-rated weekly tabloid named *Files* had continued into a sixth week, and Vince Harding, the managing editor, did not enjoy presiding at the helm of this slowly sinking *Titanic*. He refused to stand by and watch while circulation fell and ad revenues slacked off.

Something had to be done. Vince's rescue plan required an increase in the editorial budget, and that meant negotiating with British expatriate Max Owens, the owner of *Files* and the stingiest man England had produced since Scrooge. Max was going to be a hard sell, but Vince and his assistant, Connie, had packed up their arguments and gone to Max's condominium on Chicago's exclusive Gold Coast.

Vince stood at the floor-to-ceiling windows and looked out at Lake Michigan, where sailboats fluttered and the waves reflected the shimmer of glass skyscrapers. He turned his gray-eyed gaze onto his employer and launched his offensive. "I want this woman, Max. And I want her now."

Max Owens poured Earl Grey tea into translucent china cups. "Tell me again, which woman?"

"She's a photographer. Her name is Mary Theodora Edwards. Teddy Edwards."

"She's absolute magic," said Connie. Vince's assistant was a wiry, grandmotherly woman who chewed gum with jaw-breaking vigor. "She did a UFO abduction story that would break your heart. It was awful to see what happened to those poor, tragic people."

Vince shot her an annoyed glance. Though Connie was an ace professional who never missed a deadline, she and Vince had a serious difference of opinion. While Connie believed every word of the stories they printed, Vince trusted nothing and no one. He'd been in the news business for most of his thirty-two years, including five years as a crime reporter on a daily. Vince knew how easily facts could be manipulated.

"Another photographer," Owens mused. "I really don't think it's necessary, Vince. Photographers are so expensive."

From his briefcase, Vince produced the current copy of *On the Spot,* a competing tabloid. Its four-color front page featured two country and western singing stars entwined in a sensual embrace, a rabid wolf straining at a heavy chain, and the world champion yo-yo player. Vince pointed to each picture. "Sex. Violence. Human interest. These sell tabloids."

"Quite so," Owens agreed. Though this British gent appeared to be cultured to the core, he understood sensational journalism and had gotten his start as a feisty Fleet Street reporter in London.

Vince continued, "One woman was responsible for taking all three of these front-page photos. Teddy Edwards."

"And does she write the stories, too?"

Connie snapped her gum. "Not with complete sentences."

"She's not a journalist," Vince elaborated. "When Teddy goes out on a story, she takes the pictures and makes detailed notes in longhand. At *Spot,* they have a regular reporter assigned to writing up her features."

"Is she on staff at *Spot?*"

"She's free-lance." Vince riveted on Owens. "I want Teddy Edwards to work exclusively for us."

"Is there a problem with our usual free-lance agreement?"

The problem, Vince thought, was Teddy. He'd spoken with her several times on the telephone. He'd cajoled and complimented and offered twenty percent more per photo than she was currently receiving at *Spot.* But Teddy was a true free-lancer who refused to be tied down. She was stubborn, illogical and damned independent. She lived alone near the small town in southern Illinois where she'd grown up, and said she didn't need the security of full-time employment.

In order to change her mind, Vince had to make her an offer she couldn't refuse. "I was thinking of a correspondent position," he said. "With full salary and benefits."

Owens arched an eyebrow. "Rather a costly proposition."

"And it's going to take more than that," Connie added. "I have a feeling about Teddy. She's not going to be swayed by money. This is a woman who operates from her heart. I mean, look at her photos. She likes these people. She's sympathetic to their stories and—"

Vince cut her off. "I believe money is a good place to start."

Max Owens shook his head. "We should be trimming expenses rather than taking on more." He sighed and returned to his most familiar refrain. "If only you Americans had a monarchy. Di and Charles are always good for a bit of juicy news."

Vince had expected this response. That was why he'd saved the best for the last. He opened an eight-by-ten brown envelope and took out four black-and-white photos. Each was stamped on the back with Teddy's name and address, but Vince knew she hadn't sent them. The pictures had come with a typed note that said not to contact Teddy and that the person who sent them would be in touch.

Though Vince wasn't comfortable dealing with an anonymous informant who had, possibly, stolen from Teddy, these photos could not be ignored. He fanned them out on the table in front of Owens. "Here's her current project."

"My God." Owens handled the photographs gingerly. "When were these taken?"

"I received them five days ago."

"Hire her," Owens said.

Vince allowed himself a satisfied smile. "I thought you'd agree with me. I'll fly down to southern Illinois this evening and meet with Miss Edwards."

"Yes, yes," Owens said, "do whatever is necessary. Money is no object." Owens turned the black-and-white glossies in his hand. From a midrange distance, they showed a man, artfully shadowed. He had long black sideburns and heavy-lidded eyes. In one picture, the lower half of his face was obscured behind his hand. His fingers were loaded with showy rings. "Incredible," Owens said. "He's a dead ringer for Elvis Presley."

Vince couldn't resist a dig. "You see, Max, we Americans do have a king."

Chapter One

The shrill of a telephone sliced through the rural quiet of a May night that was so peaceful not even the dogs dared to bark. Teddy Edwards caught the receiver before the phone rang twice. She was expecting a call from Vince Harding, a managing editor from Chicago, who was supposed to arrive sometime this evening.

"H'lo?" Though it was much too early to be sound asleep, she wakened clumsily. Her legs tangled in her lightweight quilt. She kicked free and sat up. "Hello," she said more firmly. "Who is this?"

"Miz Edwards?"

"Yes, this is Miss Edwards. And who is this?"

"Don't you know me by now?"

She recognized the eerie, high-pitched squeak of a disguised voice. It was her Elvis informant. Thus far, the informant had not chosen to identify himself...or herself. Teddy couldn't even be sure if she was talking to a man or a woman.

"I've got something for you," the voice teased. "Wanna guess?"

"No, I don't." Teddy squinted at the red digital numbers on her bedside clock. It was only nine twenty-one, but she'd been up and running since before dawn, and she was exhausted. "Just tell me why you called."

"Now, don't be rude, Miz Edwards. Don't be cruel." The twang in the voice was no clue to the informant's identity. Almost everybody in these parts had an accent. The nearest town, Westalia, was near the bottom tip of Illinois—geographically farther south than Louisville, Kentucky. The voice continued, "I'm setting you up with a photograph that is to die for."

To die for? The words, spoken in a squawk that was as irritating as a scratch on an LP record, sounded like a threat. Teddy felt a prickling of the hairs at the back of her neck.

Taking a breath, she rose from her bedside and looked out the open dormer window of her second-story bedroom. The light from a nearly full moon glistened brightly. A strong breeze tossed the high tree branches, causing the pattern of moonlight and shadow to shift. But there was no one out there. No logical reason to be afraid. This was probably a harmless phone call from someone who didn't know her, didn't know where she lived...unless he'd seen her advertisements. "You didn't print my other two stories," the voice accused.

"They turned out to be unverifiable. The man took off before I could talk to him."

"But you and I both know who it was. Think on it."

Was it possible? Had she seen Elvis Presley? His jet black hair contrasted to the character lines in his face, appropriate for a man in his fifties. The second time she'd tracked down a clue from this informant, the Elvis-like man had been standing in the shadows outside a café in Jonesboro. The instant Teddy had spotted him, she'd snapped a series of photos with her long-range zoom lens. When he saw the movement of her camera, he'd disappeared—literally vanished—as she chased him down an alley.

Quietly, Teddy asked, "Was that you? Were you the man I saw in Jonesboro?"

"Course not. It was him. Elvis. Oh my, I think about Elvis a lot. Sometimes I hear him singing. His voice is rich as ever. What's your favorite song?"

"'Are you Lonesome Tonight?'"

"Are you lonesome? You live alone, don't you?"

Teddy winced. Yes, she lived alone. Yes, her house was located at the end of a road—a dark rural road with no neighbors nearby. But no, she wasn't pathetic and lonesome. "Let's get back to business," she said firmly. "I could arrange for somebody to interview you, and—"

"Nobody must know me."

"Why not? Most people love to see their names in print. And if you want to be anonymous, you can use an alias."

"We ain't talking about me. It's him. The King."

There was outrage in the voice. Teddy sensed that there was much more this person wanted to say, and she spoke encouragingly. "Come on, you can tell me about yourself. Where do you live? How did you find this man who looks like Elvis? Maybe we could meet somewhere and—"

"No. Only at night. The dark suits me. I got secrets to keep. Does that scare you, Teddy?"

"Not really." Not until this moment, anyway. The voice had used her nickname. Teddy's listings were under her full name, Mary Theodora Edwards. Apparently this caller knew that she didn't go by Mary and that Theodora was not shortened to Thea or Dora. What else did this person know? "Should I be frightened?"

"Here's all I have to tell. You won't see the King tonight, but if you hurry, you can find a clue. Go to PJ's Bar, just off Highway 13. Bye now."

The phone went dead. Teddy didn't have to look at her bedside clock to know exactly three minutes had elapsed from the time she answered to the final "bye." That was the same pattern as the other two calls. Probably this informant labored under the antiquated concept that a phone call couldn't be traced unless the line was kept open for more than three minutes, which was the standard impression given by old cop shows on television.

If Teddy had wanted to know the originating telephone number, she could arrange with the phone company to set up a tracer that worked with a click-buzz as soon as she picked up the receiver. In fact, the answering service she used during the daytime hours offered that capability. But the technology seemed unnecessary for the calls that rang through to her home...unless there really was a reason to be scared.

Teddy swung her legs from the bed. Though the night air felt pleasantly cool, her sheets were clammy with nervous sweat, a symptom of tension unrelated to the veiled threats from her Elvis informant. She had plenty of other worries, including Vince Harding, who apparently wasn't going to make it tonight. And tomorrow was the big party celebrating her sister's first wedding anniversary. Teddy was doomed to spend the entire afternoon in the company of the Edwards clan, who considered her to be the blacker-than-black sheep of the family.

Indeed, there were enough real-life problems to fret over without imagining that her Elvis informant had some kind of weird motive for dragging her out into the night. "Of course, it's a weird motive," she reminded herself as she yanked on a pair of jeans and a Southern Illinois University sweatshirt. In the past couple of years as a free-lance photographer, she'd taken pictures of people who'd seen aliens and angels and old Uncle Lester who'd been dead for thirty years. There was a cat near Paducah that had given birth to thirty-two kittens. And a watermelon in Cairo that was nearly as big as a Volkswagen. A redheaded man near Branson, Missouri, who only spoke backward. And a woman down in Jackson, Kentucky, who lost fifty-seven pounds in ten weeks on a diet of ice cream. Virtually every person who contacted her had a weird motive, which was why she found them so fascinating.

Rather than bothering to tame her mass of curly blond hair, she pushed it back behind her ears and stuck on a Chicago Cubs baseball cap, then headed down the oak staircase to the ground floor of her house. After checking her camera bag, Teddy realized that she was out of T-Max 3200, the fast black-and-white film she preferred for night photography. But there should be some in her van.

She banged out the front door... the unlocked front door. Once again she'd forgotten to take this simple precaution. Out here in the country she'd begun to feel so safe that she'd reverted to the habits of her childhood when nobody ever locked their doors and most times the neighbors marched right in without even knocking.

"Ought to be more careful." From under the mat, she fished out an extra key and locked up, then stuck the key into her hip pocket and ran across the yard. Her fingers hesitated on the handle of her Ford cargo van, which was also unlocked. It would be easy for someone—like her Elvis informant—to hide in the back of the van and overpower her the moment she stepped inside.

She glanced back at the house. Only her upstairs bed-room light, the lamp she'd left on, was shining dimly. There were no other lights, no other people within shouting range. Behind her, Teddy heard the distant gurgle of the brook that ultimately fed into the Big Muddy River. Crickets made their seesaw *chirrup.* A slight breeze whispered through the thick forest by the brook and stirred the mists that rose from humid spring soil. The earth smelled ripe, with new life bursting through layers of rotting mulch.

Alone and vulnerable, she'd be crazy not to have some glimmer of apprehension. Danger wasn't limited to the cities. Teddy had seen enough of the world to know that. The worst terror could come when and where you least expected it.

When she flung open the door of the van, the interior light came on. She climbed inside and looked around. Nobody there. Her breath came more easily, and she re-alized that her heart had been beating so fast and hard that it fairly echoed within the metal shell of the van.

She cranked down the driver's side window to allow some air to circulate, then closed the door, keeping the overhead light turned on. Somewhere in the back of her van was a Nikon, already loaded with T-Max 3200 film. Teddy picked delicately through the clutter of expensive equipment.

Usually she traveled light, but tomorrow at her sister's party, Teddy was the official photographer. She'd packed everything she would need for informal candids and for-mal group portraits—strobes, extension cords, a tripod, another camera bag with film and lenses. Using the van's overhead light, she dug behind the two silvered reflecto-sols and found the Nikon with the good fast film for night pictures without a flash.

Now she was ready in case Elvis decided to pop out of PJ's Bar, do a quick swivel of his famous hips and vanish into the night faster than she could say "Love Me Tender." Teddy climbed into the front seat and pulled out her car keys.

"Teddy?"

The baritone voice floated on night mists, summoning her, calling to her. Through the windshield she saw the faint illumination of another car's headlights. A tall man strode from her house, heading toward the van. Frantically, Teddy plugged the key into the ignition.

"Teddy, wait!"

She flicked on the van's headlights. The gravel driveway in front of her was blocked by a big yellow sedan that must have pulled up while she was looking for her camera.

And now the man was right beside her. His hand clamped on the window's edge. "Teddy, hold up. It's me. Vince Harding." Through the night mists, he materialized into a solid figure. She had never met the managing editor of *Files,* but she recognized him. A sudden overpowering awareness told her this was the man she'd been waiting for. "Sorry, Teddy. I didn't mean to startle you."

"When did you get here?"

"A couple of minutes ago. That's my cab." He pointed toward the yellow sedan, and Teddy noticed the lettering on the side that identified Dan's Taxi Service. "I saw the lights in your van right away, but I went to the front door first."

She unpeeled her clenched fingers from the steering wheel, sank back against the seat and rested her palm on her chest. The breath caught in her throat, and she forced herself to exhale. "You scared me half to death, Vince."

He smiled with easygoing charm, absolute confidence. In the reflected light, she studied him. His features, from the high cheekbones to the straight Grecian nose to the dimple in his chin, were evenly spaced. He would photograph well enough to be a fashion model. But his gray eyes shone with challenging intensity, and his jaw had a sharp, pugnacious thrust, as if he would welcome a fight.

She revised her opinion. Vince Harding could never be a model. The man didn't look as if he could stand still long enough to be photographed.

"Where are you going?" he asked.

That was none of his business. "Out," she said.

He frowned thoughtfully and took a guess. "On an Elvis sighting?"

Teddy didn't answer. She'd never been good at making things up, which was why she stuck to taking the pictures and not writing the stories to go with them. "It's too late for a meeting tonight, Vince. I'll see you tomor—"

"I'll come with you right now. We can talk on the way."

"No." All she needed was a hotshot editor from *Files,* trooping along on her lead, spooking her informant. But he'd already circled the front of the van and crossed to the cab. "Vince!" she shouted. "You can't come." He purposely ignored her. "Hey!" She leaned out the window of her van. "I said you can't come with me. It's not convenient."

"Too bad," Vince muttered under his breath. Her protest convinced him that Teddy Edwards was on her way to another Elvis sighting. Perfect, he thought, his timing was perfect. Riding shotgun in her van, he could forge a bond that would be more effective than hours of negotiating. He could gain her trust, show her that he wasn't a desk-jockey editor who sat in Chicago making decisions about what happened in the field.

"Hey! Vince!"

He turned toward her. "I won't get in the way, Teddy."

"You can't come." Frantically, she searched her mind for an excuse. "I'm going on a date." Teddy glared through the windshield. Her headlights shone on his thick, dark brown hair, swept back from a high forehead. He was tall, well over six feet. Beneath his beige windbreaker, his shoulders were broad, but he was rangy. Long legs in worn Levi's tapered from slim hips and a tight butt. Though she didn't want to think of him as a man, she admired the way he filled out his jeans.

In a quick moment, he paid off Dan the taxi driver, grabbed his carry-on bag from the back seat and returned to the passenger side of her van. He pulled open the door and cast a meaningful glance at the cameras she'd placed on the passenger seat. "Do you always take pictures when you go on a date?"

"I take pictures of everything." Inwardly she groaned. Now what? She couldn't leave him here. He probably wouldn't hesitate to break into her house, and she didn't want him going through her files. "All right, Vince. You might as well get in."

"Thanks for the invitation. Where are we going?"

"We? We aren't going anywhere. You are going to the nearest motel."

After he'd moved the cameras and settled into the seat beside her, Teddy stomped on the clutch and threw the van into first gear. "Fasten your seat belt, Vince."

Though he did as she asked, his every movement exuded an arrogance that told her it was his choice to obey. "I'm a journalist, Teddy, as well as an editor. I'd be happy to come along with you and write up the story. You can concentrate on the photos.''

''No thanks. I work alone.''

He knew that hadn't always been the case. At one time, Teddy had been half of a photographer-journalist team, but Vince decided not to mention her past. She was already ticked off, slamming furiously through second and third gear. Her eyes tightened at the corners. He could tell by the flexing of her jawbone just beneath her pink earlobes that she was gritting her teeth.

Her outrage would have been a lot more effective, he thought, if she hadn't been such a cute package. She reminded him of a grown-up tomboy with the sleeves of her baggy sweatshirt pushed up to her elbows and her baseball cap tugged down on her forehead. The silky tangle of her wild blond hair sprawled across her back as she hunched over the steering wheel. In the dim light from the dashboard, he could just see a sprinkle of freckles across the bridge of her snub nose. Her lower lip protruded slightly. Stubborn, he thought. And determined. And mad as hell.

He probably should have called from the airport to let her know he was coming. But after he'd encountered more than the usual delays in taking off from Midway and finally landed his Cessna 210 at the small-plane airport in Carbondale, Dan's Taxi Service had been waiting at the door. When Dan himself mentioned that the street where Teddy lived was not all that far from a motel, it seemed fated that Vince should come here tonight.

Fate? He scoffed silently. That was Connie's way of thinking. Not his. Vince relied on direct observation. Facts. And the fact was that he was here with Mary Theodora Edwards. He should be using this encounter to gain her trust and get her to listen favorably to his proposal.

As Teddy drove, her headlights cut a barely visible swath through the mist, which had thickened to ground fog. Though she wasn't speeding, she moved at a decent clip along the graded gravel road. Vince peered out into the fog. "Do you have any neighbors?"

"There are about ten other houses along this three-mile stretch. And a cluster of mobile homes." She glanced over at him. "Tell me something, Vince. Why did you assume I was going on an Elvis sighting?"

"Are you?"

His voice sounded too innocent, she thought. Teddy hadn't told anyone about the man she'd seen in Jonesboro. Though she'd made several copies of the photos she'd taken, she hadn't offered any of them for sale. "I cover a variety of stories. Why'd you think of Elvis?"

"We've had reports of sightings in this area."

"Is that why you're so hot to have me work for *Files?* Because you think I have an inside track to the King?"

"Why would I think that, Teddy?"

He was smooth, but she refused to go on the defensive. "I don't know, Vince. Why would you?"

"I want you because you're good. You're hardworking. You're talented." He backed off, sensing that he might be laying on the compliments too thickly. "I'll be honest with you, Teddy. *Files* needs a jolt, something new, exciting and different. I think your photos will provide fresh enthusiasm."

"And I think you're much too slick."

Vince spread his hands to show he had nothing to hide. "I'm direct. I want you."

That was direct, all right. She shook her head. "I'm taking you to the Sleep Inn before you sweet-talk me into something that I'll regret." Teddy figured she could drop him off and still follow up on the clue promised by her Elvis informant. The Sleep Inn was less than a mile away from PJ's Bar. She turned west at the intersection and proceeded on a paved road that eventually bled into Highway 13. Both the motel and the bar were between Carbondale and Westalia, maybe eight miles from the outskirts of each town.

She drove into the motel parking lot, glad to see that the Vacancy sign was lit. "Here you are."

He opened the door and grabbed his bag, but before he got out, he gazed into her eyes. "Work for me, Teddy. You won't regret it. I promise."

"Get out of the van, Vince."

"I'll see you tomorrow morning. At eight?"

"Nine," she said. "I'll pick you up."

He nodded and disembarked from the van. Impatiently, she nodded back. "Teddy, I'm sorry if I startled you earlier. I didn't mean to frighten you."

"It takes a lot more than you to scare me."

He closed the door, and she took off. Frightened? Not really. Okay, maybe she was tense. Maybe a little stressed, but she wasn't about to fly into fits of panic because of a weird phone call and an arrogant editor from Chicago. Teddy knew the difference between petty threats and life-threatening peril. There had been a time in her life when she'd faced death head-on, seen real blood, heard real gunfire.

Real danger simply didn't happen in Westalia, Illinois. That sense of safety was one of the reasons she'd come back here to live. This was home.

As she drove along Highway 13, Teddy recalled PJ's from her high school days as the place everybody wanted to go to as soon as they had an ID, real or faked. It was a forbidden hangout that looked wild and fun until you were old enough to know that PJ's was just another small-town tavern.

Outside the bar, the parking lot was nearly full, not surprising for a Friday night. A red neon arrow pointed to the front entrance. Each of the windows held a lighted sign advertising a different brand of beer. PJ's seemed older and seedier now. But then, so were her memories. High school had been nine long years ago.

Gliding into an empty slot, she cut her lights. According to her informant, there was a clue here. Leaving her van with two cameras hanging around her neck, she paused. The tavern in the fog made an interesting mood study, and she couldn't resist framing a picture of the tacky neon lights and beer signs hanging over a row of automobiles that ranged from shiny new to decrepit.

Quickly she composed a study of the shadows and fog contrasting with the glaring neon that beckoned the lonely to come inside, have a drink and be safe from the solitude of night. She adjusted the aperture on the Nikon for a soft focus foreground and clarity on the neon signs that were thirty feet away. She snapped a couple of angles quickly. That was the secret to Teddy's success as a photographer. She always acted on instinct, took her photos fast and took more than one. Rising, she readjusted the f-stop, throwing the entire scene into sharp focus.

From behind her, she heard a roar. Something was coming up fast. The air churned around her. She dodged just in time to avoid being run over by a Harley Davidson motorcycle. He didn't even bother to turn the face mask of his black helmet in her direction as he wheeled up to the stop sign at the exit from the gravel parking lot.

The fog swirled and parted and she clearly saw his license plate: TCB-1.

In quick automatic reflex, she snapped three pictures. This license plate had to be the clue her informant was talking about. TCB were significant letters to an Elvis fan. In the fog, the Harley looked like a mysterious ghost bike. It spun on the gravel and fishtailed out of the parking lot, heading west. Teddy raced to her van, strapped on her seat belt and followed.

She loved this part of her work. Other people might notice the plates and wonder. They might wish they knew the answer. Teddy's job gave her reason to dig, to explore, to turn over silent stones in a field of questions and see what crawled out from underneath.

The single taillight of the Harley glowed through the mist like an unblinking red eye. The rider was moving with too much speed for this weather and for the roads, but Teddy floored the accelerator until she was within fifty feet of him. She tapped on the horn, rolled down her window and waved, yelling for him to stop.

But the Harley went faster. He shot past a stop sign without even slowing down. Teddy gritted her teeth and tried to do the same. But she just couldn't ignore safety. She tapped the brake and slowed, peering quickly in either direction before proceeding through the intersection.

The Harley was far ahead of her now. Was this guy drunk? Was he crazy? Did he have something to hide?

Ahead of her, the taillight bobbed wildly as the bike surged over a double set of railroad tracks. Bracing herself, Teddy maintained her speed. Her van bucked violently on the tracks. If she hadn't been wearing her seat belt, her head would have banged against the rooftop.

Her foot came off the accelerator and she slowed. That slight hesitation lost her the race.

When the big Harley swung around a curve, the red taillight vanished. Though Teddy gripped the wheel and continued to follow his route, she knew the chase was over. She passed one turnoff and took a left at another. Had he gone right?

She pulled off onto a shoulder, turned off the ignition and hopped outside to listen for the echo of the motorcycle engine. She heard only crickets. Night folded around her like a damp shroud.

He was gone.

TCB meant Taking Care of Business, and that was what Teddy had failed to do. If only she hadn't wasted time with Vince Harding... If she'd arrived at PJ's five minutes sooner... If she hadn't crashed over the tracks...

Taking Care of Business had been Elvis Presley's motto, his creed, from 1970 onward. There was a TCB on the tail of his Convair jet, the *Lisa Marie*. And there was a TCB with a lightning bolt on his gravestone.

But tonight's adventure couldn't really count as a legitimate Elvis sighting. Nor would she have the chance to interview the Harley rider who thought TCB was a valid license plate. She wondered if he was the same man she'd photographed in Jonesboro. That reincarnation of Elvis haunted her. If given the chance, she would do almost anything to track him down.

Chapter Two

The next morning, Teddy's mood had lightened. She wasn't the sort of person who chose to remain unhappy. Only once in her twenty-seven years had she succumbed to a depression—one so deep that she didn't leave her cot for three days, didn't eat, didn't sleep. Her heart had been so heavy and her eyes had seen such horrors that there seemed to be no reason to carry on.

But that pain was well behind her, and she preferred not to dwell on sorrow. Last night, she'd missed the story behind the TCB-1 license plate, but there would be other stories and other leads. Besides, this morning she needed to concentrate on her nine o'clock appointment with Vince Harding.

By eight-fifteen, she was showered and dressed in an outfit that would take her all the way through the day. The beige rayon pantsuit with jungle-patterned blouse was businesslike enough for her meeting with Vince, and the addition of a gold belt, necklace and earrings made her clothing formal enough for her sister's anniversary party. Teddy sat at her kitchen table with a coffee mug in her hand and a firm determination in her mind. Above all, she wouldn't let Vince Harding talk her into anything she didn't want to do.

He might be smart and slick, but Teddy hated the idea of being tied down to just one market for her free-lance work. Especially now, when she was close to breaking an Elvis story, which could provide her with the biggest paycheck of her life. But she'd have to exercise vigilance in her dealings with Vince Harding. Even last night, when she'd been so annoyed, she'd felt his charm. She'd seen a strength in his dark gray eyes that made her want to melt.

The kitchen phone rang and she answered, "Hello, this is Edwards."

"Hey, Teddy. This is Lilibet at your answering service. You want to take a phone call?"

The service automatically intercepted all calls from eight to five every day, including weekends, unless Teddy advised otherwise. Though it might have been easier to buy a machine, Teddy preferred having her calls screened by a human voice. Even if that human was as flighty as Lilibet Chatworth.

"I'm in kind of a hurry," Teddy said. "Who's calling?"

"Let me give you a hint. She kicks puppy dogs, scares small children, and in a few hours she'll be flouncing around your sister's anniversary party in a tacky pink chiffon number."

Teddy grinned. "My aunt Harriet."

"Right on the first guess. By the way, that party has got to be the most talked-about event to hit Westalia since Willie Nelson's trailer broke down on the way to Branson and he did a free show in the high school gymnasium."

"I assume Harriet's on hold, and that's why you're talking so long."

"You're right again." Lilibet exhaled a long sigh that was as sultry as the summer in Georgia, where she was born. "Do you think I can wear red? I mean, I would never wear my strapless scarlet gown to a wedding, but this is just Whitney and Russel's first anniversary and it's fixing to be real hot this afternoon."

"Red sounds fine." The voluptuous Lilibet Chatworth in a strapless red dress with her long, shining black hair flowing around her shoulders would be spectacular enough to leave most of the males in Westalia howling at the moon. "I think we've left Harriet on hold long enough."

"One more thing. I heard Tom Burke is in town for this big affair. Have you seen him?"

"Not yet."

"I do wonder if he's as cute as he used to be. Remember when he was tight end on the football team?"

"Lilibet, I really ought to talk to—"

"Okay, it's your funeral. Here she is."

After a click and a hum and another click, Teddy said, "Hello Harriet."

"About time," her aunt snapped. "I tried to reach you last night, but you didn't answer. Where on earth were you?"

"I was out on assignment last night."

"Really? On something worthwhile, I hope."

"Very worthwhile." At times, Teddy took great pleasure in baiting her aunt. "An Elvis sighting."

"Oh, Teddy, I wish you'd get over this stupid tabloid phase. You know you're just doing it to embarrass me and the rest of the family. If you'd apologize, your father would take you back in a minute, and you could work for him, on a real newspaper."

"I'm happy with my work."

"Even if that were so, and I do not believe it for one single solitary minute, there's more to life than a career. You need a home, a family. A husband. My goodness, Teddy, if only you were more like your sister..."

Harriet was launched on her favorite topic, and Teddy held the phone away from her ear. She didn't want to hear about how sweet little Whitney was so lovely and so happy and always did as she was told. In Teddy's eyes, her sister's wholehearted obedience masked a pain and bitterness that might actually account for those ferocious headaches that sometimes kept Whitney in bed for days on end. But Teddy was the only person who felt that way, the only one who saw Whitney's veiled hostility, the only one who expected that someday her sister might erupt with awesome force.

The volcanic explosion almost happened a year ago when Whitney had run off to Las Vegas and eloped with Russel Stratton. Teddy alone had cheered, hoping that her sister had finally taken the first step toward freedom. But it hadn't turned out that way. The newlyweds returned to Westalia and asked the blessing of Teddy's father, Jordan Edwards, who immediately gave Russel a marketing job at the newspaper. Now, from what Teddy heard, Russel was like the son Jordan never had. And Whitney was left typing correspondence for both of them.

It was no wonder, Teddy thought, that Whitney had demanded this splashy anniversary party. Her sister had few occasions that were celebrated especially for her.

However... all this insight wasn't TCB, Taking Care of Business, and Teddy had to get over to the Sleep Inn and find Vince. She pulled the phone back to her ear. "Gosh, Harriet, I'm sure you didn't call for the sole purpose of giving me a hard time. What's the problem?''

"Three people we didn't expect are coming. They're all Strattons, which is so typical of Russel's family, the most inconsiderate people in the world. They're the real reason Whitney eloped, you know. *His* family.''

Teddy bit her tongue to keep from telling Harriet that the Edwards family was more than enough to drive a sane person into an asylum. After Teddy's mother had died fifteen years ago, the Edwards clan—especially Harriet, who lived only two blocks away from Teddy's father—rallied around like an invading horde. They'd meant well, but they were the most controlling, manipulative people that Teddy had ever encountered.

"In-laws can be such a pain," Harriet continued. "When you get married, Teddy, *if you ever get married,* you'll know what I mean. Anyway, I have to redo the seating for the head table at dinner. Where should I put you?''

"Don't bother. I'm going to be the official photographer, so I plan to be running around, taking pictures.'' That way, she hoped she'd avoid any creepy family confrontations.

"Running around?" Harriet questioned.

"Yes.'' It was harder to hit a moving target. "I don't need a seat for dinner.''

"Whitney suggested that you might want to sit by Tom Burke.''

"At the head table? Tom will be at the head table?''

"Well, yes. He and Russel are such good friends, you know. Whitney said that if she'd had a church wedding, Tom would have been best man.''

Teddy sensed the beginning of a major conflict. Tom and Whitney had been sweethearts in high school. He was a friend of Russel's, too, but seating him at the head table seemed to be inviting trouble. "I don't think either Tom or I should be at the head table."

"Well, I don't, either. But it's your sister's party. It's rather sweet of her to be concerned about the fact that you probably won't have a dance partner."

"What about you?" Teddy said irritably. Harriet had been widowed seven years ago. "Why don't you sit with Tom?"

"My dear, I have an escort. Mr. Merle Chatworth."

"Lilibet's ex-husband?" Teddy could already see the fireworks. "You're dating Merle?"

"Lilibet was always much too young for him. Merle needs a woman closer to his own age, someone like me, who can share his memories and who can understand his aches and pains. He was once quite famous, you know."

"Merle played backup guitar for a country and western band."

"A group that once played backup for Elvis Presley himself. And I'd expect you of all people to be gaga about that. Merle's rather surprised that you haven't contacted him for an interview."

Fat chance. Teddy thought of Merle as a no-talent slimeball who had lucked out by throwing together a couple of ballads that had gotten recorded by country and western stars, thereby providing Merle with a decent retirement income.

"If he'd had a few breaks," Harriet defended staunchly, "he could have been as big as Elvis."

That wasn't how Lilibet remembered her ex-husband's career, but Teddy wasn't about to take sides in this potential cat fight. "Well, congratulations, Harriet. Now, about this seating problem, I really don't want to—"

"For once in your life, think about somebody besides yourself. This is how Whitney wants it. Tom is in town by himself. And, *of course,* you don't have a date."

It was the "of course" that irked her. Teddy was sick and tired of all these references to her status as an old maid at age twenty-seven. "Why would you assume that?"

"Well," Harriet demanded, "you don't have a date, do you?"

"As a matter of fact, I do. A gentleman friend flew in unexpectedly from Chicago, and he will be accompanying me to the anniversary party."

"A boyfriend?" Her aunt's voice dripped with disbelief. "Does he have a name?"

"Vince Harding."

"Why, Teddy, this is a huge surprise."

"Yes, it is." Teddy's brain went numb. What had possessed her to make such a ridiculous claim? She hadn't even planned to accept Vince's business proposition, much less date the man.

Harriet babbled, "I'm so delighted, Teddy. Maybe you're finally going to settle down and start acting properly. This Vince? Are you serious about him?"

"Serious as a heart attack." How was she ever going to get herself out of this mess? "I have to run, Harriet. You can seat us anywhere."

Her aunt squealed a goodbye and Teddy hung up the phone. Now she'd done it.

On the drive to the Sleep Inn, she reviewed various ways of asking Vince to join her at her sister's anniversary party. There was no graceful approach. If she didn't ask him, she'd be embarrassed to death by Harriet. But how could she admit to Vince that she was a dateless, shriveled-up old prune who was forced to lie about having a boyfriend?

When she pulled into the parking lot of the Sleep Inn, these miserable thoughts flew from her mind. There, parked outside the very last room at the far end of the motel, was the Harley with the TCB-1 license plate.

Teddy hurried from the van. Using her favorite Nikon loaded with color film, she snapped a couple of photos of the big shiny bike. What an incredible break! Perhaps, in the cosmic scheme of things, her bad fortune in shooting off her mouth to Harriet was being balanced with finding the Harley. If Teddy's streak of good luck continued, the owner of the bike would be inside one of these rooms, waiting for her to interview him.

The Sleep Inn was a one-story L-shaped building, neat and tidy with white siding and black trim. Five rooms led down from the office and the others lined the long leg of the *L*. The Harley was parked in front of the last room of this row. The number on the door was nineteen.

She marched up to the door and knocked. This time, he wouldn't get away. A portentous excitement stirred within her, and she knocked again. The door swung inward, the opening framing a thick-shouldered man. He wore Levi's but was naked from the waist up. When he leaned toward her, she smelled the sticky odor of his sweat. He squinted. "Teddy? Is that you?"

"Tom Burke." Though she hadn't seen him in years, she recognized him immediately. His all-American blond features remained handsome, but somehow indistinct, as if he was fading from the sharp, clean focus of high school when dreams of the future were unsmudged. Teddy was possibly the only female from Westalia High School who had not dated Tom—a distinction she did not regret.

"What are you doing here?" he asked.

"I live here. And I assume you're back in town for the anniversary party."

"That's right." Tom hitched his thumbs in his belt and flashed a wide grin. He was still a good-looking thing. "Guess I would've been Russel's best man," he said. "If there'd been a wedding."

"Always a best man and never a groom. You never did get married, did you?"

"No girl's going to tie me down."

In Teddy's mind, his bachelor status did not represent a great tragedy for womankind, but she kept her opinion to herself. Nor was she rude enough to ask if he'd ever managed to find a decent job. "So, Tom, what have you been doing with yourself?"

"Spent some time in New York City, but it was too cold for me and those people don't drive cars. Not much call for a mechanic. Mostly I've been moving around, seeing the world. Like yourself, Teddy. I've seen your name on photographs in newspapers and magazines. Mary Theodora Edwards."

Her work, Teddy remembered. That was the real reason she happened to be standing at Tom's door at the Sleep Inn. "Of course, I'm glad to see you, Tom. But I'm a little surprised. Why are you out here, at the Sleep Inn?"

"There wasn't room for me at Russel and Whitney's. Or at your daddy's house." A small grimace of hurt distorted his mouth at not being invited to stay with his old friends. Tom might not be wiser, but he was surely older and jaded enough to realize that by not marrying Whitney when he'd had the chance, he had missed out on all that lovely Edwards money.

Teddy asked, "You don't happen to know anything about this Harley, do you?"

"You like it?"

"I don't know much about motorcycles, but it seems to be very, um, very clean."

He swaggered out of his room, brushing past her so that Teddy had to step out of his way. Up close, he smelled like cigarette butts and beer. He stepped up to the machine and ran his hand lovingly across the shiny chrome handlebars. "It's mine. Didn't you see the license plate? TCB-1. Thomas Charles Burke, my initials."

Teddy didn't know whether to laugh or to scream. Her Elvis informant's clue was nothing but another dead end. Last night's wild ride had been a waste of time. "You like speeding on this thing, don't you?"

"Why would you say that?"

"Because last night I was following you. You left from PJ's and took off like greased lightning."

"Did I?" He rubbed his hands across his eyes. Though he didn't deny her accusation, he said, "I don't remember. Last night's sort of blurry. Guess I was doing a bit of drinking."

He chuckled, but Teddy didn't laugh along with him. She didn't even smile. There was nothing amusing about getting so drunk that you couldn't remember what was going on.

He straightened his shoulders. "I was at PJ's. I remember that. Your brother-in-law and me were celebrating, having a little stag party."

"Do you often have blackouts?"

"Not anymore. I've got my drinking under control."

"Apparently not." She felt the same kind of dark apprehension that had risen within her when she talked to her Elvis informant. Tom Burke was dangerous. He was an accident waiting to happen. "Anybody who's stupid enough to drink and drive isn't under control."

"Don't you lecture me, Teddy Edwards. A man's got to be able to take a drink with his friends now and then."

"No, he doesn't. Not a real man."

She turned on her heel and came face-to-face with a real man. Vince Harding sauntered down the sidewalk toward Tom's room. "Good morning, Teddy."

"Vince, I'd like you to meet—"

He noticed the bike. "I don't believe it. This is a restored 1948 Harley Panhead."

"That's right," Tom said proudly. "She was a basket case. Did the work on her myself."

"Hell of a bike." Vince stared with unabashed reverence at Harley Davidson's work of art. "Suicide clutch and gearshift. Split tank. Rigid tail, seat shocks. This is the classic bike that Brando rode in *The Wild One*." He circled the motorcycle, glanced at the rear plate and looked at Teddy. "Taking Care of Business?"

"The initials stand for Thomas Charles Burke." She introduced the two men and they shook hands.

Vince said, "If you ever think about selling..."

"No way, buddy. Only way anybody's going to get their hands on this bike is when I'm dead and gone."

"Too bad for me. You look way too healthy for that to be happening in the near future." He turned to Teddy. "Shall we get started?"

"Hey, wait a minute." Tom stepped around Vince and stood close to Teddy. "You and me are probably going to be the only single people at this party. You want to be my date?"

Here was the invitation she'd never received in high school when she'd been an intense, gawky teenager who wore baggy jeans and tried as hard as she could not to be noticed. "No thanks. I'm going to be the official photographer, so I'll be busy all the time."

"Come on, babe, loosen up."

"I said no."

"Just like in high school." His laughter evoked bitter memories, turning back the clock to a time when Teddy wasn't so self-assured. "Always working. Right, Teddy? You've gotten prettier, but you still don't know how to have fun."

"Guess not."

"Come on," Tom persisted. "You and me. I could show you a good time."

Before she could reply that drinking until she passed out wasn't her idea of a special evening, Vince cut into their conversation. "Teddy already has a date."

"I do?"

"Of course you do." He casually draped his arm around her shoulder. "I'm not planning to leave you alone today."

Tom chuckled again. "You're dating Teddy?"

"I am."

"That figures. You're dating Teddy, but you're sleeping here. Good luck, man."

With a derisive snort, Tom backed off, returned to his room and closed the door. But Teddy hardly noticed. Her powers of observation had been short-circuited by the touch of Vince's hand on her shoulder. When she turned toward him, he encircled her with his other arm. She placed her palm against his chest, keeping her distance. The masculine hardness of his body filled her with awareness of her own femininity. It was such a long, long time since she'd been held in a man's arms.

Her gaze lifted slowly, lingering on the buttons of his forest green cotton shirt, the dark hair that curled at his throat, the thrust of his jaw. His gray eyes held flecks of green and gold, and it seemed exactly right to be standing here, studying the color of his eyes. It was as if she was supposed to be here, in his casual embrace. As if she'd read the future when she'd told Harriet that she had a date.

He cupped her chin with his free hand and tilted her head back. His lips, firm yet gentle, kissed her mouth. The trembling started in her stomach and spread outward, fast as wildfire. She was losing control. A feverish sensation just beneath the surface of her skin made her feel weak and pliant and totally wonderful.

She drew away from him. It took a moment to find her voice, then she blurted, "Don't ever do that again."

Chapter Three

She took another backward step and repeated her warning in a firm, no-nonsense voice. "Never, Vince. Don't ever do that again."

He nodded, but he knew he'd kiss her again. He would hold her as close and as often as she would let him. Yesterday, he'd wanted her to work for him. Now, he simply wanted her.

And he didn't know why. No woman had ever swept Vince Harding off his feet, and he was far too old and jaded to believe in love at first sight. Why was he so attracted to Teddy? His assistant, Connie, would have called it kismet. She'd have said it was fate, that he'd known Teddy in a past reincarnation and she was the woman he'd been looking for all his life. But Vince didn't believe in any of that mumbo jumbo.

The logical explanation was that he'd thrown his arm around her and promised to be her date because it seemed like the easiest way to discourage that jerk who didn't deserve to own a Harley Panhead. But the kiss? The amazing petal softness of her lips against his? He couldn't explain it.

"You look different today," he said.

She wore a jungle-patterned blouse tucked into beige slacks. Though she'd tried to pull her thick blond hair into a tidy bun at the top of her head, errant tendrils escaped and curled at her nape. Her darker eyebrows and lashes framed eyes of the deepest blue. She looked savage, he thought, and Vince wanted to be the man who would tame her.

"Taking Care of Business," she said. "That's why I'm dressed like this. This afternoon, my sister is having a huge anniversary party."

"And I'm your escort," he said.

Though that was exactly what she had wanted, exactly the problem she'd been pondering on the way over here, Teddy wondered if she'd made a mistake. She cast an appraising glance at his Levi's and cotton shirt. "Do you have appropriate clothes for a formal affair?"

"No problem." He took a step toward his motel room. "Come inside while I change."

"I don't think so." One kiss in the open sunlight had been so erotic that years of her self-control had ebbed in an instant. Teddy frankly didn't trust herself to be inside his room, near the bed where he'd slept last night, inhaling the scent of his after-shave and catching glimpses of his half-dressed body. "I'll wait out here."

While Vince went into his room, she leaned against the wall between the door and window of his room, crossed her arms beneath her breasts and tried to relax. Last night's fog had cleansed the air, leaving a dewy freshness on the grass, leaves and daffodils. A beautiful day. Yet Teddy's usual sense of small-town well-being was absent. Was it Vince? The burst of arousal she'd felt in his arms? Or was it something else, something unnamed?

Glancing toward Tom's room, she saw the window curtain twitch, as if he'd been watching her. Was he angry? Embarrassed? Would he want to get even with her?

Tom Charles Burke would bear close observation this afternoon at the party. And so would Lilibet Chatworth in her scarlet dress. And Aunt Harriet with Lilibet's ex-husband, Merle, as her date. And Teddy's father, a stern, powerful man who was given to explosive outbursts.

Poor Whitney! With this volatile mix of people, it was possible that her sister would be hostess to a slugfest rather than an anniversary festivity. Teddy closed her eyes and made a silent promise that she would not precipitate any battles. Today, for Whitney's sake, Teddy would practice extreme congeniality. She'd get along with everybody. . . even if it killed her.

When she opened her eyes again, Vince had emerged from his room. His navy blue double-breasted suit looked far too sophisticated for Westalia, and Teddy gave a long, low whistle. "Very sharp."

"And very hot." He adjusted the Windsor knot in his striped silk tie. "You're going to owe me for this one."

"Do you take Mastercharge?"

"Your payback won't be nearly that easy. I'm thinking of something long and slow and torturous."

So was she. Lord help her, so was she.

Teddy nodded toward the van. "Let's go."

With this classy man at her side, Aunt Harriet and all the other Edwards family would most certainly have to revise their opinion of Teddy as a pathetic spinster. Feeling smug and even a little bit desirable, she climbed behind the wheel and fastened her seat belt.

"Tired?" Vince asked.

"I'm fine."

"Even after working last night?"

"It was nothing," she informed him. "A dead end."

"So you didn't catch Elvis at an all-night pizza parlor."

"No such luck." She cocked an eyebrow. This was the second time he'd mentioned Elvis sightings. It was almost as if he knew about those midnight photos, but she hadn't sent them to *Files* or to anybody else. "Why would you think I was working on an Elvis story?"

"Maybe because I think of this as Elvis country. Lush greenery. Sultry heat. We're not all that far from Memphis."

Though his explanation was as smooth as caramel on a sundae, there was something he wasn't telling her. "I've only done one Elvis story, Vince. And that was a nostalgia piece, not a sighting. If you're familiar at all with my work—"

"I am." His voice took on a businesslike tone. "I've reviewed your work extensively and have spoken to Max Owens, the owner of *Files*, about you. We're prepared to offer you a correspondent position. Full benefits and regular salary."

Teddy jolted over the curb and merged into the slow-moving Saturday traffic. He'd just made her quite an offer. The position would give her financial stability and benefits, too. But why? It seemed unlikely that there was a crying need for a photo correspondent in southern Illinois. Had he somehow gotten wind of her Elvis photos? If she truly was onto the Elvis story of the century, Teddy wanted to sell it to the highest bidder.

"My current projects," she said. "What happens to those?"

"Keep doing what you're doing now, and we'll take all of it. You'd be working for us."

"On assignment?" she asked with distaste.

"If we have a lead in this area, it goes to you first. You choose whether or not you want the story."

"Oh, really?" She was skeptical. "I've never found that I could have freedom when I was working for somebody else."

"You'd be working for me. And I promise you, Teddy, I'm not like anybody else."

Very true, she thought. He wasn't like anybody she'd met before. But it would take more than a unique man with green-and-gold flecks in his eyes to convince her to give up her professional freedom. On the outskirts of Westalia, they found a table at a roadside café, drank thick black coffee and haggled until afternoon without reaching an agreement.

Teddy timed their arrival at the Westalia Country Club for an hour before the party was scheduled to begin. She explained, "I want to get some posed photos before everybody else arrives."

"No problem." He straightened his tie.

"I'm really sorry to drag you along on this."

"Go ahead and do your job. Don't worry about me."

When he gently squeezed her arm to reassure her, his touch fired a heat within her, and Teddy flushed warmer than the brilliant sunlight that sparkled on the manicured green lawns leading out to the golf course.

Preparations for the anniversary party occupied the terrace behind the sprawling, white, two-story clubhouse. Long tables covered with white cloths ranged across the flagstones and out onto the lawns. And there were roses, a ridiculous abundance of pink roses, which were her sister's favorite flower. Pink rose centerpieces decorated each of the tables, pink roses festooned the edges of the canopy tents where the buffet would be spread. A pink rose bower had been set up beside the bandstand and dance floor.

She spied Russel and waved to him. When he strode across the terrace toward them, she couldn't help thinking how much Russel Stratton had changed during the year he'd been married to her sister. Before he and Whitney had wed, Russel was just another one of the guys—not rich, not poor, but average. The prestige of joining the Edwards family had transformed him. In a town the size of Westalia—a small puddle—Teddy's family represented a group of very large frogs. And now Russel was one of them. He was her father's right-hand man. His skinny chest puffed out the ruffled front of his tuxedo shirt, and his Adam's apple bobbed up and down as she introduced him to Vince. Teddy half expected Russel to burst out with a big froggy croak.

Instead he said, "Could I talk to you alone, Teddy?"

Vince nodded congenially and drifted toward the buffet canopy where waiters in white jackets bustled back and forth.

Russel lowered his voice. "I'm worried about Tom Burke. I'm afraid he's going to screw things up, and I want this day to be perfect for Whitney."

"I'm sure it will be." Hoping to avoid a confrontation, Teddy pointed to the bower of pink roses. "I expect you're going to have some sort of ceremony in that area."

"Simple and quick. We'll repeat our vows."

"Then I should set up lights over there." She glanced around, taking professional measure of the photo opportunities. "Yes, that would be the best spot for formal photos."

"Whatever you say."

"After that, I'll concentrate on candid shots while everybody is mingling."

"Sure thing, Teddy." He patted her shoulder. Russel was a touchy-feely sort of guy, always patting and hugging. "You know, it means the world to Whitney that you're here."

It did? Teddy and her sister had only gotten together once since her marriage, and that meeting hadn't been particularly warm.

He continued, "And I'm really hoping you'll be able to do more than be a photographer. Like I said, I'm worried about Tom. Last night, we went out for some stupid stag party, and he was drinking pretty heavily. I don't want any trouble from him today."

She sighed. "What kind of trouble do you expect?"

"Don't know if I should say this." He cleared his throat and gulped. "But you're family, Teddy. You'll understand."

"Say what, Russel?"

"Well, it's like this. Tom's still in love with Whitney, and he's talking crazy, saying things like if he can't have her, nobody will." Though Russel looked concerned, he was somehow detached, as if this was really somebody else's problem. "Keep an eye on him for me. Okay, Teddy?"

"How does Whitney feel about all this?"

"Why don't you go ask her? She's in a private room of the clubhouse. On the second floor." Russel's attention focused on a man carrying trays. He hugged her shoulders and moved away from her. "Thanks for everything, Teddy."

He was gone before she could say "You're welcome."

Noting that Vince had snagged himself a tall, cool drink and looked comfortable, she went to find her sister. Inside the clubhouse, at the top of a sweeping oak staircase, Teddy located the reserved private room marked Stratton, and knocked.

Whitney opened the door with a flourish and a girlish pirouette. Her cream silk dress fell gracefully from her thin shoulders and skimmed her curveless body. Though her face was beautifully made up, her cheekbones stood out too sharply. And her smooth blond hair had no luster. Whitney was lovely, as always, but she looked like someone who was recovering from a long illness.

"Are you all right?" Teddy asked.

A vivacious spark flashed in Whitney's blue eyes. "Do I look okay?"

"Great!" Teddy lied. "You look great."

"That's good." She hugged herself. "Because I want to dazzle these small-town jerks. To show them what a real wedding ought to be like."

"But this isn't a wedding." At best, the anniversary party was a semiwedding. "This is even better, Whitney. You and Russel have been married a year. You've already gotten through the hardest part."

Whitney pulled her inside and closed the door. "Do you think that's true? That the first year is the worst?"

"Has it been that way for you?"

"Let's just say that being married isn't what I expected. I mean, Teddy, before I had this ring on my finger, Russel was so much more attentive. We went to the movies I wanted to see. We ate at the restaurants I liked. Now he's different. He's always busy with something else."

"Working for Daddy," Teddy said. From hard experience, she knew that their father could be an all-consuming boss.

"Russel hardly notices me anymore." She pouted. "I have half a mind to pull some kind of stunt, just to make him jealous."

"A stunt?"

"That's right." She primped in front of a full-length mirror. "There's plenty of men who think I'm pretty. Plenty."

"Like Tom Burke?"

"That's right." She was defiant. "Tom always liked me, and I might just go ahead and have an affair with him. That'd show Russel."

"Big mistake," Teddy said.

"As if you'd know. You aren't exactly experienced with men, are you? And Tommy isn't the only one. There's Merle Chatworth, too."

"Lilibet's ex-husband? Ugh, Whitney."

"He's not so old. And he was a big country and western star in his day. Of course, Aunt Harriet has set her cap for him, but he's not interested in her. I could have him. Just like that." She snapped her fingers.

"You or Harriet," Teddy mused. "Either way, Lilibet would be furious."

"Why should I care about her?"

"Good question, Whitney. Why should you care about anybody but your husband? Especially today. This is your day. A celebration just for you."

"You're right." The smile Whitney gave herself in the mirror was sly and secretive. "I'm going to make sure this is a day that nobody forgets."

It sounded like a threat, but Teddy was not inclined to argue. "And let's make sure we preserve those memories on film. I'd like to do some formal shots of you and Russel by the trellis before everybody else gets here."

"It's bad luck for him to see me before the ceremony."

"Whitney, you're already married. You've been sleeping with the man for a year. Don't be—"

"Let me do this my way, Teddy."

"Fine."

Grumbling, Teddy left the clubhouse and concentrated on setting up the lights for photos. As she had expected, everybody got in the way. But when the renewal of vows took place, Whitney beamed as radiantly as a new bride and Russel was sweetly solicitous. Under the pink rose trellis, Mr. and Mrs. Stratton appeared to be deeply in love.

After a few arranged family photos, Teddy put away her lights and roamed through the crowd taking candid shots. Everybody in town was here. Old friends from high school. The entire staff of her father's newspaper. Sunday school teachers. Friends and family.

Teddy was glad to have her camera to hide behind. Though she wasn't shy, she hated group scenes and silly conversations that started with "What have you been doing for the past eight years?" and ended with somebody showing her photos of their two wonderful children. The frequent "Are you married yet?" question was bearable only because Teddy could point to Vince, the best-looking man at the event, and say, "I'm with him."

Vince, however, was taking unfair advantage of the situation. Whenever they were side by side, he made comments about how "special" she was and how he was sure they would have "an enduring and committed relationship."

When the buffet was served, Teddy sat beside Vince for only a moment before Aunt Harriet began to pry into the real nature of their relationship. "How long have you known each other? Where did you meet?"

"Years ago," Vince said. "In Venice, Italy. We were both covering a story and shared a gondola."

Teddy choked on a chicken wing.

"Are you all right, dear?"

She couldn't listen to another word. "I'd better get some pictures of this."

"Sit down," Harriet said.

"No." Teddy was off, snapping pictures of the main players while they offered one toast after another. She noticed that Tom Burke was drinking from his water glass. Was it filled with vodka? Or was he really avoiding alcohol?

When the dancing began, Teddy circulated. She actually managed to halt a couple of arguments by popping up beside the potential combatants and saying, "Smile." At one point, she framed Lilibet and Whitney in her lens. The two women made a nice visual contrast. Whitney with her pale hair was swathed in creamy silk. And dark-haired Lilibet, the competing beauty, wore her strapless red dress.

Through her smile for the camera, Whitney said, "Lilibet, honey, did you run out of material for that dress?"

"It's nice weather, Whitney, honey. I thought I'd get some tan on my shoulders."

"Why stop with your shoulders? Why not come naked?"

Lilibet arched her back, pushing her ample breasts forward. "Jealous?"

"Not a bit. Every eye is on me. I suppose you've noticed that your ex-husband can't keep away from me."

"Merle?"

"Makes me wonder. Why couldn't you hold on to him?"

"I threw him back," Lilibet said. "There's no reason to tie up my line with a small fish." She sashayed away from Whitney and into the waiting arms of Tom Burke. Though Lilibet had come to the party with a guy from town, she made it clear that she didn't feel obligated to leave with him. And Tom was certainly putting in his bid to escort her into the night. While the band played "Suspicious Minds," Lilibet and Tom gave new meaning to the term "dirty dancing."

As the afternoon waned and the roses began to wilt, Teddy continued to aim her camera. Once she focused on Vince and her father. Shuddering to think what they might be talking about, she turned away.

Vince didn't like Teddy's father, Jordan Edwards. He was a ramrod-straight man with a burr of white hair. The kind of guy who always thought he was right. Vince tried to make conversation. "Well, Jordan, I understand you have a newspaper."

"The *Southern Illinois Gazette* is the largest paper in this area. Daily circulation of fifteen thousand."

"Interesting. I run a paper myself."

"Files." He sneered. "A tabloid. There's quite a difference between your rag and my newspaper."

"Indeed there is. My distribution is over eight hundred thousand."

"A waste of newsprint on Elvis sightings."

What a pompous old fool! "You're missing a sure bet on those sightings, Jordan. Teddy has a whole file folder of remarkable—"

"I don't care what Teddy is working on."

"No?"

"Teddy isn't a team player. She won't work with me."

And Vince didn't blame her one bit. He stood silently beside this inexplicably bitter man and stared at the dance floor where Jordan's younger daughter twirled in the arms of Merle Chatworth. Whitney laughed gaily, but Merle remained serious, not even cracking a smile. Vince thought he was holding Whitney a little too close.

But Jordan didn't seem to mind. "Whitney's a good girl."

"And her husband?"

"I didn't much like Russel when I first met him, but the boy grows on you. He's working for me now."

But not for Whitney, Vince thought. With her husband under her father's thumb, there probably wasn't much attention or affection left over. Vince could almost understand why Whitney was throwing herself at Merle and Tom.

Vince braced himself when he saw Aunt Harriet charging toward him with Teddy in tow. "All right, you two," Harriet said. "I want some answers, and I want them now."

Teddy's blue eyes glazed over with frustration. Vince had heard her explain to Harriet, at least three times, that they were associates. But that wasn't the story her aunt wanted to hear. He said, "Let's be honest about this, Teddy."

"About what?"

He fastened his hand at her waist and turned to Harriet. Teddy's father observed the scene through hostile eyes, and that was the last bit of motivation Vince needed. With perfect wide-eyed innocence, he said, "Teddy is my fiancée."

"Oh my Lord, this is wonderful." Without a moment's hesitation, Harriet marched up to the band and snatched the microphone from the lead singer. "Everybody, listen. I have an announcement. Our Teddy is *finally* getting married."

Teddy died a thousand deaths while everyone rushed to congratulate her. The worst moment came when Tom Burke grinned evilly and said, "Only you, Teddy. You're the only female on earth who would make her fiancé sleep at a motel."

"Only for last night," Vince said. "I got in late and didn't want to wake Teddy. Tonight is a different story. I'll be staying at her house." He glanced down at her. "Isn't that right, dear?"

"Why, certainly, *dear.*" She coiled her arm around his waist and pinched hard.

"Aren't they cute?" Harriet cooed.

"Aren't we?" Teddy gritted her teeth and smiled. "Will you all excuse us for a minute?" She directed Vince to a quiet spot away from the festivities. They were near the first tee of the golf course. "How could you?" she sputtered. "What are you trying to— What makes you think you're going to get away with this?"

"I did get away with it."

"Do you really think I'll take you home with me?"

"If you don't, Aunt Harriet will want a full explanation," he countered. "Are you ready for that?"

"This is blackmail, Vince."

"I prefer to think of it as enforced negotiation. If I'm staying at your house, you'll have to keep talking to me." And, he figured, sooner or later she would capitulate. And the moment of his victory would be sweeter than the honey color of her hair and the scent of her perfume.

"No way," she said. "There's no way I'm letting you roam freely through my house so you can check out my darkroom and review all the material I'm currently working on."

"I won't spy on you," he promised. "Not that you could stop me if that's what I planned to do."

"No? Well, how about if I hog-tie you to a fence post?"

"I'd like to see you try."

His voice was firm. His gray eyes shimmered. Too easily, she imagined him in her bed. *Are you lonesome tonight?* She had to look away from him before all sorts of inappropriate feelings overwhelmed her. "Here's what we're going to do. I've got a thermal sleeping bag and a tent and you can set up wherever you want. Outside."

"Inside." His hands rested on her shoulders and he leaned close to whisper, "Let me lie beside you, Teddy."

She should have slapped him, should have pushed him away from her. "What are you talking about? This is business, Vince. And you know it. Why pretend that you want to get into my bed?"

"Maybe I do."

"What?"

"Maybe I find you attractive, sexy, interesting—"

"Stop!" She closed her mind. "How gullible do you think I am? I might prefer to live in the country and I might have simple tastes, but that doesn't mean I'm some little hick you can sweep off her feet with a wink and a promise."

She turned on her heel and walked away from him, only looking back once and wondering. What if she did take him home with her? What if they did share the night?

The rest of the afternoon and evening passed in a blur. After hours and hours of dancing and eating, most of the guests, including Russel and Whitney, had departed. The roses were wilting. And so was Teddy.

At nine o'clock one of the staff from the country club informed her that she had a phone call. When she went inside to take it, her Elvis informant squeaked out, "Go to the Sleep Inn. Room 19. Hurry."

"Look, I know about the Harley. It's a Panhandle. Or a Pancake. Whatever. It's nothing."

"Hurry. You've got to hurry."

Might as well. She'd done her job, taken hundreds of candid photos, and couldn't put off the discussion with Vince much longer, anyway. She found him sitting quietly, listening to a young matron chat about her twins. He gallantly bid the woman good-night and followed Teddy to her van. They rode in silence until Teddy pulled into the parking slot outside Vince's room at the Sleep Inn.

"I'm not staying here," he said. "Remember?"

"How could I forget?" She sighed. "Go ahead and pick up your bags. I have a lead to follow up on."

"A lead?"

"Somebody called me at the clubhouse."

Cameras in hand, she marched down the sidewalk toward Room 19. She heard his footsteps behind her. Since Teddy really didn't expect to find anything here, she didn't mind that Vince tagged along. He might as well be as frustrated as she was about checking out leads that went nowhere.

Or maybe not. The door to Room 19, Tom Burke's room, was slightly ajar. Teddy slowed her pace and gestured for Vince to be quiet. A sliver of light from the opened door cut a swath across the sidewalk. But there was silence from the room. A deathly stillness.

Cautiously, Teddy pushed at the door, and it slowly moved on its hinges. She stepped inside.

The light from a bedside lamp shone across the shape of a woman lying motionless on the bed. Her arms were at her sides. Her ankles were neatly crossed. In the center of her cream silk dress a violent red stain spread around the handle of a knife. The blade was buried in Whitney Stratton's heart.

Chapter Four

She's dead. Without feeling for a pulse, without touching the blanched skin of her sister's thin wrist, Teddy knew that Whitney was dead.

Whitney's legs barely made a ripple under the clinging silk gown which was arrayed in a flare like an angel's robe. Her smooth blond hair coiled neatly over her shoulder. Her hands lay limply at her sides. The coral of her lipstick and rouge lent a macabre painted freshness to her skin. Her eyes were closed beneath glossy translucent lids, and her thick lashes brushed her cheekbones. Her repose was serene, except for the terrible disfigurement of the knife. And the scarlet stain of her lifeblood.

Teddy saw a flash of bright light, heard the whir of film advancing. There was other flash. Dazed, she lowered her Nikon. Had she taken a picture? Had she actually done such a thing?

Vince pushed past her and went to the bedside. "Teddy, call an ambulance. Call 911."

"But she's dead."

Vince felt Whitney's throat for a pulse, then lifted her limp hand. But there was no life in her body. Couldn't he see that? She watched him pick up the telephone receiver beside the bed. The words sounded like he was speaking from the bottom of a deep well. "Ambulance...police...murder..."

His voice echoed in her head, louder than the pounding of her own heart, louder than the drumbeats, the harsh, throbbing rhythm, warning her over and over. Louder than the monsoon rain. She could feel the jungle closing in, smothering her with verdant growth that promised life but had only brought her death and horror and pain. She tried to swallow, but her throat was too parched. *No water. Must not drink the water.* "Thirsty. I'm so thirsty."

But there was no jungle. She stood in a motel room with an ugly painting of an antebellum mansion on the pale ecru wall. Beneath her feet was a cheap carpet of mottled brown. Hideous bulbous lamps stood sentry on tacky bedside tables. Her tidy sister would hate being here. But Whitney was beyond caring, beyond thought, beyond hate and love and fear and anger. She was gone from this place.

Teddy turned away, bracing her arms on the edge of the dresser. A man's clothing littered the wood-grained Formica surface above the drawers. She saw blue jeans with the belt still attached and a garish buckle with the initials TCB. Tom Burke. He killed her sister.

At the party, Russel had warned her. He'd said that Tom Burke was talking crazy, saying that if he couldn't have Whitney, nobody could. And Teddy had seen him drinking. But how could he do this? How could he kill her sister?

A sob convulsed in Teddy's throat and she raised her hand to her mouth, holding back screams of protest. Her wavering gaze lifted to the mirror above the dresser and she confronted her reflection. She looked half-mad, on the verge of collapse. And, indeed, a heavy dark cloud filled her mind, threatening to blanket her conscious thought. Her knees weakened, and she clung to the surface of the dresser to keep from falling.

Her fingers pushed aside Tom's discarded clothing and she saw the glitter of jewelry. Whitney's earrings, cascades of diamonds. Whitney's plain gold wedding band. And the anniversary ring that Russel had given her at the party—a large pink coral flanked by diamonds. There was also a Westalia High School class ring, a man's ring that looked clumsy amid the other glittering feminine adornments.

She heard Vince speaking on the telephone, summoning the ambulance and the sheriff. Teddy wanted to stop him, to hold back the inevitable moment when her sister would be declared dead and the possibility of loving reconciliation gone forever.

"Vince, I need to step outside." Her voice sounded rational. "I need some air."

"Wait!" He was still on the telephone.

"I'm fine."

"Teddy, stay here. You're in shock. You need to sit down."

But she couldn't remain in that room for one more moment. If she didn't move, she would surely suffocate beneath the weight of her emotions. She lurched toward the door in a stiff-legged wooden gait. The camera that hung from a strap around her neck bumped against her rib cage.

Outside, the night was clear. But cold, Teddy thought, so cold that her skin felt like it was burning. Clumsily she rubbed her forearms and stamped her feet.

On the road that ran past the Sleep Inn, she watched two cars creep by. Slowly. So slow. Her perceptions distorted space and motion. The Sleep Inn sign loomed huge, blinking Vacancy. To her left was a field of weeds where she could run and hide and pretend that she was a child again, catching the lightning bugs in a mason jar and taking them into Whitney's bedroom where she would set them free and the two girls would watch their magical, flickering dance. Teddy wished everything was the same as always, that Whitney was still living and breathing and complaining about how Teddy was not a good sister. Not a good daughter. Not worthy to be an Edwards.

"I'm not," Teddy whispered. If only she'd been more understanding, she might have made a difference. She might have kept her sister alive. There might have been a chance.

The figure of a man appeared near the motel office. With wobbling steps, he strolled on the sidewalk between the parked cars and the motel doors. And he was singing "Are You Lonesome Tonight?" Loudly. It was Tom Burke.

"Bastard," Teddy said. She lunged toward him, her fingernails spread like talons. "You bastard! How could you—"

"Teddy, stop!"

Before she could attack Tom Burke, strong arms caught hold and gently restrained her. She struggled against Vince's grasp. "Let me go!"

Tom chuckled as he sidestepped around them. "Lovers' spat? What's the matter, Vinnie? Did Teddy turn cold on you again? Oh, man, you're never going to get in her bed. Not a prayer." With a jaunty pivot, he turned toward the door of his room.

"Hold it," Vince said. "You can't go in there."

"You say?" Tom showed him the diamond-shaped plastic marker on the motel key. "Room 19. My room."

"Whitney's dead," Vince informed him. "Murdered. She's in your room."

Tom pushed open the door and stared. He went inside a few steps, then backed out.

"Move away from the door," Vince said. "Close it. We need to leave the evidence intact."

"It's too late," Teddy groaned. Whitney was already dead. The realization sank into the marrow of Teddy's bones and she quit fighting. The battle was over. She had lost her sister. Whitney was dead. Like her mother. Like Jacques Louis Aubouchon, her former partner. They were dead; all of them had gone far away to an unreachable eternity.

She turned to Vince and burrowed against his chest beneath his suit jacket. "Cold," she whispered.

"It's okay, Teddy. Let's go to my room. You can lie down and rest."

"No, I have to stay here. I can't leave Whitney alone."

He felt a shiver race through her, then she stiffened. With sheer determination, she suppressed her grief and her fears, stifled the physical symptoms of shock.

Vince had never seen anyone exert such strict self-control, and it worried him. He wanted to tell her it was all right to cry, that it was all right to show her sorrow. But that wasn't Teddy's way. All day he'd watched her at the party, seen how she was shunned by her father, criticized by her relatives. Though Teddy had returned to her hometown, she was not welcomed. For reasons he didn't comprehend, she was an outsider. Different. Separate. Alone.

Her reaction to Whitney's death, he thought, was odd. Vince remembered the years when he'd reported hard news and had become familiar with the aftermath of tragedy. First came denial. Those who were close to the victim refused to believe that their loved one was dead. But Teddy had not questioned once. From the moment she entered the motel room, she had abandoned false hopes. As if she'd done this before.

Vince knew something of her history. Teddy had worked in a photojournalist team in war-stricken parts of Africa and South America. In that work, a newsperson saw the face of death in its most terrible, grotesque form. Destruction of families. Inhumanities. The suffering of children. What had Teddy seen?

Tom Burke jolted away from Room 19 and stumbled to the end of the concrete sidewalk, where he doubled over and vomited on the lawn. He wiped his mouth on the back of his hand. "I can't believe it. Are you sure she's—"

"I'm sure," Vince said.

"But I held her. Today. She was warm." He rubbed his eyes. Tears streaked the dirt on his face. "How did she get in my room? Why?" Suddenly aware of the obvious implications, his eyes widened in fear. "Oh, God, I didn't do it, Teddy."

Vince held Teddy protectively close. "Save it for the sheriff, Tom."

"Russel's my buddy. We've been buddies since way back. Sure, I liked Whitney, liked her a lot. Maybe I even loved the girl." His fingers drew into a fist. He whirled and punched the white siding of the motel. "Damn. It was Whitney's fault. I swear it. At the party, she was coming on to me. Said she was going to meet me at the Sleep Inn and she even knew what room I was in. But I thought she was teasing, you know, flirting, rubbing up against me and—" The realization hit him. He was talking about a dead woman. "Oh, God."

In a low voice, Vince asked, "How much have you had to drink?"

"What's that got to do with anything?"

"You have blackouts. You're a alcoholic, Tom."

"You think I did this?" His eyes were confused. "No way, man. Not even in a blackout. I didn't have that much. This was a party. Thought I'd have fun, let myself go."

"Be a big man," Vince said with disgust.

"Damn right." He hiked up his trousers, tried to pull himself together. "Like in high school. I played football. I could've had any girl I wanted. Even rich Whitney. I was a big hero."

"But now you're nothing."

"You shut the hell up. I have friends here. They'll believe me."

He would soon have a chance to test that theory, because the wail of a police siren cut into the night. In minutes, the parking lot of the Sleep Inn filled with emergency vehicles. Two ambulances and three police cars arrived, which Vince assumed was the sum total of law enforcement in this small town. There would be more, he knew. State police, coroners and others. But for now, Sheriff Jake Graham directed the show.

From what Vince could see, the barrel-chested sheriff was putting in a fairly competent performance as he barked out orders to his deputies. They secured the area, following standard police procedures. Sheriff Graham approached Vince and Teddy. "I understand your name is Vincent Harding," he said. "And you're from Chicago?"

Vince nodded.

"You and Teddy found the body."

"That's correct." Vince felt Teddy tremble in his arms. In the midst of all this activity, she had barely moved a muscle.

"I'm going to need statements from both of you." He leaned his big face closer to Teddy. "Are you all right? You need a paramedic? A sedative?"

"No," Teddy said. Her voice was muffled against Vince's chest. "I'm okay. I want to help."

"Good girl. Can you tell me what happened?"

When she leaned away from Vince, she swayed unsteadily on her feet. He hooked his arm around her, supporting her as the words stumbled from her lips. "I came here. We did. We came here. There was a phone call."

"Who called you, Teddy?"

"I don't know. It wasn't..." Her eyelids blinked. She was confused. "It was about Elvis."

The sheriff folded his arms across his girth. "Elvis Presley?"

"This person, the one who called me, keeps seeing Elvis, hears him singing. The caller said to come here. Room 19."

"And who the heck is this person?"

"Anonymous."

"You pulling my leg, Teddy?"

"No," she said vehemently.

Vince heard the tremor in her voice. "That's enough, Sheriff. There's nothing else Teddy can tell you."

"I'm okay," she insisted.

"Look, if this person is a witness, I need a name. And I cannot put out an APB on Elvis Presley. Now, doggone it, Teddy, don't you get all girly and mushy on me."

"Leave her alone. She doesn't know the name of the caller. The voice must be disguised."

The sheriff glanced toward Room 19, where deputies and paramedics raced, loudly and importantly, in and out. "When you found the body, what did the room look like?"

"Like it does now. We didn't take anything out of there. I used the phone, felt for a pulse." Vince remembered. "Teddy took two photos when she walked in the door."

"I see. I'll need those pictures, Teddy. Soon as you can get them."

Teddy yanked herself away from Vince and glared at the sheriff through haunted eyes. Her complexion was as white as paper, but her voice was strong. "Have you arrested Tom Burke?"

"You know better than that," he chided. "We have to do an investigation. Study the evidence."

"He did it. I know he did."

"Did you see him commit the murder?"

She shook her head. "Whitney said . . ." Teddy's fingers laced together in a white-knuckled knot as she held back her memories of the last private conversation she'd had with her sister when Whitney had talked about having an affair with Tom to make Russel jealous. If she spoke of those moments, Teddy knew she'd begin to cry. And if she cried, her emotions would gush uncontrollably. "I want to go home, Jake. I'll talk to you in the morning."

"Teddy, if you know a reason for me to arrest Tom, you got to tell me. Right now."

"I don't have facts," she said miserably.

Vince stepped forward. "Tomorrow morning, Sheriff, that's soon enough." Sheriff Graham nodded briskly, setting his double chin in motion, and returned to his crime-scene crew.

Vince gently directed Teddy toward her van. She was on the verge of a breakdown, needed to be lying down, warmed by blankets. Yet her steps were steady. She had to be running on some stubborn inner strength.

At the door to the van, she said, "I'll drive."

"Not a chance." He led her to the passenger side of the van. "You're going to sit here and rest."

He helped her inside and hurried around to the driver's side. "Give me the keys, Teddy."

"Jake was right. I should talk to him." But she made no move to get out of the van. "Right now. I'd better tell him about Whitney. He needs to know." Her voice was adamant, but her arms hung limply, and Vince didn't expect her to be capable of any decisive movement.

"When I talked to Whitney before the party…" Teddy remembered her feelings of unease, the dark premonitions that colored the day. The heavy perfume of pink roses. And Whitney, laughing slyly, teasing. "She was up to something, scheming. I should have known that she was going to get in trouble. I should have stayed with her the whole time."

"Don't blame yourself. There were lots of other people at the party," he countered. "Over a hundred, at least."

"But she was *my sister. My responsibility.*" With renewed sense of purpose, she grasped the door handle. "I can't go home and bury my head in the sand. I have to know who killed her."

She stepped down from the van. Waves of exhaustion washed over her, but she stood firm and waited for the dizziness to ebb. All her life, Teddy had searched out the action, then she'd stood by and taken pictures. This time would be different. This time, she would make a difference. Vince came up beside her. He opened her van door and closed it again.

"What are you doing?" she asked.

"I'm locking your damn van. Do you realize how much valuable equipment you have in there?"

"You don't have to stay here," she informed him. "This isn't your fight. You don't have to be involved."

"I'll be here." His hands glided down her arms, and his fingers closed around her fragile wrists. She might have the courage to take on this battle. But did she have the strength? "I'm not going anywhere."

"This won't make any difference in my decision to stay free-lance."

Hiring her was the furthest thing from his mind. The intensity in his gray eyes drove the message home. "This time, Teddy, you're not alone."

A grateful sob rose in her throat, and she swallowed it. Crying wasted time. Right now, she needed answers. There would be a lifetime to grieve.

"What did you remember?" he asked. "Did Whitney tell you something about Tom Burke?"

"She wanted to have an affair to make Russel jealous, and Tom was the most likely candidate. But there were others, too. She was ready to take off with whoever would have her."

"But she ended up here, in Tom's room. Why would he kill her? Did he have a motive?"

Teddy was beginning to think more clearly. "His whole life is his motivation. His failures. His drinking. If Tom had married Whitney right out of high school, he would have had money. My father would have made sure he had a job."

"But that didn't happen."

"No. He let her go. And I'm sure he regretted it."

Teddy watched as a sporty blue Miata skidded into the parking lot. Russel Stratton emerged. In the swirling red-and-blue lights of emergency vehicles, his expression was stricken. Russel must be feeling great sorrow. Though he and Whitney were not getting along, though Whitney had been plotting to have an affair, her husband would be devastated by her violent death after only a year of marriage. He stumbled toward the far end of the motel. Then suddenly he reached up and touched his prominent Adam's apple. He straightened his tie. Conscious of his appearance.

Teddy wondered. Was his misery a performance? Did he really love his wife? Or did he love the status of being married to Whitney Edwards, having a prestigious job at the family newspaper and belonging to country clubs? Perhaps, she thought, he never really knew or appreciated Whitney. And now he would never have the chance.

"Like me," Teddy said softly. She looked up at Vince. "I never knew her. Not really."

"Let's go home, Teddy. Leave the investigating to the sheriff."

"Jake Graham? I don't trust him to find the truth. He'll take the easiest solution and that will be that."

When Teddy strode across the blacktop parking lot, her step was steady and determined. As a photographer, she'd attended more crime scenes than weddings, but this was the first time she'd been a player in the drama. The first thing she noticed was that Tom Burke was being ushered into the rear of a police car. But he wasn't in cuffs. She saw him slump forward, a policeman at his side. Then the car door closed and the overhead light went out.

She and Vince came up beside Sheriff Graham as he said to Russel, "I hate to be asking, Russ. But where did you go after you left the party with your wife?"

"It was about eight o'clock," he replied. "We left early because we needed to finish packing. We were leaving on a second honeymoon tomorrow." His thin nostrils flared as he brought his voice under control. "A cruise. In the Bahamas."

The sheriff turned to Teddy. "If you don't mind, this is police business."

"It's okay," Russel said. "I've got nothing to hide."

Teddy stepped up beside him. She rested her small hand on his arm. "I'm sorry. We're all going to miss her."

He squeezed her hand and pulled Teddy against him in a hug. "She was so full of life. And today she was so beautiful. Did you see the ring I gave her?"

Teddy nodded, thinking of the golden jewelry on the dresser top, hidden beneath a sordid pile of Tom's dirty clothes. And the class ring.

Sheriff Graham cleared his throat. "Let's get this over with, Russ. Then I won't have to bother you again. After you went home and packed, what happened?"

"Whitney said she needed to pick up a couple of things from the drugstore. She left."

Before he released Teddy, she sensed a tension in him. Was Russel lying?

"That was the last time I saw her," he said. "A little after eight-thirty. I sat down to watch TV and fell asleep. Next thing I knew, I got a call from your deputy."

From out of the night, Aunt Harriet swooped down upon him, enveloping him in a pink chiffon embrace. It wasn't clear to Teddy whether Harriet was comforting Russel or vice versa because Harriet's round shoulders shook with sobs and she sputtered unintelligible half sentences.

Merle Chatworth slouched behind her, and Vince stepped back a few paces to stand beside him. Merle's weathered face stuck in a perpetual squint, narrowing his eyes into slits. "Whitney was just too damn beautiful to live. Like a butterfly."

Vince couldn't believe they were all talking about the same woman. Didn't anyone notice that Whitney Edwards Stratton was as skinny as a rail, all elbows and angles? The thinness sharpened her features, making her look hard. Her dull blond hair showed the overdyed effects of too many trips to the stylist's shop. Teddy was the real beauty in the family.

"Elusive," Merle said.

It seemed like an unusual word for this rugged old Southerner to be using until Vince remembered that Merle fancied himself a potential singing star. He probably had a lyric for every occasion. "She was murdered," Vince said.

"I know." His gaze shifted. His eyes were the only part of his body that moved. Merle had a talent for standing as still as a statue. "The guy who did it is going to pay."

"How do you know it was a guy?"

"Had to be. Women don't do things like that. Leastwise, not the women in this town. They're ladies. They been brought up right." His tongue flicked out and moistened his lips. "Except maybe for Lilibet."

"Your ex?"

"Parading around at that party in her red dress with her bare shoulders. You know she left with Tommy Burke?"

Vince nodded encouragingly.

"They went to PJ's, a little tavern up the way. But she picked a fight with him and took off. Lilibet's a great one for picking fights."

So was Teddy's father. Jordan Edwards cruised into the parking lot in his big gray Lincoln Continental with the horn blaring. The deputies and assembled watchers had to scramble quickly to get out of his way. Jordan stormed out of the car. He scanned the parking lot and homed in on the sheriff like a heat-seeking missile.

Strangely, his first words were the same as Teddy's. "Have you arrested Tom Burke yet?"

"I'm sorry, Jordan." The sheriff puffed out his big barrel chest, using his bulk to increase the distance between himself and Jordan Edwards. "But I do need some proof."

"What else could you possibly need? She was in his room. She was stabbed with his buck knife."

"Whoa," the sheriff said. "How did you know that?"

"I'm a newspaperman, you idiot. I've been listening to your stupid deputies yammering on my police radio. If it was his knife—"

"We don't know that it was Tom's knife. It was a buck knife. Lots of motorcycle guys use buck knives. They carry them in leather cases on their belts."

"I know that. I have a cycle myself."

"So you know that buck knives are carried in most cycle accessory shops."

"On the radio, your deputy said it was Tom's knife." He paced, unable to contain his fury. His skin blazed a deep, dangerous red, contrasting with his burr-cut white hair. Even his eyes were bloodshot. "It's obvious what happened here. Any fool could see it. Tom Burke kidnapped my daughter. He dragged her into his room and killed her."

The sheriff drawled, "I'm afraid the evidence doesn't support that theory."

"Then she was waylaid by a thief. Whitney was wearing several hundred dollars' worth of jewelry."

"Far as I can tell, nothing was stolen."

"Damn it, man." Jordan Edwards looked like he might explode. "My daughter would not come here voluntarily. She was a married woman."

"I'm aware of that, Jordan."

"Has it also occurred to you that somebody might have killed her to get back at me? I have a lot of enemies."

"Yes, sir. I'm sure you do."

Vince realized that Teddy was no longer beside him. She'd disappeared through the headlights and the milling crowd. He knew she couldn't be in the van because he'd locked it and had the keys. On a hunch, he went toward Room 19. In the doorway, he paused.

In contrast to the sound and fury in the parking lot, the room was silent. The police photographers and paramedics stood away from the bed, and Teddy knelt beside it. She held Whitney's hand. Slowly, she rose to her feet. With a light touch, she stroked the hair from her sister's forehead and placed a soft kiss on the cold flesh. "Goodbye, Sis. Now you'll be with Mother."

Abruptly, she turned away. When she saw Vince in the doorway, she let go with a heavy sigh.

"I'll take you home now, Teddy. You can rest."

"And drink a cup of tea." If she had the strength, she would have laughed. The mechanism for consoling was always the same. Kind words, gentle solace and a cup of sweet herbal tea. "Time to care for the living."

For the dead were beyond hope, beyond help. For the third time in her life, Teddy experienced the terrible, irrational guilt of a survivor.

Chapter Five

From the outside, her isolated house in the country looked like an unremarkable two story with a sloping roof and dormer windows. Inside, it was pure Teddy. Soft, Vince thought, and comfortable, with her subtle sense of humor evident in the mushroom footstools and the coatrack shaped like a cactus with extended green arms. The rare beauty of a handwoven Tibetan rug in shades of teal-and-gray set the color theme for chairs and sofa. The walls covered with photographs bespoke a varied life experience.

Taken altogether, the living room showed the confidence of a woman who was comfortable with herself, and when Teddy stepped inside her home, she seemed to draw strength from her surroundings. She went immediately to a round-back chair beside a halogen lamp, kicked off her shoes and tucked her feet under her. "I want my tea, Vince." Her lips curved in an ironic grimace. "That's what I need. Lots of tea, oceans of tea, to calm me down."

"Okay, Teddy. Sure."

After the long ride home during which she hardly spoke a word, her voice sounded unnaturally calm. "I must sit and drink my grieving herbal tea. Not coffee,

because caffeine will keep me awake and I need my rest."
She looked up at him. "Don't worry, Vince. I'll be fine.
I won't fall apart."

He wasn't so sure about that. "Why not?"

"Because I did that before."

"When was that?"

"Another time. Another place." Sharply she demanded, "Are you going to fix the tea or not?"

"Let's get something straight." He braced his arms on
the chair and stood over her, completely surrounding her
so she couldn't escape and couldn't look anywhere but at
him. "I don't take orders, Teddy."

"I'm sorry. That was rude of me."

"Yeah." He stood upright and dragged his hand
through his hair. God, it had been a long day. "I'm not
the soul of politeness myself. I'm not much good at consoling people."

It was her turn to ask. "Why not?"

"You know how it is. Before I was a managing editor,
I was a journalist. I couldn't get involved in the problems of the people I was covering. That's how it is. You
observe, you write the story, you go home and try to get
a good night's sleep."

He headed in the direction he thought would lead to
the kitchen and turned on the light. His last assignment
as a correspondent had been in the Persian Gulf, where
he'd seen the devastation of cities and the aching tragedy of human loss. Mothers who lost their children.
Wives who held their dying husbands.

He hadn't been able to comfort them, either.

He found the silvery teakettle, filled it with water and
placed it on the burner. When he returned to the front
room, he asked, "Where should I put your cameras and
film?"

"Darkroom. It's across the front hall. In back of the dining room." She rose suddenly. "I'll do it."

"It's okay. I'll take care of it."

"Oh sure, and you'll also take a look at all the photos I have in there. You'll check out my progress on several stories." She took the cameras from him. "I haven't decided to work for *Files,* Vince. Not yet."

He deserved her mistrust, Vince thought, remembering the Elvis photos.

She continued, "There's something I've been wondering about, Vince. The very first time you saw me, you assumed I was going out on an Elvis story. And you've taken an unusual interest in my Elvis informant."

He shrugged. "Elvis is hot news for a tabloid."

"If you're looking for an Elvis expert, there are a lot of other photographers, especially in Memphis near Graceland, who know more about him than I do." She sat up straighter in her chair. "Tell me the truth, Vince. Why do you associate me with Elvis?"

He sank to the center of the sofa and leaned forward. "The truth?"

"You claim to be a journalist. You should know something about the truth."

Sooner or later he would be forced to tell her. Might as well be now. "I've seen the pictures, Teddy. Four photos of a guy who looks like he was born to sing 'Hound Dog.' They were sent to our offices in an envelope without a return address. The postmark was Westalia. Your name and address were stamped on the back of each picture."

"Why didn't you call me?"

"There was also a note. Typed. It said that you didn't know these pictures had been sent, and the sender would contact us later with more information."

"Somebody stole photos from my files? I can't believe it. I work alone. I don't know who—"

"Come on, Teddy. Even when you do remember to lock up, you leave the key under the mat. Anybody could come in here."

"Now I understand why you're so interested in me."

The accusing expression in her eyes shot right to his heart. He reminded her, "You wanted the truth."

She swallowed hard. "All this time you've been after a story. That was the reason you lied about being engaged to me."

"You're wrong about that, Teddy."

"Did you really think I was that desperate? Did you think I was a pathetic old maid who you could sweet-talk into trusting you? Did you think you could—"

"If I'd planned to seduce you, you would have been in my bed last night."

While the teakettle whistled in the kitchen, he watched her stride across the room. Her full-cut slacks, belted at her slender waist, showed the flare of her hips and buttocks. She sure didn't look like a desperate old maid as she bent down to scoop the camera bags off the floor and proceeded across the front hallway into a dining room. He heard the decisive slam of a door.

Vince went to the kitchen and removed the teakettle from the burner. He'd blown it. He might as well leave right now and continue negotiations with Teddy via telephone and fax—not that she'd ever work for him now.

Did he care? Hell, yes. He wanted Teddy Edwards on his staff. But he wanted more than that. He hadn't been thinking of *Files* when he'd kissed her. He wasn't acting as a managing editor when she'd been in shock and he'd shielded her from the sheriff's heartless interrogation. When they'd danced at the party and he'd felt the supple movement of her body against his, Vince had been responding like a man, not an editor.

He circled the house and found a closed door at the rear of the small dining room. Without knocking, he opened it and stepped inside. Teddy was perched on a high stool beside a clean white countertop. Her unzipped camera bags lay on the floor at her feet. Several rolls of film were strewn in front of her. "You're not welcome in here, Vince. My darkroom is private."

The only way he'd leave was if she physically ejected him. Vince meant to have his say. "Teddy, I want you to work as a correspondent at *Files*. And I promise the highest bid on your Elvis-sighting story." He cleared his throat. "But that's not why I'm still here."

She refused to look at him. "You don't have to stay here tonight. You're free to go."

"I'll stay."

"There's no reason to. People are going to talk whether you're here or at the Sleep Inn." Her expression darkened when she mentioned the hotel where her sister had died, but she rallied immediately. "There aren't many people in Westalia who approve of anything I do."

"I've noticed," he said. "Why is that, Teddy?"

"Because I'm different." She shrugged her shoulders. "There's no deep dark secret in my past, except that I fought with my father. When he wanted me to be a good little girl and work for him, I said no. I wanted to take my own pictures and find my own stories, but he didn't want me to have that kind of independence."

"Talent is threatening for an editor," Vince said. "Star reporters and photographers can be a difficult breed to handle."

"So why do you want me?"

"You're worth the trouble." Teddy Edwards represented the most difficult, delicate negotiation of his life. He'd rather face a screaming roomful of union officials from the Newspaper Guild. "My offer stands. You know that, don't you?"

"Yes."

"Good. Because there's something else you need to understand." He paused. They were dealing with emotions here, not facts. And that was always uncomfortable for him. "I care about you, Teddy."

She gave a disbelieving scoff, but her gently accented voice remained as soft as a moist breeze off the Big Muddy. "I don't believe you care, Vince. Not any more than I believe you really are my fiancé."

"The truth," he said, "is that I can think of worse things than being your fiancé." Startled, she stared across the room. "Hey, I'm not proposing marriage," he said quickly. "I'm offering to stay and give you a hand. You're going to need someone with investigative skills, and I was a damn good reporter once. Spent four years on a crime beat. I want to help."

"Why?"

"Maybe because I miss the excitement. Maybe because I'm intrigued." Those reasons fudged the truth, and Vince was determined to be honest. "It's because I like you, Teddy, and I don't want to think of you going through this alone."

She assessed his offer and said, "Thank you, Vince. I'd appreciate your help. But don't even think about coming into this darkroom again without my permission."

"Agreed." He extended his arm for a businesslike handshake, but when he felt her small, soft hand in his, Vince knew that it was going to be a trial to keep his mind on business.

"So," she said, "this is my darkroom. How much do you know about processing film and developing photos?"

He glanced around the large, clean space. "Enough to know that you've got some fancy equipment here."

"Over there is the wet side." She pointed to the wall that bordered the kitchen. "I have a color-film processor in that lighttight booth. Then there's the developer, stop bath and fixer for black and white." Proudly she indicated another area that bordered the rear wall. "Here's the dry side with two enlargers. One for black and white, one for color. And my paper supplies."

Vince glanced toward the other two walls of the room. The space was filled with mat white cabinets. "And this?"

"This is where you are forbidden to go." She opened a cabinet front to reveal a series of small drawers. "Here's where I store negatives and slides." On the wall nearest the door, she flipped open another cabinet front. "Here are finished photos." Frowning, she pulled out a manila folder and rifled the contents. She tossed the black-and-white pictures of the man who looked like Elvis on the countertop beside Vince. "I had three sets in here. Now there are only two."

"What about the negatives?"

She picked through the shelves which were not, as far as Vince could tell, labeled in any sensible order. Teddy easily located a drawer, removed a glassine envelope, took out the negatives and held them to the light. "Nope. These are still here."

"So whoever took the photos sent them only to *Files*."

"An obvious choice," she said. "You run an Elvis Sighting Hot Line at least twice a year."

"True. The King always boosts our readership."

She returned to her stool. "Okay, Vince. You've had the grand tour. Now I need to get organized. I've got all those photos of the party to process into negatives. Six rolls of color and two of black and white. That's almost three hundred exposures. I need to get them into proof sheets so Whitney can decide which ones..." Her voice trailed off. Whitney was gone. The realization stung like a sharp slap in the face, and Teddy stiffened. "Aunt Harriet will have to decide, won't she?"

"Or Russel."

"No," she said decisively. "Russel wouldn't know what Whitney wanted. They weren't getting along."

"Worse than most married couples?"

"I think so." She crossed the room, went into the booth and turned on the color processor to let it warm up. "Before the party, Whitney told me—" Her words halted as she remembered her sister, twirling in front of the mirror. "She was planning to have an affair to make Russel jealous."

Gently Vince nudged her memory. "Did she mention any names?"

"Merle Chatworth for one. And Tom. Damn him." A dark, sordid picture formed in Teddy's mind. She could almost see Whitney in her lovely silk dress and her jewelry. Teddy could easily imagine her sister laughing and dancing down the sidewalk to Tom's motel room. "That must have been why she was at the Sleep Inn. She went there to meet Tom."

"What do you think she told Russel?"

"Some excuse." Teddy frowned, remembering her impression that Russel was lying when he gave the reason Whitney left. "Or maybe they had a fight. Oh, Vince, it'd be just terrible if the last time Russel saw her, they'd argued." She shuddered, imagining how Russel must be feeling right now, lying in bed, feeling the impression of the place where Whitney had rested beside him. He would be alone tonight and forevermore. "I'm glad you're here, Vince. I'm glad for the company."

"I'll stay as long as you want me." Though he'd met her only twenty-four hours ago, Vince felt like he'd known Teddy Edwards all his life . . . or maybe in a past life. He grinned, thinking of Connie.

"Why are you smiling?" Teddy asked.

"Do you believe in fate?"

"Kind of." Her thoughts shifted away from Whitney, and Teddy breathed more easily. "Fate, huh? Well, if I'm feeling real lucky, I do sometimes believe that something like fate has led me to my good fortune. Like with those Elvis photos."

He nodded encouragingly.

"But, Vince, I'm not going to tell you about that meeting. There's really nothing to tell. I didn't get enough information to make a story."

He noticed a subtle shift in her manner, a relief from the burden of her sister's murder, and he encouraged her to think of other things. "Consider fate and Elvis," he said musingly. "Is that why he became a megastar? Was that his fate?"

"Partly," she conceded. "But it was talent, too. He put his whole heart and soul into his performances. I never did see one of his live shows, but I've watched the videos." She sighed. "He was incredible."

"You think he was sexy?"

"You bet! Wearing that black leather? With his raven black hair, and those heavy-lidded blue eyes? He was more than sexy. He was combustible."

"A hunk of burning love?"

"He was the King. Larger than life, and I guess that's why he'll never die. People don't want to lose that excitement."

"And you? Do you believe he's still alive?"

"I'd like to. The man might be declared dead and buried at Graceland, but there's a part of me that doesn't believe it. I want to wake up one morning and read that Elvis staged his own death to escape the intensity of his fame. Or that he's been working on an underground scheme to foil the bad guys of the world, just like in his movies. I want to believe in magic."

"You're not alone," Vince said. "Thousands of our readers feel the same way."

"What about you? Do you believe in fate?"

"No. I believe in logic. In cause and effect."

"Then why?" Fast as quicksilver, her mood changed. Her fingers tightened into fists. "Why did Whitney die?"

"She was murdered, Teddy. There's a motive and a method and a killer."

"But none of those things mean she had to die. She could have escaped. Or been rescued. If I'd stayed with her, Vince, maybe she'd still be alive."

"Or maybe you'd be dead along with her."

"No, that's not my fate." Teddy knew this clearly. "I'm meant to always stand by while the people around me, the beloved people in my life, are killed by viruses and cancers and stray bullets. When Jacques died, it could just as easily have been me. The poacher never took aim. He fired into the brush and we started running. We made it to the Jeep and I had photos of that bastard, standing over his kill, a silverback gorilla. I didn't know until I started driving that Jacques had been hit. Only a flesh wound, he said."

Abruptly she stopped talking. Teddy had never spoken of Jacques's death before, except to the authorities in Africa. She'd given them the photograph of the killer. But there had never been an arrest.

"Jacques Aubouchon," Vince said. "He was a great journalist."

"He was my partner." And the only man she'd ever truly loved. Though they were together for almost three years, they did not choose to be married. Jacques was twenty years her senior, and he had insisted that someday she would find a man who was closer to her own age, someone who wanted children and a home. Jacques never comprehended that love was enough for her. All she had wanted was to be with him day and night for the rest of her life. "When he died . . . I wanted to die, too."

Her heart was breaking all over again. Why, damn it, why? Could she blame fate?

Clumsily she gathered up the rolls of color film. "You'll have to step outside, Vince. I need total darkness to unload the color film into the processor."

"I thought your booth was lighttight?"

"Yes. But I don't like to take chances with the negatives."

"When you come out, you're going to have that tea, then go to bed."

She didn't argue.

He closed the door, and she went into the booth, checked all the settings and lined up the film. The routine should have soothed her, but when Teddy turned off the lights, the blackness resonated with memories, specters of grief. Her fingers trembled as she pried open the cassettes and guided the film onto the rollers.

The first cassette, thirty-six color exposures, fed in smoothly. *Don't make a mistake. These are the last pic-*

tures of Whitney. In the years to come, the photographs would be a comfort. But now? A fresh pain stabbed her heart. She couldn't stand it. Not again. The hellish depths of grief were all too familiar. She'd been there when her mother died, when Jacques was killed... and now, Whitney.

The second and third rolls went smoothly into the machine. Pretty pictures. From this darkness Teddy would conjure bright memories of Whitney dancing, laughing. Her gold jewelry would shimmer forever in a photograph. In the total inky dark, time stood still. Her color processor was fast and reliable. It took less than five minutes per roll to feed, but each second was a trial. She didn't want to be alone.

When she finished with the last roll, the barricades she'd erected to control her emotions finally crumbled. A single drop spilled from her eye and traced an indelible path down her cheek, a trail that would be marked by endless tears. She blinked to stop the flow. No, she couldn't start crying. She mustn't. There was too much pain, too damn much sorrow.

Stumbling from the booth, she reached for the light switch, then allowed her hand to drop to her side. She never wanted to see again, wished to be blinded by tears. A pained cry tore from her throat. She stood in the darkness, disoriented.

"Teddy? Are you all right?" Vince was at the door. "Can I come in?"

She fought for control, and forced her voice to be calm. "You can come in. The film is all fed in. It doesn't have to be dark now."

He entered, and turned on the lights. Squinting at the glare, she shielded her eyes with her hands. But her arms were so awfully heavy. Vince was beside her, holding her.

He didn't patronize her with easy words of sympathy. Instead he pulled her against him, entwined his hand with hers and squeezed hard, infusing his will into her.

"I'm sorry." She couldn't see him through her tears. "I loved her. I did. I never told her how much."

"I know," he said.

And she believed that he did. He knew her.

Harsh sobs rattled through her body, drawn from the aching depths of her own regret. Vince made no comment or demand; he simply accepted her. Nobody had done that before. When her mother died, people told her to be brave for her sister and her father. And she had tried. Constantly she tried to be a good girl. But she couldn't be. She angered her father, annoyed her sister. She was never good enough to please the angels.

She'd tried to run away. But misery had found her again. In Africa.

At the moment of Jacques's death, she had been a woman alone, confused and heartbroken. Terribly alone. She'd left his remains to be dealt with by the head of the news agency they had both worked for. Then Teddy had returned to their small encampment in the high mountain plains. She had stayed on her cot in her tent, waiting for a kindly fate to kill her, too. Though she succeeded in becoming deathly ill, she had survived.

All of the sorrow flooded back over her, stealing her breath, breaking her heart. She gave up the fight, allowing the years of silent grief to wash over her. Never had she wept like this before. Never had she poured out her soul in tears. She stood against Vince, sobbing, until her body felt limp and utterly empty. Her knees buckled and she sank to the floor. Then she sobbed even more.

She felt him lifting her, holding her against his chest. At the darkroom door, he paused. She heard him turn the key in the lock. "What are you doing?"

"Basic security," he said. "That's something you're going to start doing."

He carried her upstairs and placed her on the bed, where she curled into a fetal position and whimpered weakly. "I never had my tea."

"It's okay, Teddy."

"If I'd had my tea, I would have been fine."

"You're still fine. It's all right."

She didn't want him to leave her, and he must have understood because he stayed by her bed, stroking her back, holding her hand, until she felt consciousness fading. Sleep, blessed sleep, would not heal all wounds, but it would provide respite from conscious pain.

Vince saw her eyelids flutter closed and felt her body begin to relax. Her breathing became steady and sonorous. Teddy was asleep.

He smoothed back the strands of damp hair from her forehead. Her face, though swollen from crying, was lovely in repose, and he wished he could ease the pain that tortured her sensitive heart. Now he was better able to understand why a woman who had built an international reputation had decided to bury herself in the stifling small-town atmosphere of Westalia.

After the death of Jacques Aubouchon, it seemed that Teddy had lost her taste for living, much less for pursuing the adventures of an international career. And so she returned to her roots to find solace. Instead she was battered by provincial hostilities as well as Aunt Harriet pestering her about getting married and settling down. And her father? Vince had disliked Jordan Edwards at first sight.

Why did Teddy stay here?

Vince looked at her, curled up on her bed and sleeping. Much like Teddy, he had no earthly reason to remain in Westalia. He could finish their business transactions on the phone, and send a field reporter to follow up on the Elvis story. And yet Vince knew he would stay. He'd promised. For as long as she needed him, he would be here for her.

He stretched out on the bed beside her. If she wakened in the night and was frightened, he would offer the comfort she needed.

Hours later, he felt her gaze. His eyelids opened, and he saw Teddy's luminous blue eyes watching him. "You're still here," she said.

"I didn't want to leave you alone." Vince propped himself up on his elbow and squinted through the dark at her bedside clock. It was seventeen minutes past three. "How are you feeling, Teddy?"

"Sad. Confused. I keep smelling roses. Dead pink roses."

Reaching toward her to feel her forehead, his hand brushed through the chaos of honey blond curls that spilled across the pillows. Her hair was silken, enticing, but Vince did not allow his fingers to dwell. He felt her head, relieved to find that she was neither feverish nor chilled. Her temperature seemed normal.

Nothing else about her was . . . normal. She was an extraordinary woman, someone he enjoyed waking up beside. He was aware of the lingering fragrance of her perfume, faint now after the rigors of this day.

Her fingers dallied over the front of his shirt, lightly playing across his chest. "I've missed this. Being in bed with a man. It's been a long time."

When she unfastened the first button of his shirt, Vince experienced a duality of emotion. Making love to Teddy would give him tremendous satisfaction—of that he was sure. This morning when he kissed her, he tasted passions that ran deep, intense and erotic. Oh, God, yes, he wanted to kiss her again and again, to hear her moan with passion, to feel her come alive in his arms. But not now. Not like this. He knew enough about women to know that this wasn't the right time. Later she'd think he'd taken advantage of her. Gently he disentangled her hand. "No, Teddy."

With a quiet sigh, she snuggled into the crook of his arm, and he lay back, holding her. As she rested her head against his chest the sound of his heartbeat, steady and strong, reassured her. Life went on. Every sunrise brought new deaths and births in an eternal cycle as unchanging as the seasons. And she had no control over any of it. She could only accept. And hope.

Teddy realized that, in a way, her bout of weeping had cleansed her. Now the instinct for survival rose triumphantly within her. She would need to be strong in the coming days, to deal with her family, to accept Whitney's death. "Vince? Do you think it was Tom who killed her?"

"I don't know."

"Had to be. She was in his room. They must have been planning to meet there."

"Don't think about it, Teddy. Go back to sleep."

But she was completely awake. Her body surged with a tension that she remembered from long ago. With Jacques. A churning stimulation sent ripples through her muscles and teased the tips of her breasts as she pressed herself against Vince's hard masculine chest. He was so much bigger than she, so much stronger. For a moment, she was tempted to give her problems to him, to let herself be protected and taken care of.

As she glided her legs close to him, thigh to thigh, she felt the hardness of his arousal, and it excited her. More than ever before in her life, Teddy needed loving. "Vince." Her eyelids closed. "Kiss me."

He wanted to respond. Badly. But she was still fragile. He couldn't risk hurting her. "You need sleep, Teddy."

"I need you, Vince. Right now."

He shifted his legs away from hers and sat up on the edge of the bed. Though he didn't want to leave her alone, he couldn't stay in bed beside her. Vince stood. He turned on the bedside lamp, bathing the cozy room in a golden glow. "I'll sit over here," he said. "In this rocking chair."

Her hand caught his, and he turned toward her. Teddy rose to her knees on the bed. Her eyes smoldered with unmistakable sexual heat. "Don't leave me, Vince. I need you."

Trailing her fingers down her throat, she undid the buttons on her blouse and pushed the material aside, revealing a lacy white bra. There was nothing subtle in her seduction. Her actions demanded, challenged, insisted that he give her the satisfaction that a man can give a woman. His resolution to dissuade her was fading fast.

Teddy released his hand, then slipped her blouse off her shoulders and discarded it. She needed loving, the most perfect affirmation of life. Quickly she slipped off her belt, wriggled her slacks and panties off in one movement, and unhooked her bra. She was naked.

Gracefully she climbed off the bed and approached him. A heat radiated from deep within her. The urge to make love consumed her. She coiled her arms around his neck and kissed him with a ferocious, primal passion.

Her tongue probed the interior of his mouth, stimulating him. And when she felt him move against her, she knew the battle had been won.

"Teddy." His breath came in hoarse gasps. "I can't resist you."

"Then don't."

With unleashed strength, he crushed her slender body against his. His mouth hungrily bruised her lips, and they collapsed together on the disheveled sheets. Every movement of her silken body against his aroused him more intensely. He struggled to hold back his own pleasure.

She tore at his clothing, needing to feel the rough male texture of his chest hair, a thick patch of shining black that arrowed down his muscled torso. She groaned with pleasure as he stroked her body, fondled her breasts. Even before he entered her, she could feel herself rising to the verge of trembling orgasm. And when he thrust hard into her damp, waiting flesh, she cried out. Each stroke, each pulsating throb drove her higher and higher until she thought she would die from sheer ecstasy.

And then it was over. She was as limp as a newborn kitten, freed from sorrow and grief and emotion. Fulfilled.

She felt Vince's body go tense beside her.

He whispered, "Did you hear that?"

Dazed, she shook her head.

"Did we lock the doors, Teddy?"

"I don't know."

From downstairs, she heard the scrape of a chair against the hardwood floor and the unmistakable shuffle of footsteps near the front door.

Chapter Six

Silently, Vince left her bed. Through glazed eyes she watched as he moved with strength and purpose. His back muscles flexed as he reached down to pull on his trousers. Then he stood erect in the moonlight. His body looked powerful, strong and dangerous.

Teddy's sensation of perfect well-being after making love evaporated. What if something happened to him? She couldn't bear it. She couldn't stand to lose one more person in her life. "Vince," she called to him, frightened. "Vince, no. Come back here."

When he turned toward her, his eyes reflected a hard, silver gray light. He placed a finger across his lips in a gesture for silence.

She tugged at the pale flowered sheets and covered her breasts. Too much was happening too fast, and her mind didn't seem to be functioning with its usual alacrity. She was only certain that she didn't want Vince to risk his life by going downstairs to confront an intruder. "Please stay here," she begged. "Don't leave me."

"Call 911. When I leave, lock the bedroom door."

"But there's no lock."

"That figures." He kept his voice low, hoping the person below wouldn't hear them. The timing of this break-in was far too coincidental to be random. It had to be connected with Whitney's murder. "Call 911 and hide."

"Where? Hide where?" Tangled in sheets, she got out of bed. "I'm going downstairs with you."

He didn't take time to argue. He could only hope that by the time she got dressed, he'd have the situation under control. "If you want to help, stay here. Call the police."

Moving as silently as possible, he crossed the bedroom in his bare feet. In the hall he stayed close to the wall to avoid becoming a clear silhouette in the moonlight, an easy target. At the top of the stairs, he stood and listened. He heard a small scratching sound coming from the dining room to the left of the front door. The darkroom, he thought. That explained the break-in. This person wanted something from the darkroom, which had, ironically, the only locked door in Teddy's house. At least Vince had done that right. The darkroom key nestled safe in his trouser pocket.

In the stillness of the house, Vince doubted that he could make it all the way down the stairs without alerting the intruder, but he had to try. Staying near the wall where the floorboards would be least likely to creak, he went down one stair. Then another.

One factor in Vince's favor was the layout of the house. The darkroom had only one door, leading into the dining room. The intruder would have to come past the front stairs to get out of the house. And then Vince would have him.

Teddy appeared at the top of the staircase, wraithlike in a white nightshirt, with her slender legs exposed. She'd taken the time to slip on a pair of loafers. He gestured her back, but she stubbornly shook her head.

He sighed, leaning slightly backward. His shoulder brushed the wall and caused one of the framed photographs hanging there to fall from its place. The glass shattered. Immediately a corresponding noise resounded from the rear of the dining room. The crash of a window breaking. The sound of someone escaping.

"Damn." Vince charged down the stairs, no longer mindful of silence. He flew around the corner of the stairs and into the dining room. The intruder had already fled. A chair from the dining table lay on its side by a broken casement window. Vince dashed toward the front door. Teddy was right behind him. "Stay here," he yelled.

"Not unless you stay with me."

Outside, Vince leapt down the two stairs of her porch in a single bound and ran to the left side of the house, past the broken window. In the light of a waning moon, he saw a dark figure not more than twenty yards away, heading toward the thicket of trees by the brook. If the intruder made it into the forest, there would be no way to catch him. Not at night.

Even in bare feet, Vince was gaining on him. Running hard, he closed the gap, coming near enough to see a black shirt and black cap. The intruder halted, pivoted, braced his arms and aimed. He had a gun. The moonlight gleamed blue on the barrel. My God, where was Teddy?

He turned and saw her racing up behind him. "Down!" He dived toward her, pulling her to the cold, wet ground as she shouted a protest. The sharp retort of gunfire cracked the night. He held her down. They were both breathing heavily. "Damn it, Teddy." He pulled himself up into a crouch. "Stay here. Stay down."

"What are you going to do?"

"I'm going to get that son of a—"

"Oh no, you're not." She panted. "If you're dumb enough to chase an armed man, I'm dumb enough to follow." Vince rose higher, peered into the darkness of the woods near the brook. "Let him go," Teddy said. "He's not worth dying for."

"He's gone."

There was no sign of movement except for the rustle of wind in the tree branches. Their intruder had disappeared into the forest. Still, Vince exercised protective caution, guiding Teddy to her feet and warning her to bend low as they ran back to the house.

In the kitchen, he flicked on the light. The bottom half of the windows had small wood shutters. No one could get a clear shot unless they were standing on the porch. And he didn't figure that would happen. If the intruder had meant to harm them, there had been plenty of opportunity. They could have been killed in the bedroom before they were aware that someone had broken into the house. They could have been shot when they ran down the stairs. Whoever had broken in had been after something else, possibly something connected with Whitney's murder.

"Vince, you have to sit down."

"Why?" He felt like pacing, like breaking something. He wanted to charge into the forest and hunt this person down. "Why should I sit?"

"Because you're bleeding all over the floor."

He looked down and saw smears of blood in his footprints. "I must have stepped on something. Damn it, if I'd been wearing shoes, I probably could have caught that guy. Do you have a gun, Teddy?"

"No, of course not. I don't like—"

"Of course not," he said bitterly. "And I don't, either. I didn't bring my revolver with me."

"How could you be carrying a gun?" She directed him to a chair and pushed him down onto it. "You can't take weapons on an airplane."

"I flew my own plane."

"You can fly?"

She looked at him with wide-eyed wonderment, as if he'd sprouted wings. "It's not like walking on water, Teddy. Flying a plane isn't even as hard as driving a car."

"Would you teach me how?"

"It would take months." And Vince didn't have months to spare. Time lines and schedules flashed through his mind. Normally he was a busy man with a weekly tabloid to manage. He had a subscription slowdown to overcome. Promotions to run. Deadlines to meet.

Somehow, none of this seemed important anymore.

"Then it can't be that easy," she said.

"What?"

"Flying an airplane can't be that easy if it takes months to learn."

Calmly she went to the sink, filled a pan with warm water, and tended to the cut on his foot. "You're amazing," he said.

"Actually I'm not very good at nursing. I've taken CPR classes and basic first aid, but I'm clumsy."

"Teddy, somebody just broke into your house and shot at you. How can you chat about CPR and airplanes?"

Teddy shrugged. Amazing? Not her. She certainly wasn't more courageous than other people. In fact, she might be a greater coward because she chose to put her fear aside to think about later. Tonight, she might dream of shadowy figures. Tomorrow, she might hear the backfire of a car and break into a cold sweat. But for now, she closed her mind. "I'm glad neither of us was hurt."

"What kind of life have you led, Teddy? How did you get to be so brave?"

"I'm not." If she allowed herself to think about what had happened, she might cry again. She might run and hide in a closet and never come out. "Please, Vince. Let's talk about airplanes."

He didn't understand her, not at all. "Airplanes," he repeated. "Are you sure you're all right?"

"I'm fine. Tell me about flying."

"You can learn the basics in one afternoon. But it takes months to be certified as a pilot. And a lifetime to prepare for all the little problems that can occur." He grinned. "You'd probably make a terrific pilot. You don't panic."

It was easy to imagine Teddy beside him in the cockpit of his single-engine Cessna. Her intelligent blue eyes would sparkle with excitement. Her long hair would tangle in the earphones.

"Ouch." He pulled his foot away from her.

"You must have stepped on a shard of glass from the window." She placed his foot back in the water and stood. "I'll get some ointment and bandages."

"It's only a cut, Teddy."

"Until it's infected and gets gangrene." She went into the bathroom beside the kitchen. "Months, huh? I'd love to learn how to fly."

Though she wasn't asking him to make that commitment, Vince realized that he was all too willing to take her back to Chicago with him and teach her to fly his airplane. Having Teddy in his life on a semipermanent basis was not an unpleasant prospect. But he didn't say any of those things. When she returned with a bottle of disinfectant and a handful of bandages, he suggested, "Let's get this place cleaned up before the sheriff gets here, okay?"

"The sheriff?"

"You did call 911, didn't you?"

"I didn't have time, Vince. I couldn't put on a shirt, follow you and use the telephone all at once."

He groaned. "You couldn't pick up the phone and punch three numbers?"

When she drew herself up to retort, she looked so damned cute that he would have forgiven her anything. The tail of her nightshirt skimmed the tops of her slender thighs. The front was soiled where he'd pushed her to the ground and her chin, also dirty, jutted sharply. "I'll handle this my way, Vince. This is my life. My hometown. And if anything happens here, it's my story. You got that?"

"I'm not after a story. We don't do break-ins and local news stories at *Files.*"

"Not even when they're related to Elvis?"

He blinked in astonishment. "How?"

"You've got to be thinking along the same lines as I am. The person who keeps calling and telling me they saw Elvis is the same individual who must have known about the murder. Might even be the killer."

The murder? How could she have referred to her sister's death as *the murder?* It was *Whitney's* death. Her sister. Was she so distanced from the event? The calm she felt inside was almost frightening. As if she were detached and floating away from the whole scene. She needed grounding, needed this man to hold her, to bring her down to earth. "Vince?"

"I'm right here, Teddy."

She wasn't going to cry again. "Never mind."

When she looked at him, she could see that his gaze had turned inward as he considered the Elvis aspect of the story. She could almost see the headlines flashing across his brain: Elvis Witnesses Crime. Elvis Guides Police Investigation. Elvis Goes Undercover.

Had she really made love to this man? Clearly she couldn't begin to consider all that had happened this day without going stark raving mad.

She concentrated on treating his wound, daubed on the ointment and applied a bandage. Then she stood. "I'm going to take a shower and go to bed," she said. "Tomorrow is early enough to call the sheriff."

"Suit yourself."

"What's that supposed to mean?"

He hobbled over to the phone on the kitchen wall and lifted the receiver. "I tend to be fairly unforgiving when somebody shoots at me. But maybe that's just my own big-city hostility."

"Don't call 911. We'll end up with ambulances and police cars all over my front yard." She picked up a thick leather-bound book lying beside a standard telephone directory, flipped to a number and handed the book to Vince. "This is a direct line to the local police station. And if you don't get an answer there, look under Graham, Sheriff Jake."

Without looking back, she marched up the stairs, went into the bathroom, and proceeded to indulge herself in a long shower that used up every drop from the hot-water heater. She slipped on a clean nightshirt and crawled into bed, rearranging the light quilt and flowered sheets that smelled like Vince and passion. Guiltily Teddy savored the fragrance, closed her eyes and slept.

When the morning sunlight shone full through her dormer window at eight o'clock, she wakened with a start. The nightmare she'd been having was forgotten as soon as she opened her eyes. Vince lay beside her on the bed. "Oh, my God." Memories flooded back, and Teddy covered her eyes with her hands. Last night. "Oh no."

Last night, she had wept. She had mourned. Last night, there had been danger in her home. An armed intruder had crept inside as stealthy as a shadow. She remembered the snap of gunfire, the feel of cold earth as Vince threw her to the ground. Last night . . . she'd torn off her clothing and demanded that Vince Harding, the managing editor of an international publication, make love to her.

"Oh, my God." Teddy peeked through her fingers at his masculine features. His dark brown hair fell boyishly across his forehead. Though it was still only spring, his complexion was tanned. A dark stubble roughened his jaw. He was amazingly handsome, she thought. Though she was thoroughly ashamed of her unbridled desire, Teddy didn't regret their lovemaking. Last night had been wonderful, fulfilling a need she wasn't aware of. Vince was a skillful, talented, inspired lover.

But now, it was morning. In the harsh light of day, Teddy could not delude herself into believing that last night's passion meant anything. It was but a moment, a temporary fulfillment. It was not love.

Lazily, Vince opened his eyes—a soft morning gray in color—and smiled at her.

"I won't apologize," she said.

"Okay."

"It's as much your fault as mine, anyway. With all your talk about being engaged and staying the night at my house. In any case, what happened just, well, you know, it just kind of happened.''

"Teddy, what are you—"

"You know what I'm talking about."

He closed his eyes. "That's scary."

"What?"

"I almost understand you."

She left him in her bed and went to brush her teeth, splash water on her face and run a comb through the tangle of her hair. The night's sleep had renewed her energies, and Teddy was ready to take action. Cracking open the bathroom door while struggling to bring some semblance of order to her hair, she called out to Vince, "Did you call Sheriff Graham last night?"

"Yes."

She poked her head into the bedroom. "And?"

"He asked if we were all right and if anything was missing. I said no, not as far as I could tell. He said our intruder would wait until morning."

Teddy had expected as much. Sheriff Graham wasn't exactly a member of the Mary Theodora Edwards Fan Club, not since she'd followed him around for a couple of days when she was in high school in the hopes of understanding the business of law enforcement. Instead, she uncovered the secret of his girlfriend, a secret she never revealed to anyone but Jake Graham himself. Understandably, he was not terribly fond of Teddy and her snooping.

Most likely, if the sheriff heard a psychotic mass murderer was on his way to Teddy's house, he'd be obliged to respond. But anything less wasn't going to get a rise from him.

She returned to her bedroom, gathered up fresh underwear, a pair of jeans and a blue cotton shirt. Then she went back to the bathroom to change. After last night's intimacy with Vince, it seemed ridiculously prudish to worry about showing a glimpse of her thigh, but she wanted to avoid a repeat performance of last night. Or did she?

With her hair in a ponytail, she tucked her blouse into her full-cut jeans and returned to the bedroom where Vince had propped pillows against the headboard and was sitting up. Her pastel flower-patterned sheets covered the lower half of his body, but his chest was disturbingly bare. Her fingertips tingled with remembered sensations of gliding her hands through his chest hair.

She liked the way he looked in the morning. A little rumpled. More calm. It was as if sleep had emptied the tension from him. "Did you rest well?"

"If you don't count the break-in and being shot at, it was a perfect night." Before she could remark, he continued, "I did a little checking around last night, and there were scratches on the darkroom door lock."

"Makes sense. I keep a lot of expensive equipment in there. It's the first thing a thief would go for."

"A thief? Come on, Teddy. Your break-in last night must be related to the pictures you took yesterday."

"I guess it had to be," she said with heavy reluctance. "Otherwise it's too much of a coincidence."

"Your intruder was after negatives or photographs. And he's somebody who knows you well enough to know where your darkroom is located. How many people have been to your house?"

"Not very many." Teddy didn't encourage a stream of visitors, and her house was situated inconveniently for casual dropping by.

"How about Tom Burke? Has he ever been here?"

"Not on a bet."

Though Teddy was a morning person who was alert within minutes of waking, this was complicated thinking—extra complicated because she couldn't keep her mind off sex. Even if she didn't look at him, the sound of his voice seemed to set off vibrations within her. She walked across the room to sit in a rocking chair, putting distance between them.

"Let me get this straight, Vince. Are you saying that the person who broke into my house is the same person who killed my..." Teddy swallowed hard, trying to think of Whitney's death as a case to be investigated and photographed. But that was impossible. It was too soon.

"I'm saying it's likely. There must be a clue in the photographs, some piece of evidence."

"Like what? It was just a party."

"What else could the intruder have been after? Are there other stories you're working on? Any other rolls of film that need to be processed?"

Teddy concentrated for a moment. She seldom left undeveloped film lying around because the task of sorting and filing became overwhelming if she allowed herself to fall behind. "Some random shots. A sweet birthday party for hundred-year-old twins. A turtle race in Murphysboro. A couple of bogus Elvis-sighting pictures near PJ's Bar." A chill slithered down her spine as she flashed on the moment she and Vince had discovered her sister's body. "Those pictures I snapped in the motel room."

"Right," he interrupted before the remembrance had fully formed in her mind. "Last night, at the Sleep Inn, I told the sheriff about those photos."

"Which means that everybody in eight counties knows about them. Even Tom. Who doesn't, however, know where to find your darkroom."

"How hard could it be to figure out? This house isn't exactly Tara-size. You could guess which room is the darkroom by taking a good look at the outside of the house because I've got the window blacked out. If somebody came lurking in here and found a locked door—"

"That must have surprised them." He indulged in a smug chuckle, imagining the intruder's surprise at encountering a lock. "I would assume that your habit of not locking up is fairly well-known."

"And what does that have to do with anything?"

"The guy was prepared well enough to bring a gun. But had no tools for breaking into a locked room."

"Therefore," she concluded, "he expected all the doors to be standing wide open. Good grief, I'm an idiot."

"Never say that about yourself. You're not stupid, Teddy. Careless, maybe, but not an idiot. If anything, you're too smart for your own good."

He didn't want Teddy to think of herself in derogatory terms. He didn't want her to believe all the negative comments that the good people of Westalia shoveled in her direction. When he gazed across the bedroom into her wide blue eyes, Vince saw questions, confusion and self-doubt. "Don't let them grind you down, Teddy."

"They never have."

"Good." Because her strength and character were appealing to him, even exciting. He patted the sheets. "Come here."

She rose from the rocking chair and went to stand next to the bed. Hands on hips, she frowned down at the sheets. "How...how's your foot, Vince?"

"It's fine." Her hesitant manner indicated that now might not be the best moment for him to attempt a seduction. She needed time, and he would give it to her. But not for too long. Vince was anxious to make love to her again. The next time, he would proceed slowly, without the pressures of last night's frantic need. "Have you got any coffee?"

"Sure." She turned on her heel and fled toward the door. "Breakfast will be coming up in a minute."

Downstairs in the kitchen, Teddy placed a call to her answering service. Lilibet immediately offered condolences. "I still can't believe it," Lilibet said. "Whitney murdered. Teddy, I feel so bad for you and your family."

But not for Whitney? If the pain of her sister's death had not been so fresh, Teddy would have smiled. There was no love lost between Whitney and Lilibet. Those two beauties had competed since high school. At the anniversary party, they'd almost come to blows. Then, Lilibet had been dancing with Tom. Would she be his alibi? "Lilibet, you mind if I ask you who took you home last night? Was it Tom?"

"He tried." She heaved a sigh. "Tom Burke is one handsome devil, but I can't abide a man who drinks. I had heard he was in some kind of alcohol treatment program and had been sober for a year. But I guess I heard wrong."

"Did you leave with him?" Teddy persisted.

"About eight o'clock, we went over to PJ's. But I drove my own car, and I left the very minute he ordered something stronger than soda pop."

"And you went home?"

"Honey, that strapless bra was killing me, and I had to get out of my dress. I did go back out a little later." Her dulcet Southern voice shifted to a lower key. "But it was too late."

"Too late for what?" Teddy probed. There was something Lilibet wasn't telling her.

"When I got back to my house, Merle was there."

Her ex-husband? Teddy couldn't believe it.

"Can you believe the way he was behaving at the party? I declare, he made a fool of himself, playing up to your aunt Harriet and drooling over Whitney. When he showed up on my doorstep, begging to come in, I gave him a piece of my mind. Honest to Pete, if he's going to be acting like a tomcat, he could do better than to hitch up with Harriet, and he had no business fooling around with a married woman like Whitney. Not that she was acting like a married lady at her own anniversary party." She paused. "Sorry, Teddy. I shouldn't have said that."

"It's okay. I thought the same thing."

"Yesterday was a black day for Westalia," Lilibet pronounced. "There hasn't been a murder around here in years. Not since that fat old Mr. Mike who operated the Standard gas station shot those boys who were trying to hold him up. And they weren't from here. They were—"

"Lilibet," Teddy interrupted, "have I had any messages this morning?"

"Yes, indeed. Your daddy called three times. And Russel Stratton. And Jake."

"Sheriff Jake Graham?"

"Ri-i-ight." She drawled the word into several syllables. "Oh, and something else."

"What?"

"I'm assuming that Vince Harding is staying at your house."

"That's correct."

"He's supposed to call somebody named Connie at his office."

"Thanks, Lilibet."

"That's one gorgeous man," she said wistfully. "Looks like he's got money, too. If you decide to throw him back, Teddy, you be sure to let me know."

"Sure will."

Before returning her calls, Teddy started the coffee. She wasn't looking forward to talking with her father, or to Russel, either. Both men, the most important men in her sister's life, would be grief-stricken. Teddy didn't really know Russel well enough to know how he would behave, but she remembered her father's reaction when her mother died. He kept the pain buried deeply within and presented an unruffled exterior to the world. Other people had admired him, Teddy recalled. They'd said that Jordan Edwards was so brave, that he was dealing with the tragedy so very well. But Teddy knew otherwise.

All the sunlight and laughter had gone from their home, leaving a cold, dark silence. Her father had erected a barrier between himself and his emotions, between himself and his daughters, and Teddy had spent her teenage years battering at that wall, trying to get a rise out of him.

Looking back, she could see the source of her rebellious nature. She'd wanted to do something, anything, to catch her father's attention. But he had never comprehended. From early on, he'd branded her a headstrong troublemaker and never changed his opinion.

The irony, she realized, was that she'd emulated his behavior. In spite of her emotional nature, Teddy forced herself to remain cool in the face of tragedy. When Jacques had died, she'd suffered alone, not seeking the solace of friends and family. She kept to herself, hiding her pain and never ever talking about his death. Until last night.

What had happened last night? Until that moment, she'd succeeded in restraining her tears. And then, all of a sudden, it seemed as if she'd been caught in a raging fire storm of emotion. The hot tears. Uncontrollable weeping.

Had that really happened? If it weren't for the persistent ache behind her eyelids, Teddy wouldn't have believed that she'd sobbed her heart out. If it weren't for the tenderness between her legs, she wouldn't have believed that she'd made love to Vince with a craving that surpassed desire and passion...though she'd felt those things, too.

And now, she was in a quandary.

How would she explain to Vince? Last night had been a once-in-a-lifetime occurrence, a catharsis. What would she say if he wanted to make love again?

"Just say no," she murmured as she started digging in her refrigerator, looking for something that might become breakfast. Her supplies were pathetic. Though Teddy was a decent cook, she didn't much care to whip up a fancy meal for one so she usually grabbed something to eat while she was out. The idea of grocery shopping seemed ridiculous. Vince probably wouldn't even be here tomorrow, and she'd be stuck with food that would go uneaten and unprepared.

She pulled her head out of the refrigerator when she heard a knock at the front door, and straightened. Was it the sheriff? Teddy hurried through the living room to the front door and opened it. Standing there, on the other side of the screen door was the last man in the world she wanted to confront.

"Tom Burke." Teddy's voice was ice cold. "What are you doing here?"

"You've got to help me. Please."

Chapter Seven

Teddy stared through the screen at the man she suspected of killing her sister. He didn't look like a murderer. In his short-sleeved starched white shirt and his hair neatly slicked back, Tom Burke seemed intent on making a good impression. But when she peered directly into his face, his eyes slid away from hers as if he didn't want her to look too closely. He was scared. The taint of fear clung to him. *Be careful,* she warned herself. Frightened men sometimes take desperate chances.

"Don't slam the door. Teddy, please. You got to listen to me."

"The only thing I want to hear from you, Tom Burke, is why Sheriff Graham hasn't arrested you. Last night you were in the back of a police car."

"They had to let me go."

"What time?" she asked, thinking of the break-in.

"Early." He couldn't keep the bragging tone from his voice. "They didn't even have enough evidence to take me down to the station house and book me. It was before midnight."

"They didn't keep you long enough." He'd had plenty of time to get on his motorcycle and come to her house.

Plenty of time to creep to her darkroom, to scratch at the lock, to run, to pull out his gun, to shoot.

"I didn't kill her, Teddy. I swear it. I liked Whitney a lot. I wouldn't hurt her."

Teddy remembered the way her sister had been laid out on the bed—neatly, with the fond respect of a gentle lover. She hadn't been beaten or bruised. Her delicate gown had not been torn.

Teddy's grief weighed heavily upon her. The darkness of her anger dimmed the morning sunlight. And yet, there was a glimmer of curiosity. Why was Tom here? If he had tried to break into her darkroom last night, why had he returned, acting so humbly?

"Maybe," he said, "I even loved Whitney."

"Loving her doesn't mean you're innocent." Her sister had not struggled before dying. Whoever murdered her was someone she trusted enough not to fight until the killer was close enough to plunge a knife into her heart. "Maybe you were jealous," Teddy said. "Maybe you never got over the fact that she married Russel. Maybe you couldn't stand the thought of Whitney in another man's arms."

"I made my peace with that a long time ago." He swallowed hard. "Please, Teddy. At least hear me out."

She didn't want him in her house, but Teddy couldn't turn him away. If there was the slightest doubt that Tom had murdered her sister, she needed to know who did. "You wait for me here. Outside." She relented. "I'll bring some coffee. Black?"

"Thanks." A tentative smile curved his dry lips. "I knew you'd want to find out the truth."

Before going into the kitchen, she raced up the stairs and found Vince, standing over the sink and rinsing the traces of shaving lather from his chin. The sight of him sparked a glow of intimacy within her. There had never been a man in this house before—not a man who'd stayed the night.

Standing in her peach-colored bathroom, he seemed too large and too tall, an alien, masculine presence in a feminine world. He had to bend over to reach the sink, to be careful when he turned his broad shoulders. His brown leather shaving kit looked clumsy and out of place beside her glass and porcelain bottles of lotion, perfume and makeup.

When he caught sight of her in the bathroom mirror, his welcoming smile faded. "What's wrong, Teddy?"

"Tom Burke is out on the porch. He says he's innocent."

"I'll be right there."

By the time she'd returned to the kitchen and poured two cups of coffee, Vince was coming down the stairs. He grabbed his own mug and followed her outside where Tom paced back and forth on the wooden porch. "Good," Tom said. "You're here, too."

"Why is that good?"

"You're smart. Both you and Teddy are smart enough to help me set things right." His hand trembled when he took the mug, and he set it down on the porch railing. Though there was a swing suspended at the end of the porch, none of them sat. "I'm being set up," Tom said. "Framed. The only reason that Sheriff Graham hasn't hauled my butt off to jail is that I have an alibi for the time when Whitney was killed."

"What's your alibi?" Vince asked.

"I was at PJ's Bar. I went there right after the party." He scowled. "Only problem is that the bartender can't guarantee that I was there all the time. He's saying that I might have slipped out for a few minutes—maybe even long enough to go over to the Sleep Inn and back. If I rode my Harley.''

"When you came back," Teddy said, "after Whitney was dead, you were walking."

"I was too drunk to get on my bike." He grabbed the coffee and downed a scalding sip. "I might have fallen off the wagon since I've been in Westalia, but I sure don't need any more DUIs. I know enough not to drink and drive."

"Not the night before last," Teddy said, remembering her first encounter with the TCB license plate. "You were flying like a bat out of hell."

"Was I?" He shook his head. "I don't recall. But then I was pretty much drunk that night."

"Blacked out?" Vince questioned.

"Guess so." Tom's full lips pulled into a frown. "I never felt like that before. Sure, it was the first drink I'd had in a long time, but it was only beer. Only a couple of beers, then I don't remember nothing."

"You must have ridden your bike," Teddy observed, "because the next morning, it was parked in front of your motel room."

He rubbed his forehead and squinted his eyes, trying to dredge up memory. "You're right," he said. "Guess I must have been that stupid."

"What about last night?" Vince probed. "Was it the same blackout feeling?"

"Not a bit. Sure, I was drinking at the party, and later at PJ's, but I remember everything one hundred percent clear."

"When you left the party, what happened?"

"I was feeling low, even though Lilibet Chatworth had decided to come home with me."

Teddy knew from her phone conversation that Tom was lying. Lilibet had not consented to a one-night fling. If he lied about this, what else would he lie about? "You and Lilibet, huh? Doesn't surprise me."

"Well, it should, because nothing happened. I couldn't even get that right."

"What do you mean?"

"She wouldn't go back to the motel with me. Said she didn't hang out with drunks." He winced. "She also accused me of having the hots for Whitney. Then she informed me—that was the exact word she used—'I would like to inform you that Lilibet Chatworth don't play second fiddle to nobody.' And then she went strutting off."

"Why'd she think you were interested in Whitney?"

"That wasn't my fault, Teddy. Whitney was coming on to me all day at that party. I think she was sorry she married Russel, and she really wanted to be with me."

Teddy remembered her conversation with Whitney and how she'd planned to use Tom to make her husband jealous. She was laughing and posing in front of the mirror. It was very much like Whitney to come up with such a scheme, pitting one man against another. But would she have followed through?

Tom continued. "At the party, Whitney came sidling up next to me, so close I could smell her roses and gardenia perfume, the same stuff she wore in high school. She said she would see me later, in my room. I believe she said nine o'clock, but I wasn't listening real good because I thought she was playing. So I teased back. I grabbed her and kissed her hard, so she'd remember it. I told her she was the prettiest woman I've ever known."

When his face relaxed in a smug male grin, Teddy almost believed his story. Nobody could pretend to be quite this insensitive and stupid. "Then what happened, Tom?"

"She and Russel left. I danced a little. Me and Lilibet made plans, I got on my bike and went to PJ's."

"On your bike?" Teddy questioned. "But you were drunk."

"A little buzz. Nothing I couldn't handle." He cleared his throat. "But maybe I'm wrong. This is the first time in almost a year that I've had any alcohol."

Vince dragged him back to his first statement. "Why did you say you were being framed?"

"Because they found her in my motel room. *My room.* And the sheriff says he knows we had a date for nine o'clock. Me and Whitney. I don't know why he's saying that, but it's a lie. An out-and-out lie."

"How did Whitney get into your room?" Vince asked. "The door was ajar when we got there, but there weren't signs of forced entry. Did you leave the door unlocked?"

"I don't think so."

"If you didn't open the door for her," Vince persisted, "who did?"

"I don't know."

Vince put on the pressure. "What about the knife? Last night, I heard that the murder weapon was your knife."

"That's what the sheriff thought, because it was a buck knife, like a lot of motorcycle guys carry." Tom slipped his hand into his back pocket and pulled out a flat pewter-colored pocketknife, four inches long. He flipped it open. The steel blade, well honed and polished, had a dangerous gleam. "But the sheriff was wrong." He held the knife so Teddy could see the grip. "Can you see what it says?"

"Your initials. TCB."

"Got it in Memphis," Tom said. "At a cycle shop where Elvis used to get his bikes."

There was a lightning bolt through the initials. To Elvis, the jag of lightning meant "Taking Care of Business, in a Flash." According to legend, Elvis liked things done fast. Immediate gratification. If Tom had the same leanings, and Whitney turned him down... It had been a dangerous game Whitney played with Tom, like teasing a rattlesnake.

His hand dropped to his side with the handle of the open blade clenched in his fist. "I'm the victim here. That's how it's been all my life. You know that, don't you? You know how the people in this town are. They decide you're bad and they never let you be anything else."

"I know," Teddy said.

"When I was growing up, I was always the one to get the blame. I took the rap for Russel Stratton more times than I can remember. And now I'm not good enough to stay in his house. When he called me up a month ago and told me about the party, I promised to come. Then he puts me in a motel. A dumpy motel room is good enough for Tom Burke."

Vince encouraged him to continue talking. "You were teed off."

"You bet I was. My good buddy, Russel, treated me like dirt. But I guess he made up for it that night at PJ's. I mean, I asked him, but he paid for all our drinks." He took a deep breath. "Teddy, are you going to help me? I got nobody else to turn to."

"I'll find the truth," Teddy said. She would not allow her sister's death to go unsolved. "If you didn't hurt Whitney, then you have nothing to fear."

"You know it's not me," Tom said.

"I don't know anything for sure."

"I didn't do it." His body tensed. His fingers tightened on the buck knife, and the tendons on his forearm stood out. Though Tom Burke hadn't played football in years, his body was muscular enough to be physically intimidating. He snapped the knife closed. "You got to believe me."

"We'll believe it when we have the proof," Vince said. He stepped forward. Though he didn't touch Tom, he managed to direct him down the two porch steps. "You go back to the motel. Don't drink. Cooperate with the sheriff."

"Lay low," Tom said.

"That's right."

"Why? Are you thinking I'd better get used to living in one room? Better get used to a cell?"

"I'm thinking you'd better shut your mouth before you get into any more trouble."

Tom strode to his Harley, took the black leather jacket off the seat and shrugged his arms into it. Unexpectedly he laughed. "Hey, Teddy, you remember this?" He struck a wide-legged pose and sang the first line to the Elvis hit, "Suspicious Minds."

"Halloween party," she said. "Senior year in high school. You came as Elvis. And Whitney..."

"She wore one of those big round felt skirts."

The bittersweet memory of happier days knotted Teddy's throat. It seemed impossible that Whitney was dead.

"Guess I ought to pay attention to that song," Tom said. "I'm caught in a trap. Just like Elvis. You remember in his movies how he was always getting blamed for something he didn't do?"

"Those were movies," Teddy said. The story lines bore little resemblance to real life, where the most likely suspect was usually the guilty party.

Tom swung his leg over his bike and started the motor with a roar. When he popped the clutch, the big bike took off with a buck.

Vince let out a long sigh. "He might be an idiot. An alcoholic. A jerk. But I don't believe he's a murderer."

"Why not?"

"A man with a bike like that has heart."

Vince sat on the porch steps and longingly watched the Harley pull away. In some ways, he envied Tom Burke, one of that dying American breed of loner, heading out on the highway with no responsibilities. Calling his own shots. Answering to no one.

Teddy sat on the step beside him. When her thigh pressed against his, she quickly inched away, putting distance between them. She cleared her throat and said, "You raised a good question about the motel key. If Tom didn't give Whitney the key, how did she get into his room?"

"Think twice, Teddy, before you start asking questions." Playing sleuth could be a dangerous game. Vince had a feeling that Westalia had more than its share of skeletons in the closet. "You might not like some of the things we uncover."

"I'll never find answers if I don't ask. And I've never shied away from the truth."

He nodded. "Then we need a plan."

"First," she said, "I should gather up those color negatives and make contact sheets. If the person who was here last night was after the photos, I'll feel better when the sheriff has a set."

"While you're doing that, I'll set up a tracer with the phone company so that the next time your informant checks in, we'll know his number and we can record the call."

"On a Sunday? You are so naive. I'll bet you don't handle the phones in your office. You have secretaries who do that work."

"Most times," he admitted.

"Well, let me tell you. It's easier to negotiate a lasting peace in the Middle East than to get the phone company to perform an extra service outside their regular business hours." She grinned. "Setting up tracers and recorders is a job for Lilibet's answering service."

Teddy didn't mention the additional professional reason. She communicated regularly with editors from *On the Spot*, and she wanted to make sure that whatever equipment was installed would not allow Vince to overhear those conversations.

"By the way, Vince, Lilibet gave me some messages this morning, and you had a phone call from someone in your office named Connie."

"My assistant."

He stretched and yawned. The workday world was calling, but he would have to put it on hold while he sat on Teddy's porch, absorbing the warmth of the morning sun and listening to the gentle, rushing sounds of the brook hidden behind the forest at the edge of her property. The day might have been idyllic if they hadn't been making plans for capturing a cold-blooded murderer.

Teddy's voice sounded relaxed, with a faint trace of Southern twang that he found charming. "I'd guess that Lilibet has some kind of tracing equipment for calls that come directly to her answering service. But the evening calls come to my house, and that's the only time my informant has called.''

"Hmm. Only at night.'' The timing worried him. "Do you think it's someone who knows you?''

"I'm sure it is. He—or she—calls me Teddy, and all my listings are as Mary Theodora.''

She remembered the distinct edginess she felt during the call when the night skies had misted over with fog and the stillness had held an unnamed threat. The voice had asked if she were scared. Not then, she thought. Not as much as now, when death was a reality.

The safe decision, she knew, would be to back off and allow the sheriff to do his job. No matter what she thought of Sheriff Jake Graham personally, he had an excellent arrest record. He was competent. What made her think that she could do better? "I could even do worse,'' she murmured.

"What are you talking about?''

"I don't want to screw things up by meddling in Sheriff Graham's investigation. Who do I think I am? Sherlock Holmes? Hercule Poirot?'' She rested her elbows on her knees and peered toward the thicket where last night's intruder had vanished. Could he possibly still be here? She remembered the dark figure in black. He could be waiting for them to leave, watching their every move. "But I can't sit back and wait. It's not my nature.''

"Not mine, either,'' Vince said. "So, we agree. We won't get in the way of the sheriff, but we'll do some poking around. First, we should stop by the Sleep Inn and have a talk with Mrs. Klaus, the manager, about the motel-room key.''

"You know her name?''

"Hey, I stayed at her place. I'm a friendly guy.'' He nudged her in the ribs. "Jealous?''

"For your information, we used to call her Mrs. Santa Klaus, because when she laughs her tummy shakes like a bowl full of jelly."

"Ah, the cruelty of children. Let's discuss that topic over breakfast."

"I've got some bad news on that front. I inventoried my food supplies, and we'll have to go out."

"Should we go," he mused, "before Sheriff Graham rushes out here to fingerprint the handle of the darkroom door?"

"Twenty hours after the fact," she said.

"Might be a new record for negligence in answering a 911 call."

"The sheriff probably isn't even going to run prints. He's not going to take a serious forensic interest in a simple intruder when he's got a major murder case."

"However," Vince said, "in the interests of preserving any possible evidence, we should take all your undeveloped film with us."

"Consider it done."

But once she was in the darkroom, Teddy would not be rushed. She gathered the negatives from the wire basket they'd been automatically fed into by the developing machine, checked several for quality and murmured her satisfaction.

"Could you hurry?" Vince asked. "I'm starving."

"I don't want to mess this up. There might be a clue in here."

"Can I help?"

"How much do you know about photography?"

He stepped over to the dry side of her darkroom. "I know how to use the enlarger to make contact prints. And I have developed black and white before, but I'm not sure I recall all the steps."

Teddy seemed satisfied. "Gather up all my black-and-white rolls of film, and help me get these color negatives into protective glassine envelopes."

With his assistance, the job went more quickly. Teddy filed everything in a camera bag along with her ubiquitous Nikon. When Teddy stepped onto the porch, she shot a surreptitious glance toward the thicket. If the intruder was still lurking, she hoped he would know that he'd been outsmarted. The film was with them. There was nothing else in her house that he would want.

"And I need to stop by the hardware store," she said as she climbed into the driver's seat, "to pick up glass for the broken window."

"Do we need measurements?"

"No, I've broken windows before when I was putting in the darkroom. They're all the same size."

Though the only stoplight in Westalia was seventeen miles from Teddy's front door, the distance seemed farther to Vince, probably because the route followed slow-traffic, two-lane roads.

As small Midwestern towns went, Westalia represented the essence of typical. At the outskirts, the frame houses varied from ranch-style to two story with peaked roofs. The square green lawns, marked off with neat sidewalks and curbs, sported the beginnings of spring gardens, with blooming bulbs and lilacs and brilliant yellow sprays of forsythia.

"Where does your father live?" Vince asked.

"Well, let's take ten minutes and do the grand tour, shall we?" She passed the stoplight and continued north for five or six blocks, then she turned. "This street is named Elm, but there aren't any more mature elm trees after Dutch elm disease wiped most of them out. You'll notice that this part of town is on a hill which—appropriately enough—is where most of the Edwards clan has settled. On the hill. From that elevation, they can more easily look down on the rest of the local population."

Her glib narrative masked a certain bitterness, and Vince tried to imagine Teddy as the little rich girl from the hill. The image didn't suit her. Teddy, he suspected, was a tomboy with skinned knees, straggling hair and freckles. He could almost see her on these quiet streets, racing her bike up and down the hill like the wind. "You don't act like a rich kid."

"Don't I know it? I used to drive my aunt Harriet crazy. The poor woman would get me all fancied up, and I'd have torn my petticoat before I even got out the door." She started a laugh that shattered abruptly. "When we were kids, Whitney was much better at genteel behavior. She was a perfect little lady." Pressing down on the accelerator, she tried to outrun her memories. "That house on the corner is where my dad lives."

The two-story blond brick house featured a spectacular entrance with four tall pillars. As soon as Vince saw the place, he grinned. "No wonder you're fascinated with Elvis. Your family home looks like Graceland."

"Never thought of it that way." She glanced through his window. "There is a resemblance. But Graceland is fieldstone, not brick. And the shutters are gray."

"Green," Vince corrected. "Forest green."

Teddy raised her eyebrows. "You've been there?"

"What kind of tabloid editor hasn't seen the monument to the King? Of course I've been there. Like a Muslim to Mecca."

"Or a swallow to Capistrano."

Around the corner, she pointed out a similar structure in white that belonged to Aunt Harriet. The house across the street, a less-imposing ranch-style, had several cars parked in front. "That was Whitney's house. Looks like Russel has plenty of people around to help out."

"Do you want to stop?"

"No," she said quickly. Teddy didn't think she could stand being around her family. Likewise, the Edwardses and Strattons wouldn't be delighted to see her. Everyone would feel uncomfortable, and there was no point in raking up old hostilities. "I'd probably just cause trouble," she said.

When she turned back toward the center of town, Teddy seemed to breathe more easily, and Vince wondered how stifled she had been in her childhood. Glancing in the rearview mirror attached to the passenger side of the van, he noticed a Lincoln Continental with tinted windows behind them.

Teddy continued her narrative. "This, of course, is Main Street, complete with barbershop, drugstore, a couple of boutiques and three churches, the most attractive of which is the United Methodist, that big white one on the corner. No stained glass but a lovely bell tower that chimes the hour, every hour. Donated by an Edwards, of course."

Outside the local café on Main Street, Teddy noticed several familiar cars, and had second thoughts about venturing inside. "I don't think I'm up to facing the gossip."

He nodded. "Is the grocery store safe?"

"Let's try it."

When they pulled into the parking lot, Vince lost track of the big Lincoln sedan that had stayed with them throughout the latter part of the tour. Had to be a coincidence, he thought. There weren't that many thoroughfares in Westalia. Everybody had to drive the same routes. Then three rows over, he saw the Lincoln pull into a space. Nobody got out.

In the supermarket, Teddy shopped with enthusiasm, filling her cart with more food than she could possibly eat in a month. And Vince encouraged her, insisting on buying a pot roast, which he promised to fix for dinner. "That's ridiculous," Teddy insisted. "You and I can't eat a whole five-pound roast."

"Has to be that big. I don't know the recipe for less."

They argued pleasantly over coffee brands and squabbled about the difference between ground beef and ground turkey. Altogether, the shopping trip represented more domesticity than Teddy had experienced in her whole life. While she was living with Jacques in exotic locations overseas, they usually stayed in hotels or pension with limited cooking facilities.

In the parking lot, as they piled bags of groceries into the van, she said, "So this is what it's like."

"What?"

"I always see couples wandering through the aisles with their shopping carts, picking and choosing. It's kind of fun."

"Oh yeah? But think about doing it week after week. Month after month. That's got to be the height of boring."

Or of comfort, she thought. Sameness could be pleasant, as could pursuing a weekly ritual, always knowing that the other person would be there. Apparently Vince Harding wasn't the sort of man who enjoyed being settled down.

When they came around to the front of the van, the noise of a Harley distracted them. Tom Burke squealed into a space only a few yards away. He pulled off his helmet and marched toward them. "Why didn't you tell me you got broken into last night?"

"Why should I?" Teddy asked.

"The sheriff was asking me questions about where I was last night after he released me. If I had known I needed an alibi, I could have made something up."

"What are you suggesting?" Teddy angrily demanded. "That I help you hide the truth?"

"Hell, no. But you're on my side now and—"

"Get this straight, Tom." She jabbed a stiff index finger at his chest. "The only thing I want to know is who killed my sister. I'm not on anybody's side. Now, get away from me."

"You bet I will. You're going to be sorry about this, Teddy." He turned on his heel and stalked off.

Before he could mount his Harley, the Lincoln pulled up, blocking his exit. Teddy's father, Jordan Edwards, leapt out. An errant ray of sunlight glistened like a platinum crown in his short white hair. His golfer's tan had deepened to a dark, dangerous red. He waved his fist and shouted, "I've been looking for you, Tom."

"Why's that, sir?"

"You know why." Jordan slammed his car door and marched toward them, militarily erect. Another car pulled up behind him and tooted impatiently, but Jordan ignored the ruckus. All of his attention, all of his bitterness, focused on Tom. "You know what I want."

Vince spotted the revolver in his hand. Before the older man could raise the gun and take aim, Vince was beside him. "Don't do it, Jordan."

"I will have my justice." He dropped to one knee and lifted the gun with both hands.

"No," Teddy shouted.

Vince slammed into Jordan's shoulder, driving him to the ground before he could pull the trigger. Jordan tried to roll away, but Vince was on top of him, straddling his wiry body. With muscular ease, Vince pinned his gun hand against the asphalt of the parking lot. "Give it to me, Jordan."

"Make me, you son of a—"

"My pleasure." Vince tapped him on the chin. The light blow was sufficient to distract Jordan's attention, and Vince wrestled the gun from his grasp.

Shoppers stopped and stared and whispered. A mother pulled her small children close to her side and ran with them toward her car. Horns blared.

Holding the revolver, Vince stood. He dusted off his Levi's, not trusting himself to speak until he brought his anger under control. What the hell had Jordan Edwards thought he was doing? This old man must be crazy with grief.

The instant Jordan regained his feet, he stuck out his hand and demanded, "My gun, sir."

Vince fastened the safety, stuck the handgun into his waistband and pulled out his shirttail to cover the handle. "You can thank me later."

"You'll be lucky if I don't sue you for assault." He rubbed his jaw, apparently oblivious to the crowd that had gathered around them. "Damn lucky."

Teddy ran up to them. "Dad, are you all right?"

Her father ignored her. He pointed to Tom and shouted, "I'm coming after you, sonny. Every time you look over your shoulder, I'll be there."

"You don't scare me, old man."

"Get in the car, Dad," Teddy encouraged. "I'll drive you home."

"I don't have to leave. This is a public place."

Teddy made placating gestures toward the crowd. "It's okay now, everybody. Everything's under control."

"Nobody's going to arrest me," Jordan said. "This is my town. Things are going to work out my way."

"Don't be so sure," Tom yelled.

Vince left Teddy with her father and went toward Tom. In a low voice, he advised, "Go back to the motel, Tom. And when you talk to the sheriff, you might mention that Jordan came after you with a gun."

"Won't do any good," Tom muttered. He kick-started his bike. "Jordan Edwards is somebody important in these parts. He could get away with murder."

As Tom dodged his motorcycle around the big sedan, Vince wondered. If Jordan had known that Whitney planned to embarrass him by having an affair with a low-class scum like Tom, what would he do? Though it was hard to imagine that any father could hurt his own child, Jordan Edwards was one cold, selfish piece of work.

Vince watched as Teddy escorted her father back to his car and safely tucked him into the passenger side. She ran around the front and tossed the van's keys to Vince. "Meet us at Dad's place."

He didn't like the fact that she was driving off without him, didn't like that Jordan had been following them. Would she be safe? Could he protect her? "Be careful, Teddy."

Inside the big Lincoln, Teddy felt like she was in another world, a plush cocoon encased by tinted glass. Her father's world. She cruised away from the supermarket. "I was going to stop by and see you," she said.

"As if you give a damn about me." He sounded as petulant as a child.

"I'm sorry, Dad. Can I do anything to help?"

"Harriet's taking care of the funeral arrangements and the flowers and the notices. I gave her my checkbook. She'll pick out a fine coffin, just as she did for your mother. I don't need your help, Teddy."

Couldn't he forget his grudge against her for one minute? "What about Russel? Is he okay?"

Her father shrugged. "I suppose so."

"Dad, I'm worried about you." She was more concerned than she liked to admit. Until now, Teddy had never seen her father out of control. She longed to comfort him, to share their sorrow. "Maybe I should stay with you for a couple of days."

"You and me?" He barked a laugh. "Hell, Teddy, we'd probably kill each other within forty-eight hours."

His words stung, but she held back her tears. Her father was the only real family she had left. Her mother was gone. Whitney was gone. "We could get along, Dad. I know we could."

"If you really want to make me happy, you wouldn't have let your boyfriend stop me."

"What?"

"I should have killed Tom Burke. He's nothing but worthless trash. He deserves to be dead."

"Damn it, you are the most unreasonable—"

"Hah!" He pointed at her. "We've been together five minutes, and we're already fighting."

When he lifted his chin, she saw the bristling stubble beneath his country-club tan. He hadn't yet shaved this morning. For a fastidious man like her father, lack of grooming was a frightening revelation. And yet there was something deliberate about his anger. Above all, her father was logical. "How do you know he's guilty?"

"Get with it, Mary Theodora. You know as well as I do that Tom Burke lured Whitney to his motel room. He set it up at the party. I know. I saw her putting his room key into her purse."

"Whitney had a key to his room?"

"That's right. It did not escape my attention that she and Tom were making eyes at each other during the party, and I knew he was staying at the Sleep Inn. So when I saw her with the key, I asked her if that was the key to Tom's room. And I warned her that there had better not be any hanky-panky between her and that ne'er-do-well."

Brilliant move, Teddy thought. In the rebellious mood Whitney had been in, her father's warning practically guaranteed that she'd fly into Tom's arms at the first opportunity.

"This was an anniversary party," Jordan grumbled. "To celebrate a marriage. Not a divorce. Besides, that Russel Stratton is all right."

"There was a time when you didn't think so," Teddy gently reminded. When Whitney had first announced her possible engagement to Russel, their father had countered with vehement opposition. Jordan's objections were the primary reason they'd eloped.

"I'm an open-minded man. I came to accept him. Even to like him. He's on his way to being my right-hand man at the newspaper." He stared at her. "I'd always thought that would be your job, Teddy. Even when you went traipsing around the globe with that foreigner, I thought you'd come to your senses and apologize."

"I have nothing to apologize for." Teddy stopped herself before they became embroiled in a very old argument.

"If I can't count on my girls to do what I want, who can I count on? Whitney used to pay attention to what I said. Once upon a time, she used to be a good girl. And I will avenge her death.''

''But you can't take the law into your own hands. Leave Tom Burke to the sheriff.''

''What about my law? My authority as your father? You should stand ready to support me, Mary Theodora. You should obey me, right or wrong, because I know what's best for you.''

''The hell you do.''

''Oh, that's right. Challenge me. That's just perfect, Teddy.'' He crowed triumphantly. Once again, her father had succeeded in angering her. ''You don't like it when I act the way you do.''

''What does that mean?''

''I'll say to you the words you've always said to me. Don't get in my way.''

''Tell you what, Dad. I wouldn't dream of interfering. And when you wind up in jail, I'll bake a cake with a file inside. Is that obedient enough for you?''

When she pulled up in front of her father's house, the front door opened and Harriet stood there. Good, Teddy thought. Let Harriet take care of this madman.

''Both of you,'' he said. ''Both of you girls disappointed me. But at least Whitney was a good girl.'' He flung open the car door. ''You tell that young man of yours to return my gun.''

''Dad, I'm sorry. I didn't mean to—''

''You take care of your own self, Mary Theodora.''

She looked up, wanting him to say more, wishing he would forgive her for whatever transgression she had committed. But he stiffened and marched slowly toward the portico where Harriet was waiting. Leaving her father's keys in his car, Teddy went to the van, where Vince was waiting. Her father's unrelenting disapproval was the same. She would never be able to please him. Never in a million years.

When she opened the driver's side, she said, "We've got a couple of other stops, Vince. I'll drive."

"Teddy, are you all right?" His eyes shone with compassion, and she gazed yearningly at his strong, broad shoulder. A nice shoulder to cry on. It would be lovely to rest her head against him, to have him stroke her back and tell her that everything would be fine.

But Teddy couldn't do that. Last night was a mistake she could not repeat. If she became attached to Vince Harding, dependent upon him, she would be hurt again. Vince had a job and a life in Chicago and he had never promised to be here for the long haul. There had been no commitments made, and she knew better than to attach herself to a man who had no plans for sticking around.

Chapter Eight

Teddy eased the clutch into first gear and pulled away from the house on the hill, not looking back. "My dad wants his gun back."

"I'll be happy to return his piece," Vince said, "as soon as there's a hockey team in hell."

"Don't be ridiculous. He's not dangerous."

"Maybe not in more usual circumstances." Vince tried to be sympathetic toward Jordan Edwards. The man had just lost his daughter. He was grief-stricken.

"He didn't mean to kill Tom. If he'd been serious about murder, my father could easily have picked Tom off his motorcycle. Dad's an excellent marksman."

"All the more reason to keep his gun right here in my briefcase." Vince patted the leather case. He'd also taken the opportunity—when he was alone in her van—to transfer Teddy's color negatives and undeveloped black-and-white film from her camera bag into his briefcase. Twice in as many days, he'd been threatened by gunmen, and he wouldn't make the mistake of underestimating the rampant craziness in Westalia. Vince wanted as much control over the situation as possible. And that meant holding on to the film.

Apparently Teddy did not share his concerns. She was annoyed, glowering over the steering wheel. When she flicked the turn signal, it almost came off in her hand.

"My father is usually a reasonable person."

Somehow, Vince doubted that. "Even a reasonable person can be driven to commit an irrational act."

"Irrational? How can you say that? Don't you have any sense of—"

"What? Respect for the great Jordan Edwards? No, Teddy, I don't. I didn't grow up in this town knowing that I was supposed to be impressed." He stared through the windshield. "I don't like the way he treats you."

A somber chord sounded within her soul. Teddy didn't like it, either. "He's my father."

She couldn't settle a lifetime of problems in a few insightful minutes. Right now, other concerns were more pressing. Driving with extra caution, Teddy passed PJ's. They were only a mile from the Sleep Inn.

Seeing the scene of Whitney's death might trigger a fresh emotional onslaught, and Teddy prepared herself. "We're going to talk with Mrs. Klaus," she said. "I'm going to figure this out, Vince. I haven't changed my mind." When she glided into the parking lot and cut the engine, he reached over and took her hand. His gesture calmed her as she turned and confronted the black-and-white exterior of the motel. Yellow crime-scene tape marked off the last room, the room where Whitney had been killed.

Tom's Harley was parked in front of the room where Vince had been staying. He was here, Teddy thought. How could he bear to stay here? She squeezed Vince's hand. "It's just a motel, isn't it? No ghosts."

"None as far as I can see."

"Do you believe in them? In ghosts?"

"No. And before you say anything about that, I know that *Files* runs a good number of ghost stories. My assistant, Connie, handles the supernatural nonsense."

"It's not nonsense." Teddy disagreed. "Not all of it."

In the motel office, they found Mrs. Klaus, round and pleasant. "Hi, Teddy," she said. "I'm so sorry about your sister. Whitney was a lovely girl." She turned to Vince. "Mr. Harding, are you coming back to us?"

"No, ma'am. But we did want to ask you a couple of questions."

"Ask away. I haven't been interviewed this many times since I was a beauty-queen contestant back home in Indiana. And that was more years ago than I like to count."

"We're curious about the extra key to Room 19," he said. "Can you tell us about that?"

"Is this going to be a story in *Files?*"

"Could be."

Mrs. Klaus primped her brown curls. "No photos, Teddy. Not unless I have a chance to freshen up."

"Whatever you say."

"Well, here's what happened," she began. "Last night was the murder, and oh my, it's been such a mess since then, but the funny business with the key happened the night before. It was fairly late, after the ten o'clock news. And Tommy Burke came riding up on his motorcycle—rip-roaring drunk, I might add. He told me he'd lost his key and needed another."

"So you gave him a duplicate," Vince offered.

"That's right. I told him he had to pay a twenty-dollar charge for the lost key when he checked out, and he stuck his hand in his pocket and threw a twenty on the counter."

"Thanks, Mrs. Klaus." Vince smiled his appreciation, and the lady smiled right back. "That explains how

Whitney got into his room. I don't suppose you noticed what time she arrived.''

"Didn't see a thing. They say she parked down the road a ways and walked back here. I don't approve of clandestine meetings in my motel, but I know it happens." She glanced at Teddy. "I'm so sorry, hon."

"You know, it's strange. Tom had his own key when he came back here," Vince said.

"Don't I know it. He told the sheriff that I was lying, that he never did come in here and ask for another key. As if I made it all up. As if I didn't see him and his fancy motorcycle and his big black helmet. Looks like a space monster in that thing. But he changed his tune."

"Did he?"

"Marched himself in here and apologized to me. He said he didn't remember anything about that night at PJ's. The poor boy fell off the wagon real hard."

They thanked her and promised to give her plenty of notice if they needed a photograph. As Teddy drove away from the motel, she breathed more freely. The sight of the place had not thrown her into hysterics, but the memory stuck in her mind. And her nostrils seemed clogged with the faint scent of roses, a fragrance she would always associate with Whitney. She steered the van back toward town, driving silently for a distance while she gathered her thoughts.

Finally she said, "Tom had two motel-room keys, and he gave one of them to Whitney. My dad said he saw her with a key at the party."

"Did he witness Tom giving the key to Whitney?"

"I don't think so."

"Then we can't assume that's what happened. All we know is that Tom had two keys in his possession. Then

Whitney had one of them." He paused. "Was your father angry about the key?"

"Furious," she said. "Why would anybody other than Tom give Whitney a key to Tom's room?"

"As Tom pointed out, the murderer had reason—if the murderer was, in fact, planning to frame Tom."

"As Tom said?" Heavy sarcasm coated her voice. "Him and his convenient blackouts. I really don't think we should listen to anything Tom Burke has to say."

"Oh? But we should listen to your father, right? We should pay attention to his abusive ranting and raving."

"Abusive? What do you mean? He's never laid a hand on me."

"There are other forms of abuse, Teddy. Don't you read the papers you take photographs for? Haven't you taken a hard look at your life and wondered why a brilliantly talented woman like yourself has hidden herself away in her hometown, a place where she's miserable?"

"I'm not miserable." Teddy pulled up in front of a quaint, two-story white house with red-and-yellow tulips lining the sidewalk. She unsnapped her seat belt and flung open her door. "I'm doing perfectly fine."

Vince followed her up the walk. "You weren't doing fine last night."

"I'll thank you not to mention last night. If you were a gentleman, you'd forget it ever happened."

"It did happen, Teddy. Don't deny it. You cried as if your heart was breaking. And we made love with a passion that came from—"

"Hush, Vince. I do not intend to stand here on Lilibet's doorstep and talk about my indiscretions." She jabbed the doorbell. "Last night, I was not myself."

He caught her arms and turned her toward him. Before she could warn him to get away, his lips claimed hers with a searing, possessive heat that shot straight to her heart and melted her resolution never to touch him again. She moaned. Forbidden pleasures tasted sweet, and she kissed him back. Her arms encircled him.

When Lilibet opened the door, they were locked in an embrace, their bodies pressed tightly together. "Well now," she drawled, "if this is a business call, you got the wrong number. I don't do phone sex."

Teddy disentangled herself. Her heart was beating fast and her cheeks felt flushed and warm. "I'm sorry, Lilibet. I needed . . . we were . . ."

"Don't apologize. I do believe that kissing is what fiancées are supposed to do." Her knowing glance swept over both Teddy and Vince.

Vince followed the two women inside. He hadn't planned to kiss her. He'd intended to give her space. But he'd be damned if he allowed her to dismiss last night's incredible lovemaking as a fluke. He would never forget the feel of her satin skin, the scent of her hair or the perfect fit of her body against his.

Last night, her desire had risen from a deep, compulsive need he didn't fully comprehend. The next time they made love—and he vowed there would be a next time— he hoped the sole motivation would be that she wanted him.

He was so consumed with thoughts of Teddy that his observation of Lilibet was indifferent in spite of the fact that this very sexy female wore tight cutoffs that displayed long legs, and a halter top that showed off her cleavage. The only evidence of her business was a telephone headset with a long, dangling cord.

While Teddy explained to Lilibet what she needed, he was pleased to notice the breathless quality of her speech and the warm glow that flushed her cheeks a warm, soft pink.

"Can you arrange it?" Teddy asked. "A tracer and phone tap."

Lilibet nodded, sending a shimmer through her shiny black hair. She was attractive, Vince thought. Maybe even beautiful. But Lilibet didn't affect him the way Teddy did. Possibly no woman had ever affected him so profoundly.

"With the equipment I've got right now," Lilibet said, "I can do both those things for you."

"What about after business hours when the calls come directly to my house?"

"I'll talk to the phone company. But it's going to be tomorrow before they can set up a trace. In the meantime, I can lend you a recorder that activates as soon as you answer."

Teddy smiled. "You're terrific."

"You are right about that, honey. Terrific and efficient. I've got messages for both of you." She handed three messages to Teddy and five scraps of paper to Vince. "All these are from Connie. And they range from 'please call' to 'urgent.'"

"Thanks, Lilibet." Vince wondered why Connie was so frantic to talk to him on a weekend. Their offices were closed on Sunday, and Connie never took work home with her on the weekends. Something must have come up. Something important.

In a workroom at the rear of Lilibet's house, Vince sat down to use one of the phones beside a large console, which was, appropriately for a Sunday, silent. Even before he punched in the number of Connie's home telephone, he had decided that no matter what crisis had occurred, he would not leave Westalia. He couldn't abandon Teddy. Whether she wanted him here or not, he would stand beside her.

Connie answered on the second ring. "Finally! Vince, you're not going to believe this. I didn't believe it myself. *He* called."

"What are you talking about? Who called?"

"Elvis."

Vince closed his eyes and slowly opened them to gaze through the window into Lilibet's backyard. *Elvis called?* Well, sure. Why not? Why not Elvis?

Near the newly planted garden in Lilibet's backyard, a huge black crow strutted across the grass and hopped up onto the window ledge. Vince half expected the creature to croak, in the immortal words of Edgar Allan Poe, "Nevermore."

"Everybody is going crazy," Vince muttered. "Do you want to tell me about this, Connie?"

"He insisted on talking to you, and the receptionist transferred him to me." Her ever-present wad of chewing gum crackled. "Anyway, I was real impressed with his impersonation. I had a sense, you know, that this call was more than just somebody goofing. It was like fate, you know?"

Not fate. Please not fate. "Go on, Connie. What did he say?"

"He was passing through Branson, Missouri. You know, the place where all the country and western singers have their own theaters."

"I know."

"And he heard talk of a really excellent photographer, Miss Mary Theodora Edwards, who lived somewhere nearby. That's Teddy."

"I know," Vince said impatiently.

"And this guy, who sounded—I swear, Vince—just like Elvis, he said he was thinking about doing an informal shoot with Miss Mary Theodora. But—"

"Let me guess," Vince interrupted. "First he wants a million dollars in small, unmarked bills."

"He didn't mention money. He wanted to talk to Teddy and to you. When I gave him her phone number, he said he already had it, and he wondered if I might know where she lived."

Vince sat up a little straighter. This "Elvis" could be a cover-up for something else. But what? Everybody in Westalia knew where Teddy lived. "You didn't give him her address, did you, Connie?"

"Of course not. He was quite irritated. Polite, but mad. He said that maybe he ought to go to another paper, someplace that cared. And that really ticked me off. You know how I hate being threatened. Anyway—" she paused "—I made kind of a big decision. I probably should have run it past you first, but it just seemed right."

In Lilibet's backyard, Vince saw a tall man leap over the fence and duck behind a forsythia bush. He crouched there, unmoving.

"Vince? Are you still there?"

"What did you do, Connie?"

"I called the printers last night and told them to run the Elvis Sighting Hot Line on page one."

Only half-listening to her, Vince kept watch on the man in Lilibet's backyard. He had not moved.

"I can still cancel," Connie said.

"It's okay. We haven't run the Hot Line for nearly eight months. It's probably time."

Her sigh of relief whooshed through the phone. "Oh, good. I put the last place he'd been spotted in as Branson. The 900 number will take the calls, and what should I do with the ones that need follow-up?"

"Great. That's fine."

"You're not listening to me, Vince. Should I send down a reporter?"

"No, I'll respond to the calls myself. Run them through this number." Vince watched the man in the backyard stand erect, straighten his showy silver belt buckle, then stroll toward the back door as if he owned the place. And possibly he did. Vince recognized Merle Chatworth, Lilibet's ex-husband. "Got to go, Connie."

"Vince, I don't think you understand how many of these calls we get. You're going to be running all over—"

"Bye." Vince hung up the phone.

He entered the front parlor in time to see Merle Chatworth saunter across the living room, frowning. He nodded toward Teddy. "How are you holding up?"

"All right. Thanks for asking."

Merle picked a daisy out of a flower arrangement on an end table, twirled it in his hand, and stuck it back before he assumed a pose, thumbs hitched in his pockets. He glanced at his ex-wife. "Plastic flowers, Lilibet?"

"I've learned to purchase things that last." She glared at him. "What are you doing here, Merle?"

"I been consoling Harriet. But I had to get away from all those people. Just for a while. I escaped."

Vince grinned. From Merle's creeping approach through the backyard, he guessed that "escaped" was a literal description.

"I'm wondering..." Merle said. "Teddy, have you heard any news about..." He swallowed hard. There was a poignant note of sadness in his voice. "About the death?"

Vince stepped into the room. "Why ask Teddy?"

Merle shifted his gaze, noticed Vince, and nodded once. Not a single wasted motion. Though Merle Chatworth was a healthy male, only slightly past his prime, he gave the impression of being much older because he surrounded himself with absolute stillness. Immobility. And yet when he'd danced at the anniversary party, his agility had been impressive. And when he'd hopped the fence and dodged through the backyard, he could have been a teenage boy playing hooky.

"You're Teddy's beau," Merle recalled in his musical Southern drawl. "Well, I'll tell you. I'm looking to Teddy because she's got more brains in her little finger than Sheriff Jake Graham has in his whole fat body. I'll tell you all, there was one time when that pig of a sheriff poked his snout into my—"

"That's enough," Lilibet interrupted firmly. She turned to Vince. "Did you reach Connie?"

"I did. And I should warn you, Lilibet, that she's going to be calling a lot in the next few days. We're running a hot-line number in *Files* and Connie will be calling me with legitimate follow-ups."

"What kind of hot line?" Teddy asked suspiciously.

"You know, the Elvis Hot Line." Vince remembered what Connie planned to run on the front page. "Elvis has been sighted in Branson, Missouri."

Teddy started slightly, as if she'd been hit with a sudden and unexpected gust of wind. This was her story, damn it, the story of the century.

"I knew it!" Merle actually broke down and smiled. "I just knew it! The King is alive! Don't that beat all, Lilibet? And he's in Branson."

"Don't be a fool, Merle."

"I knew Elvis when he was first starting out. Way back when he called himself the Hillybilly Cat. He was something special. And the way those women would scream and carry on? Best darn job in the world was to play backup on a bill with Elvis. Those ladies, they were—"

"Oh, Merle, put a sock in it." Lilibet glanced from Teddy to Vince. "If he gets started with talking about the good old days when he used to play backup guitar for the country and western greats, we'll be here all day."

"Watch your mouth, Lilibet." Merle's voice was hard. "A little respect for your elders wouldn't hurt you none."

"Respect is something that's earned, and you're not likely to get my respect by running around with the likes of Harriet and Whitney."

Teddy looked up sharply. *The likes of Whitney...* That wasn't fair. Lilibet and Whitney had always been enemies, and Whitney wasn't perfect, but Teddy wanted to remember the good things about her sister. With half an ear, she heard Lilibet apologize and heard Merle defending.

"Whitney Edwards Stratton was a lady," he said. "You will not speak poorly of her in my presence."

"Get out of here," Lilibet ordered. "In the divorce papers, it says this house is mine."

"I paid for the damn place. I think I have the right to walk through here every couple of months or so."

"Then walk on through. Close the door on your way out."

Merle strode across the parlor to the front door, then pivoted. With a long, callused finger, he pointed to Teddy. "If you need anything, anything at all, you call me."

"Thanks, Merle."

He expelled a short laugh. "Elvis is back. Don't that beat all."

The moment he was gone, Lilibet let out a long-suffering sigh. "I ought to have that man locked up. I mean, we've been divorced for almost a year and a half, and he still thinks he can park his nasty motorcycle in the alley, hop the fence and walk in like he owns the place."

"You could get a restraining order," Teddy said.

"It'd be a waste of time and money. By the time the sheriff got here, he'd be gone." She ruefully shook her head, sending strands of her thick black hair astray. "He's no big deal. Just a pest, and it don't make good sense to call out the marines to swat a flea."

"Do you think he's serious about Harriet?"

"I don't care. He's not my problem. But I would say he's a little long in the tooth to be acting like such a ladies' man." She glanced at her wristwatch. "I've got a part-timer coming in, then I'm off for the rest of the day. Teddy, do you want me to come out to your place and hook up this recorder?"

"I think I can handle it." What else was left on their plan? They'd seen Mrs. Klaus and Lilibet. And purchased food. They needed glass from the hardware store to fix the broken window. Though Teddy knew she really ought to go over to Russel's house and see if she could help out, she didn't feel up to it. "To tell you the truth, all I want to worry about in the immediate future is a nap."

"Good idea," Vince said with wholehearted enthusiasm. "We need to get you into bed."

She peered meaningfully into his eyes. "Alone."

"Fine with me." He turned to Lilibet. "Maybe you could help me out."

Teddy stifled the automatic protest that rose to her lips. She had no claim on Vince's time. After all, he wasn't really her betrothed. That had only been a ploy to dispel the gossip. He was his own man, free and unencumbered by any relationship with her, except for a vague promise to help her find her sister's killer.

However, while she drove back to her house alone, Teddy felt abandoned. For some reason, Vince had thought it imperative to obtain his own rental car, and Lilibet had been only too happy to take him to the airport to pick one up. "Terrific," Teddy muttered as she turned down the road that led to her house. Good old Lilibet was terrific, and she'd come through with the equipment Teddy needed. But she was also too cooperative when Vince had needed a ride. Too willing to help. And much too pretty.

"Stop it," Teddy chastised herself. "You have no right to be jealous." In spite of what had happened last night... in spite of that knee-weakening kiss on Lilibet's porch... Teddy wasn't kidding herself about the impossibilities of a relationship with Vince. The logistical barriers to such a coupling were massive. He lived in Chicago and loved it. She lived here.

"But he has his own plane," came the response from a rebellious corner of her brain. "He could always fly down here to see me."

"However," she argued with herself, "he'd probably rather be showing the plane to Lilibet. I'll bet they're doing that right now, snuggling up, at this very minute, in his cockpit."

Gritting her teeth, Teddy told herself that she was much too adult and too experienced to confuse last night's frantic passion with a more enduring attachment that absolutely, positively could not be. She and Vince had different temperaments. He followed logic. And Teddy led with her heart, basing her perceptions on intuitions and feelings.

And right now, as she pulled up in front of her house, she was feeling low. Tired. Depressed. Her mind flashed disturbing memories of Whitney, and Teddy knew that the long grieving process had begun. There would be sorrow and pain. Anger. And the need for revenge. Whitney, like Jacques, had been murdered. Someone had stolen her breath, her dreams, her hopes, her joys, her life.

Teddy shook away those thoughts. Though she wanted to sleep, to rest and heal, she had practical concerns and mundane tasks to attend to. Her stop at the hardware store to pick up replacement glass for her broken window had taken forever. She had to unload her van, which was filled with an inappropriately domestic assortment of groceries. She never should have let Vince talk her into shopping. At this point, food was the furthest thing from her mind.

As soon as she parked in her driveway, she heard the first explosion. Then another and another. It was the unmistakable sound of gunfire. She cranked the key in the ignition, flipped into reverse, and did a one-hundred-and-eighty-degree turn so that she was facing back toward the road. There was a drag on the rear tires, and she knew they were flat. The bullets had been aimed at her van. Someone was shooting at her.

Through her windshield, she glimpsed a figure in black. Armed with a handgun. She ducked beneath the dashboard. A bullet slammed into the front of the van. Would the engine explode? Damn it, the bullets could ignite the gas into a ball of flame. She had to get out, had to run, to escape with her life. But how? There was somebody out there waiting to kill her. She had to stay here, inside.

Her brain relayed a terse message. *The doors. Lock the van doors.* She hit the front-door locks and scrambled between the seats to the rear of the van to lock the side door. *Just in time.* She saw the handle jiggle. The rear doors locked automatically, so those were already tight.

Now what? She waited in silence. Not for a second did she delude herself into thinking that this van was an impregnable fortress. Nothing stood between her and this dark-clad attacker but a thin sheet of metal and glass. He was toying with her, she realized. Getting inside the van would be easy. All he had to do was break a window and pop open the lock.

But he was waiting, holding back. Why?

The first thundering blow rocked the van on its axles, and Teddy gave a small, surprised yelp. The force felt as hard as a battering ram. Another earsplitting crash resounded against the side door. Would the lock hold? Would the catch loosen?

The banging echoed, and her equipment jolted, tumbling around her in chaos. The van pitched wildly. As Teddy huddled on the floor between the seats, she imagined the van closing in upon her. The walls twisting in grotesque shards, immobilizing her. The sharp metallic edges slashing her flesh.

"No," she cried. That couldn't happen. He couldn't destroy the metal shell. Not even firing bullets against the walls was an effective assault. "Think, Teddy."

The windows. He would break a window and come after her. Her best chance for escape was to go to the rear of the van and wait, bide her time until he was almost inside the front of the van. Then, run. Toward the shelter of the thicket. Run faster than his damn bullets.

The film. That had to be what he was after. She grabbed her camera bag. On hands and knees, she crawled through her scattered equipment toward the rear of the van. It lurched violently as if her assailant was hanging on to the side and rocking the vehicle. My God, did he plan to turn the van on its side? If so, there was nothing she could do about it. She was helpless.

Teddy stumbled and fell hard against the cold metal wall. The shatter of window glass awakened a new terror in her. Her fate—whatever it might be—was almost upon her. She took deep breaths, filling her lungs with life. She needed to make her escape, not tremble here like a scared rabbit.

A baseball bat poked through the driver's-side window. Efficiently the thick wood knocked the bits of glass away. *Not yet.* Teddy waited, her muscles cramped with tension. She watched a gloved hand reach inside the van, unfasten the door lock. *Not yet.*

The van door was flung open. He lunged inside.

Now.

Teddy shoved open the rear door and ran. *Not to the house.* She'd be trapped in there. Through the grasses, through the shrubs, her feet pounding the ground, she raced into the woods. Her camera bag slung across her shoulders, she fled for her life. A branch whipped across her face, but she kept running. She'd explored every inch of this land. She knew where the squirrels hid their caches and where the night cats made their lair.

It wasn't until she leapt across the stream that she halted and turned. No one was pursuing her. She stood, poised to run, breathing heavily. The driver's-side door of her van hung open on its hinges. He must be inside, digging through the mess of groceries and camera equipment.

Her assailant was a man. The force of his blows with the bat had been too powerful for a woman's hand. And the brutality of the attack was male. Violent and terrifying. Would he come after her? After he realized that she had taken the camera bag containing the film, would he look for her?

Of course, he would. The man was desperate. A vicious creature. A murderer.

There was a cave in the woods. Not a real cave, but a shallow hiding place between tumbled-down boulders. She could go there. She could hide until this was over.

But what about Vince? He might be on his way back here right now. *Go to the road.* She could catch Vince before he interfered with this desperate man with the gun.

Running through the high bushes and darting between slender swamp oak and the stinging boughs of pine, she made a wide circle. Ahead was the road. Up a slight incline. Bursting through a prickly shrub, she came out at a curve in the road.

The man in black was there, his back to the sun that his face obscured. His gun was raised, waiting to sight on her. There wasn't time for a scream. She dived backward into the brush. A bullet whizzed over her head, slicing the leaves.

Now he was following. She could hear him thrashing the leaves of shrubbery. She imagined his gloved hand reaching out, catching her shoulder, tripping her ankles. Doubling back, she made it to the graded road and started sprinting for all she was worth. Her breath tore through her throat. Her lungs burned with the effort of running full-out. She ignored the stitch in her side, the throbbing ache of her legs and arms as she pumped furiously, fighting her way onward.

Gunfire.

No.

She turned and saw him standing not twenty yards away. There was only one way to escape with her life. She tore off the camera bag and threw it to the ground. And then she continued, her legs thrusting in long strides, putting distance between herself and the man.

"Vince," she whispered hoarsely. Where was he? She needed him. He would help her. She couldn't do this by herself. Tears streaked down her face. Where was he?

She stumbled, skinning the palms of her hands on the road. Forcing herself up, she kept running. Forever. Running forever. A blue car, a shimmering royal blue, appeared before her on the road. Through the windshield, she saw Vince. But he wasn't alone. The car swerved to avoid her. Who was with him? She thought it might be Whitney. But her sister was dead. Gone.

Teddy felt the last of her stamina give out. She couldn't think. She collapsed to her knees in the middle of the road. Vince came toward her. In his hand was a gun, her father's gun. "No," she gasped. Vince must not go after the man. He would be killed. She couldn't stand to lose him, too. "Let him go."

"It's okay, Teddy." He was beside her. "I'm here."

"I didn't see his face."

He stroked her shoulders, soothing their agonized heaving. She couldn't get enough breath. Her throat was closing. She was on the verge of unconsciousness.

"It's okay," he repeated gently. "Everything is all right. You're going to be all right."

The world slipped away. Sounds faded in white noise. She looked up at the black branches of trees against a whitening sky. And her mind went blank.

Chapter Nine

Teddy suddenly regained consciousness. She bolted upright, shivering. On the wall opposite her bed, the shadows of wind-tossed tree branches made wild, erratic patterns.

Instinctively she clutched at Vince. Her fingernails dug into the muscled flesh of his forearm. Just as quickly, she felt a throbbing pain and released him. She held up her hands. Her palms and the heel of her right hand were swathed in gauze pads and adhesive wrapping. Her fingers trembled when she tried to flex and extend them.

What happened to me?

Sinking back against the pillows, she remembered running with all her might. She'd stumbled. Skinned her hands. Her knees ached, too. And her throat burned. But she was still alive. Teddy inhaled and exhaled slowly, deeply, allowing sensation to return to her body, feeling the pain. "I'm all right," she said.

Vince looked deep into her eyes. He must have seen something there that pleased him, because he smiled. Then he dabbed at her cheek with a damp washcloth.

"What are you doing?"

"You've got a scratch on your face. About a quarter of an inch away from your eye."

She regarded her hands again. The first-aid supplies must have come from her own medicine cabinet. "Did you do this bandaging?"

"I had help. Lilibet came out here with me."

"Lilibet was in the car with you. The blue car." Not Whitney. Teddy had not seen her dead sister, and that was a relief. At least she wasn't losing her sanity. Not yet, anyway. "I think I remember now." Every wretched detail. She closed her eyes against a pain that went far deeper than bruises, scratches and scrapes. "I've ruined everything. The film, Vince. When he was coming after me, I gave him the camera bag."

"It's all right, Teddy." He reached down beside the bed, flipped open his briefcase and spilled the contents of a large padded envelope across her lap: glassine envelopes and undeveloped rolls of black-and-white film.

"Thank God." Her bandaged hands fumbled with the small, delicate envelopes, not quite able to grasp. Frustrated with her clumsiness, she said, "Help me pick these up, Vince. We have to take good care of these negatives. I need to print the contact sheets right away."

As soon as he'd cleared off the negatives and film, she pushed aside the bedclothes. Though she still wore her filthy shirt, her other clothing had been stripped off. Darkening bruises showed on her knees. She moved stiffly, easing her legs over the edge of the bed. "I'm going down to the darkroom to get started."

Vince stood before her, blocking her way. "You're not going anywhere. There's a doctor on the way, and you're going to stay in bed and wait for him."

"I don't need a doctor."

"You passed out," he reminded her.

"I fainted. I can't believe I fainted."

Gently he eased her back into the bed and pulled up the covers. "You need to rest."

"I can't, Vince. I don't want to."

She couldn't give in to her fear, couldn't allow weakness to rule her decisions. That was what Jacques had always told her. Working together, they'd lived at the razor edge of danger covering poachers in Africa, a student riot in the streets of Paris, a coup in Central America where she had seen men die at her feet....

And yet she was more terrified by the man in black who had attacked her van with a baseball bat. He was too close. His violence was not a phenomenon to be observed and recorded through a telephoto lens. He had been coming after her, stalking her. Even now, in memory, the terror rose within her like a scream.

She jerked her head up sharply. "Did you catch him? Did the sheriff arrest him?"

"No."

"Then he's still out there."

"Yes."

Vince saw the struggle behind her eyes. He heard the panic in her voice. The attacker had shaken the most essential part of Teddy—her courage. He gently stroked her hair back from her warm forehead. Her temperature was still high. "Do you want to tell me what happened?"

"Not yet." She shivered. "Did you see him, Vince?"

"No. We didn't see anybody."

"And how did I get back here?"

"You fainted on the road, and I loaded you into the car. It was like you were half-asleep. You walked into the house and up the stairs on your own steam, but you collapsed across the bed and couldn't move."

A loud shout came from outside the bedroom window. "What was that?" she asked.

"The sheriff and two of his deputies are here. They're sifting through the back of your van, but the groceries are a mess. Smashed eggs and spilled milk."

"There won't be any fingerprints. He was wearing gloves." She remembered his hand reaching through the broken van window, and trembled. "Oh, God, I was scared."

"So was I."

"You?"

"You were bleeding, hurt. I was scared for you. Every time I looked into your eyes, you weren't there. You were awake, but there was no life." His easy smile vanished. His jaw tensed, and there was steel in his dark gray eyes. "I should never have left you alone."

His protective urge sparked a primitive sense of satisfaction within her. For once in her life, it might be nice to have someone else take care of her, watch over her, protect her from harm. Teddy felt a small quiver of pleasure. "I'm going to be all right, Vince. Really."

"That's what Lilibet said, too. You ought to heal up and be as good as new in a few days."

"Sooner than that." She threw off the covers. "All I really need is a hot shower."

As she lurched from the bed, her steps were shaky. Vince caught hold of her arm and supported her. He could have argued, insisted that she stay in the bed. *Stay safe, Teddy.* But this time he would acquiesce.

"It had better be a quick shower. If you're not out in five minutes, I'm coming in after you. I mean that."

"What if I lock the door?"

"The bathroom door locks?" He feigned surprise. "You actually have a door in this house that can be locked?"

"I don't know," she admitted. "I've never locked it."

When she closed the bathroom door in his face, her eyes shone with lively obstinance, and Vince felt his residual tension begin to uncoil. She was going to be all right. Teddy had encountered another nightmare and bounced back.

Someday, he feared, her resilience would reach its limit. He rested his palm on the cool wood of the bathroom door and listened for the water to start running. In a moment, a steady splashing reassured him that she hadn't fallen unconscious to the tiled floor. He paced across the bedroom, reluctant to leave her unguarded, even to take a shower.

While he and Lilibet had been driving back here from the airport, Vince had felt an urgency, almost as if Teddy had been calling his name. He'd sensed that she was hurt. It seemed crazy at the time, like some kind of hocus-pocus telepathy. But he refused to stop, as Lilibet wanted, to pick up a burger and fries. His foot had pressed down harder on the accelerator. Her need came through to him loud and clear. Yeah, sure, ESP? Thought transference? *Good thing he didn't believe in that stuff.*

He stood at her bedroom window, looking down at the sheriff's men as they studied her beat-up van. Another car pulled up and a white-haired man with a black doctor's bag came out, waved to the deputies and hustled toward the front door. Vince checked his wristwatch. Five minutes had elapsed since she went into the bathroom.

He tapped loudly on the door. "Time's up, Teddy. The doctor's here."

The rushing noise of the shower stopped. "Would you get me a nightgown, Vince? Look in my second bureau drawer."

In the dresser, he confronted an array of silky fabrics. A filmy black thing appealed to him, but he selected a more conservative gown. Pale blue and cotton. He opened the bathroom door a crack and held it inside.

"Thank you," she said.

He left her in the care of the doctor, but Vince still wasn't ready to put much distance between himself and Teddy. He stayed in the upper level of the house, within earshot. There was only one other room up here. Leaving the door open so he could hear when the doctor was finished, Vince meandered into Teddy's office.

It had a phone and a desk and file cabinets—the usual office equipment. Two enameled African masks hung on either side of the window. In nooks and crannies, there were statuettes. A brass turtle. A plastic deer. A fuzzy teddy bear wearing a blond wig. Vince smiled as he picked it up. "Hello, Teddy." He'd seen the bear's expression on her face. Curious eyebrows raised above round blue eyes. And the bear's stitched mouth showed a slight overbite. Just like Teddy's.

On a hook by the door was a pink sweatshirt. Vince held up the soft cotton fabric so he could read the legend on the back: Ladybugs. That might be the name of the softball team. Or, knowing Teddy, it might be a statement of sympathy for insects who needed to fly away home.

From a sorting bin, he picked up a flyer printed on bright yellow paper. Below a cartoon sketch of a photographer taking pictures of a carnival, the single sheet advertised Mary Theodora Edwards, free-lance photographer. "What's your story?" the flyer asked. "Did you invent a better mousetrap? Sight a UFO? Shake hands with Elvis? I WANT TO KNOW YOUR STORY." Then came a straightforward listing of some of Teddy's more spectacular credentials, including private sittings with celebrities, followed by her phone number and a post office box in Westalia.

If he'd never met her, Vince would have taken an immediate liking to Teddy based on this flyer. Her advertising showed an understated sense of whimsy. And yet she was businesslike and qualified. And so much more.

"Mr. Harding?"

A brief conference with the doctor reassured Vince. Basically, Teddy was fine. Her cuts required no stitches. Her scrapes and bruises would heal. And she didn't have a concussion. In fact, she had no head injury at all.

"Then why did she keep passing out?"

"Probably exhaustion. I'll do a more thorough exam in my office when she's ready. Right now, she needs rest, Mr. Harding. After she has something to eat, be sure she takes this mild sedative."

"That's not going to be easy, Doc. Not if she doesn't want to."

He nodded. "I'm aware of her stubbornness. Mary Theodora has been my patient since she was a little girl, and she wasn't much different then."

In the bedroom, Teddy sat up in bed with pillows at her back. Her professionally bandaged hands were folded neatly in her lap. The blue cotton nightie covered her shoulders, and the scalloped lace neck looked soft and pretty. Without a trace of makeup, she looked more delicate and feminine than he had ever seen her. Her wan smile tugged at his heart.

But she spoke with a hard edge to her voice. "I was wondering, Vince. If you didn't catch the man who attacked me, how did you get my film back?"

"He never had it, Teddy."

"What do you mean? I threw the camera bag right at him."

Vince reminded himself that her appearance of sweet delicacy was only skin-deep. He braced himself for an eruption. "Back in town, when I was driving your van, I took the negatives and film from your bag and put them in my briefcase."

"You did what?" She sat up straight, discovering a new set of aches and pains in her back and shoulder. "That's my film. Nobody, not even you, touches my film."

He raised a hand to placate her. "This was right after your father pulled out the gun in the parking lot, and I—"

"You didn't think I could take care of the negatives by myself, did you?"

"I meant to talk to you about it."

There was a tap on the bedroom door, and Sheriff Graham stuck his head inside. "Teddy? Are you awake?"

Her jaw stuck out. "Come on in. I'm afraid I can't tell you much, but I'll try."

Perfect timing, Vince thought. When the sheriff advised him that he'd prefer taking Teddy's statement alone, Vince gladly escaped her wrath. He grabbed the padded envelope and took it downstairs into the darkroom. Though every surface in the room gleamed cleanly, there were signs that the room had been searched. A couple of cabinets hung open. Drawers were slightly ajar. The intruder had been in here first, and he had jimmied the lock, which was now useless.

Vince slipped the envelope into a cabinet near the enlarger, closed the door and went into the kitchen where Lilibet was busily rescuing the groceries that had not been demolished.

"How's our Teddy feeling?" Lilibet asked. "The doc said she was going to be fine."

"Yeah, fine." She was recovering fast enough to want to rip his throat out. "I need to make her something to eat."

"I'll do it."

He sat at the table and watched as Lilibet cleaned and sorted and put things in order. Before Vince could ask, she poured a mug of fresh coffee and placed it on the table in front of him. To some men, Lilibet Chatworth fulfilled the fantasy of a perfect wife—beautiful, sexy and efficient at housework. "How long were you and Merle married?"

"Four years. We've been divorced for a year now."

"Why'd you get divorced?"

"Well, I don't know if that's any of your business." She spread out the fixings for sandwiches on the countertop. "You and Teddy are the perfect match. Both of you keep sticking your noses where they don't belong."

"So? Why the divorce?"

She plunked the bread knife down on the countertop and whipped around to face him. Her long black hair swirled around her shoulders. "He wanted babies, and I didn't. There. I've said it. I am an unnatural woman who doesn't want to get stuck raising nine kids the way my mama did."

"What about one? Or two?"

"Maybe. Someday."

"Merle wasn't willing to wait?"

"He's in a hurry," she said. "He's in his fifties, you know. At that age a man spends a lot of time looking back, trying to catch hold of those sparkling moments in the past. That's why he bought that stupid motorcycle. I hated that thing. Never did get on the back of it." She erased the unpleasant memories with a toss of her head. "And he also wanted to leave some legacy behind. Said he was going to name our firstborn Elvis, whether it was a boy or a girl."

A mid-life crisis, Vince thought. Merle had the classic symptoms. However, like everyone else in Westalia, his behavior was a little off center. Like Lilibet's. She was hiding something. "If Merle wants children, why is he courting Harriet?"

"Because she's so dang impressed that he was almost a country and western star." She turned back to the sandwiches. "But he'll never get serious about marrying her."

"He wanted Whitney," Vince said. He'd seen the desire in Merle's eyes when the older man had danced with Teddy's sister. And he'd held her much too close.

"You're right about that." She tore lettuce and slapped mayo on ham sandwiches. "That crazy old fool thought he'd win the heart of Whitney Edwards Stratton. Hah!"

"But Tom Burke got there first."

"Her husband got there first," Lilibet corrected. "If Russel Stratton had one sliver of backbone, he would've stood up to those two. I tell you, Vince, I was so tired of hearing about Whitney that I was ready to kill her myself."

"Who do you think did?"

"Tom," she said without hesitation. "I know he did. But you didn't hear it from me, and the sheriff won't, either."

"How do you know?"

She paused. When she turned and looked at him, her eyes were dark and sultry. "Woman's intuition."

But Vince wasn't buying her femme fatale act. Lilibet knew something about Whitney's murder that she wasn't telling. "If he killed her, Tom's dangerous. You saw what he did to Teddy. What he did to her van."

"I can't imagine Tom did that. The boy just ain't that smart. He's more likely to just say, 'Gimme the film.'"

"If he thinks you know something, Lilibet, he might come after you."

"Let him come."

"Tell me what you know."

"Honey, I didn't see nothing. I just know in my heart." She finished the sandwiches and opened the cabinet in search of a plate. "I'm going to take these upstairs to Teddy. Then I'm going to make some lunch for the sheriff and his boys. And then, I have got to get back home. Sunday's the only day I really have to myself."

"I'll take the food upstairs," Vince said. He wasn't getting anywhere with Lilibet. Might as well go back to Teddy's bedside and have her lecture him about touching her film.

As he climbed the stairs, balancing a tray laden with sandwiches, a banana and orange juice, he decided that he never would understand women. Lilibet was hiding a piece of material evidence for some unknown Southern-belle reason. Or, possibly, she didn't really know anything and simply enjoyed the pretense of having a secret. Or, she was out to get Tom Burke. Vince couldn't guess. *Woman's intuition?*

When he stepped inside the bedroom, Sheriff Graham mirrored his own baffled expression. He sat silently in the rocking chair beside the window. Teddy scowled. The sheriff grumbled, "She didn't recognize the guy. When he started attacking her van, she hid in the back and didn't see a thing. And that's a damn shame. I'd like to lock this guy up."

"So would I." Vince placed the tray on the bed in front of Teddy. "Have your men found any fingerprints?"

"Sure. We lifted a bunch of prints off the van, but Teddy tells me the guy was wearing gloves. And we've got a couple of footprints. Sneakers. We'll figure out from the tread pattern what brand name." He considered the situation. "Not that it'll do much good. I don't expect he's going to be dumb enough to hang on to those shoes."

"Basically," Teddy summarized, "we've got zip. And I can't help because I didn't see his face. All I saw was a man, average build, average height, dressed in black."

Sheriff Graham gazed longingly at Teddy's food. "You think there's any more where that came from?"

"Lilibet's making sandwiches for you and your men," Vince replied. "So, Sheriff Graham, did you find tire tracks?"

"Not exactly. But one of my men is a bona fide, amazing coon hunter and he trailed this guy's path through the forest to the other side where there's another road. That must have been where he parked his vehicle."

"A motorcycle?"

"Can't tell. The road's paved. We'll ask around with the neighbors, but nobody lives nearby, so there ain't much chance that anybody saw him."

"Zip," Teddy repeated through a mouthful. Despite her bandaged hands, she was managing nicely.

But Vince wasn't ready to give up. "What about the autopsy on Whitney?"

"Nothing yet. Coroner is still working on it." He stuck out his lower lip. "All we've got are those pictures Teddy took at the party. They must be important, because this guy wants them pretty bad. But Teddy is telling me that she's not going to surrender her film or negatives."

"Not without a court order," she said. "I will not have some klutz police photographer messing with my film."

"I'm of a mind to get that order, Teddy. I could confiscate that film."

"I'll fight you every step of the way."

"I don't like that attitude. As long as you have that film in your possession, you're in danger, young lady. And I can't spare a man to stand guard."

"You'll have to," she said.

"In a pig's eye. Not unless I take you into protective custody and bring you into town where I can keep an eye on you."

Vince knew that wouldn't work. Teddy was too stubborn. No matter how scared she was, she wouldn't accept protection that threatened her independence. "I have a plan," he said.

"Glory hallelujah!" The sheriff turned toward him. "I'm listening."

"We'll make those contact sheets today. You keep a set. Teddy keeps a set and the negatives."

Teddy interrupted. "Aren't you forgetting something?" She held up her hands. "I can't do developing work today. I'll screw up everything."

"But you're forgetting..." He held up his own hands. "I know how to use an enlarger."

"I'm not leaving you in my darkroom alone with all my negatives and my stories-in-progress. How do I know you won't mess up my equipment?"

"You can supervise," he said.

"Come on, Teddy," the sheriff said. "Whatever's in there is important. Plus, when you get rid of those pictures, the bad guy's going to stop coming after you."

"I'll think about it." But she was dubious.

Vince continued with his plan. "Sheriff, we'll need a guard for this afternoon while we're in the darkroom. When it's done, we'll give a set of contact sheets to him."

"That seems mighty reasonable to me." He bustled toward the door. "I'm going to see what Lilibet has rustled up."

Vince came around to the side of her bed. He shook two small blue pills into his hand and placed them on the tray beside her juice. "The doctor said for you to take these."

"I'm coming to the darkroom with you." She dutifully popped the pills into her mouth and swallowed. "These won't make me tired, will they?"

"Not any more tired than you need to be."

The effect of the pills was fairly quick. When she finished eating, Teddy gave him a brief lecture on the use of her enlarger. By the end of her talk, she was yawning. Vince removed the tray and sat on the bed beside her. "It's been a hell of a day, Mary Theodora."

"Yes, it has."

He took her bandaged hand in his and lightly stroked the pale skin of her inner wrist. "Relax," he said. "You can take a nap."

"But I promised to print that film." Her eyelids half-closed, heavy with the need for sleep. "Got to be tough."

She looked anything but tough, he thought. Her features softened as the tension flowed from her. Though she was still sitting up in the bed, she slumped lower and unconsciously pushed at the quilt, revealing the swell of her breasts beneath the light blue nightgown. He wanted to touch her. Someday, he knew, they would explore the incredible passion they had shared. Someday.

When he lifted his gaze, he knew that she'd been watching him. She'd been reading his mind. "We can't," she said. Sleepily she dragged out the words. "We can't make love."

"I know. You need rest."

"Never again, Vince."

"Never say never again."

She tried to scowl, but she was too tired. The resulting pout was adorable. "You and me? Oh no, it won't work. Not at all. There's no future."

"We'll talk about this another time, sweetheart."

"Don't call me sweetheart," she managed to object softly before her eyes finally closed. "I'm nobody's sweetheart."

She was wrong about that.

Vince waited until her breathing flowed steady and calm, until she slept. Then he lightly kissed her smooth forehead and whispered, "Rest well, sweetheart."

TEDDY REACHED FOR the telephone before she was fully aware that it was ringing. Even while she was sound asleep, she had anticipated this call. "What do you want?"

"Teddy? Teddy, is that you?"

The disguised voice of her informant did not surprise her. The strange tone sounded appropriate for the darkness that had gathered outside her bedroom window. She stiffly rose from the bed and stood staring into the night, wondering if she had been caught in an Alice-in-Wonderland nightmare where the absurd made sense and the sensible was absurd. She demanded, "Why did you call?"

"I owe you an apology, honey. Got to say sorry. I never meant to scare you. I was only funning with you."

"Fun?" Teddy controlled the urge to yell at her informant. She needed to encourage this person to continue with his gibberish, to keep him on the line as long as possible so she could find out who he was and what he—or maybe she—had seen. Had she hooked up the recording equipment? Teddy couldn't remember. "Tell me your idea of fun."

"Long cool glass of limeade on a hot day," the voice squeaked. "I sit back on the porch. I listen to the King. To Elvis. 'Crying in the Chapel.' Or 'Love Me Tender.' There weren't ever any other like Elvis."

"I need to know about my sister," Teddy pressed. "Tell me what you saw at the Sleep Inn."

A low keening trailed through the telephone receiver.

Teddy asked, "Are you crying?"

"She's dead. So beautiful. And she's gone now. All the good people die young."

Teddy covered her mouth with her clumsy, bandaged hand and squeezed her eyes shut to keep back the tears. The voice of her informant was an echo in her head, a mad reminder of her own fears and suffering. "You loved her, too," Teddy said. "You loved Whitney."

"And she loved me. I know she did."

"We have to meet."

"Oh no, honey. We can't do that."

"But you can help," Teddy said.

"I just called to tell you one thing. You listening?"

"What did you see?"

"Pay attention, hear? You got to be careful, Teddy. Don't trust nobody, hear?"

Teddy feared that her informant was going to hang up. "Don't go," she pleaded. "Please, oh please, help me find the man who killed my sister."

"You watch your step, Teddy Edwards. That's all I got to say to you."

The phone went dead. The contact was severed. Uselessly, Teddy shouted into the instrument, "Wait! Come back. Please." She gripped the receiver so tightly that her hand throbbed. She shouldn't have pressured the caller. After all these years of handling difficult subjects, Teddy knew better than to push. She should have kept her mouth shut, should have listened instead of making a demand. This person, she knew, was a witness. But what had they seen? What did they know?

The phone beeped in her hand, reminding her to hang up, and she did. Why hadn't she hooked up the recording equipment? Why hadn't she been ready for this call?

"Teddy?" She whirled around, startled that she wasn't alone. Vince spoke softly. "Was that your informant on the phone?"

The hall light shone behind him, casting an eerie shadow across his shoulders and picking out the highlights in his dark brown hair. She must have still been half-asleep because, in the semidark, lounging against the doorframe, he reminded her of Elvis. He had the same brooding sensuality. The deep voice. That essential male quality. A seductive strength that beckoned from an era when men were kings, the unquestioned lords of their domains. An era when sensitivity referred only to skin care. The good old days when men were men and women were...chattel.

"What's wrong, Teddy?"

His voice held a commanding note, and she longed to rest in his arms, confide her problems and allow him to take care of everything.

"I'm all right," she responded. Her fingers clutched the thin fabric of her nightie, and she wished for a more substantial barrier of clothing between herself and Vince. At the same time, she wanted to be naked, to be taken into his arms and crushed against him. She wanted to be comforted and consoled.

Teddy reached over to her bedside and turned on the lamp, erasing the night and banishing her fantasies. She was a modern female who knew her own mind. Massaging her temples, she said, "Wow! That was some sedative. You drugged me."

"I followed the doc's orders."

The fog in her brain dissolved as she got a grip on the reality of her situation. The man who stood before her was Vince Harding, managing editor of *Files*. His presence was, on the one hand, reassuring. On the other hand, she couldn't trust him. Her informant was correct. There was no one she could trust.

"Who was your midnight caller?"

She glanced at the beside table where her telephone rested, and noticed the black console beside it. A tiny red light was flashing. "Vince, did you hook up the recording equipment?"

"Sure did."

"How do I play it back?"

He came around the bed to the space between the window and her bedside. Though his approach was casual and nonthreatening, a shiver bristled the fine hairs on her forearms as she sat back on the bed, allowing him room to work the recording equipment she'd gotten from Lilibet.

"It's like an answering machine," he explained. "But voice activated to start recording as soon as you speak into the phone."

He sat down on the edge of her bed and punched a rewind button. In the silence of her room, the whir and click of the machine sounded strange and out of place. Teddy's instincts urged her to move closer to him, but she held back, kneeling behind him in the center of the bed with the covers in disarray around her. Fetching herself a robe might have been prudent, but it would also have been an admission that she couldn't trust herself when she was near him, that she wanted him in ways that were too exciting to contemplate.

"Now," he said, "I touch this button and we have playback."

"Wait!" When she touched his arm to restrain him, her breasts brushed against his back. He turned his face toward hers, and her self-control slipped several more notches. She scooted away from him as quickly as if she'd been burned.

"Why should I wait, Teddy?"

"I don't want you to hear this caller."

His gray eyes flared. "You can't be serious."

"But I am. This person might just lead me to the photograph of the century." She could see his anger building. "And I'm not going to give it away to you."

"This person," he said, "is a demented lunatic who knows something important about your sister's murder."

"But I can't—"

"This lunatic might be the same lunatic who trapped you in your van and beat the hell out of it with a baseball bat."

"Oh, I don't think so." She shook her head. "This informant might be as wacky as a walrus, but not violent."

"Why not, Teddy?"

"I can sense the gentleness. This person doesn't want to hurt me. Not like the man in black who smashed up my van."

"You can sense how these people were feeling?" His disbelieving attitude was reflected in his voice and in his posture as he pulled back from her.

"I'm analyzing. There was something methodical about the way that man terrorized me. Like he could think one step ahead of what I was doing. The way he shot out the tires, then fired into the engine, then banged on the doors until I went to the back. When I ran to the road, he was standing there, waiting. Very efficient. Very controlled."

"Like your father?"

"Don't start that again." But Vince was right. The assault on her vehicle was exactly the sort of maneuver that Jordan Edwards might pursue if he wanted to get his hands on the film. Still, she said, "It was not my father."

"Then who?"

"Vince, I would appreciate it if you'd leave the room so I can replay that tape."

"I'm not going anywhere. You're going to have to get it through your head that I'm not here for a scoop. I'm here for you."

She wasn't ready to hear that he was here because he cared about her. Even after their incredible lovemaking, she couldn't believe that she held him in thrall.

"I promised to be here," he continued, "and that's what I'm going to do."

"So it's a male ego thing," she decided. "You promised to be here to slay the dragon for the pitiful little damsel in distress. Is that it?"

"Just play the damn tape, okay?"

She stretched out and touched the Play button. As always, when she heard her own voice on tape, she cringed. Did she really have that much twang? Was her voice really that low? Her informant sounded like Alvin the Chipmunk, all squeaky and squawky. Teddy's responses came as a desperate counterpoint.

She rewound the tape and played it again. There was something about the beginning moments that intrigued her. When she'd answered the phone, she recalled a disturbing familiarity. Replaying the beginning again and again, she finally heard it. "Did you hear that, Vince?"

"No."

"Listen real close. Right at the beginning, there's a sound." She played it again. "You were right about this being a midnight caller. Almost precisely at midnight."

"A bell?"

"A chime. From the Westalia United Methodist Church downtown. When I was growing up at home, I heard that clock marking off the hour every day. And I'll bet that little bit of reverberation was the last stroke of midnight." She drew the conclusion that was already at the edge of her consciousness. "This is somebody I know. Somebody I know very well."

Chapter Ten

Without the phone tracing equipment, they could only guess at the originating number. Which of Westalia's residents was Teddy's Elvis informant?

"Lilibet will have the trace arranged with the phone company tomorrow," she said.

"Damn." Vince sat on the foot of her bed, then sprawled backward and stared up at the ceiling. "We keep missing by inches."

"This person knows me. He calls me Teddy. He knew how to reach me at the country club at Whitney's party. He lives in downtown Westalia. Why can't he say his name?"

"He?" Vince questioned.

"You heard the voice. He or she?"

"Don't know."

She pulled up her knees so she wouldn't be touching him and immediately felt a twinge of pain. Her calves were sore. Her thighs were sore. Even her butt ached. "I feel like I ran a hundred miles, but it wasn't that far. Maybe I ought to start working out. Jogging or something."

"Yeah, you never can tell when you'll need to run for your life again."

He rubbed his hand across his eyes. Spending the day in her darkroom making contact sheets from the color negatives left him with heavy eyestrain. That, and the lack of sleep. He hadn't trusted himself to lie beside her on the bed, and her sofa was too short. Before he heard her on the phone up here, Vince had seriously contemplated taking one of her little blue pills and getting some solid rest. He closed his eyes. Her bed felt wonderfully comfortable.

"Okay, Teddy, let's go about this logically. Is there anybody we can eliminate as the caller? Anybody who lives too far from the bell tower to hear it ringing?"

"It's loudest on the hill where my father, Harriet, Russel and a bunch of other relatives live. But I've heard it at Lilibet's house. And Merle's place is fairly close to hers." She brightened. "Tom Burke. You can't hear the bell as far away as the Sleep Inn."

"But I assume there's a public phone booth in Westalia."

"Sure. At the gas station. But we can still eliminate Tom. I started getting these calls before he blew into town."

"And who were the other people you rattled off?"

"Harriet or Lilibet . . . I don't think it's Lilibet. Playing games on the phone isn't her style."

He remembered Lilibet's secret, a mysterious piece of evidence that made her certain that Tom Burke was the killer. But Vince agreed with Teddy's assessment. Lilibet might play coy with him, but she'd blab to Teddy.

"Could be Merle," she said. "He's an Elvis fan."

"What about Russel or your father?"

She stretched and yawned and nodded. "I doubt that either of them could name three Elvis hits, much less tell you what he looked like. But I could be wrong."

"Could be." His eyelids remained closed.

"Are you tired, Vince?"

"Are you?"

"I can't decide if I'm more tired or hungry. Should I eat or should I sleep?"

"I vote for sleep." Vince sighed.

"Tomorrow, we'll find my informant," she said. "We'll go into town and root this person out. After we do the contact sheets, of course."

"That sounds like a good plan." He lay still, hoping she wouldn't ask directly about the film. He wasn't up to an argument.

"And I need to get the van fixed. First thing." Carefully, she wiggled her fingers. The scrapes on the palms of her hands were still painful, but the doctor's effective bandaging had increased her flexibility enough so she could manage the darkroom work. They could start right now. Though she wouldn't attempt anything artistic or do retouching, she could handle the enlarger. Especially if Vince was standing by, ready to help.

But that didn't appear to be likely. His breath rose and fell in sonorous cadence as he lay at the brink of unconsciousness. He was almost asleep. She leaned over him. What a sweet, lovely man he was! He'd been so terribly worried about her, and more fiercely protective than a lion guarding his pride.

Teddy took a breath and blew lightly across his forehead. His eyebrows twitched, but he didn't open his eyes. Such a handsome man. His face, in repose, fascinated her. He had a strong chin and character lines etched around his eyes. She stared down, taking an indelible photograph with her mind. Did other people think he was as attractive as she did? Or was this face created especially for her, to fulfill her own idea of masculine perfection?

Tomorrow, she decided, would be soon enough for more plans and more actions. For tonight, she was content to curl up beside him and drift into a calm, healing sleep.

THE NEXT MORNING, her tender feelings toward Vince turned brittle, shattering the moment she walked into her darkroom and saw the finished contact prints. He must have done them yesterday while she slept. How could he? He'd promised to wait!

Teddy felt like racing back upstairs to the bedroom where he was still asleep, grabbing him by his broad shoulders and shaking him. He had no right to touch her cameras, her film. No damn right at all to use her darkroom. That red-lit space was the private core of her existence. It was her heart—the place where she could always retreat and discover the magic of pictures spreading across blank paper. In the years she'd been with Jacques, she'd never let him work with her photos. Yet Vince had marched right in and taken charge.

Though he'd left the work space tidy, the organization was all wrong, and a renewed anger flared within her. If he'd messed up these negatives, she would wring his neck.

He'd printed about sixteen exposures to a sheet. That was good. The prints were clear enough to make out some detail. When she squinted at the pictures, her eye was caught by a full-face shot of Whitney holding a long-stemmed pink rose. Teddy remembered taking the picture a few moments before Whitney and Russel stood beneath the rose bower and renewed their vows.

A good portrait. Pensive. Whitney's blue eyes were wide and thoughtful as she looked into a mysterious distance beyond the lens of the camera.

Teddy blinked to keep herself from crying. She would give this photograph to Russel, perhaps blow it up to portrait size for display at the funeral so people could remember Whitney's moments of sweetness, her zest for living. So they wouldn't think of her only as the victim of a murder.

Glancing through the other prints, she was not displeased with Vince's handiwork. If she were truly objective, she couldn't complain. "Not bad at all."

"Thank you." Vince leaned against the doorway. His hair was still tousled from sleep, but the aura of exhaustion was gone.

"You know I'm angry," she said.

"I kind of expected that." Immediately he changed the subject. "I was thinking about your informant. If it's not someone who knows you personally, how did they get your phone number?"

"I'm in the yellow pages under Photography, and I also do flyers." She shot him a barbed glance. "But you probably know that. I'm sure that during your sojourn in my house, you've gone into my office. Surely you checked out my flyers."

"I saw them, and I liked them."

"What else did you paw through? Back files? Old family pictures? I'll bet you got a laugh out of those."

"Hey, I didn't go through the drawers. And in the darkroom, I only used the equipment. My plan wasn't to spy. I wanted to eliminate the threat."

"So you did this yesterday?"

"While you were asleep. I made two sets of contact prints. One for the sheriff and one for you."

"And you figured that as soon as the sheriff had these prints in his possession, the man in black who came after me would quit."

"He's after the pictures," Vince said.

"I hope you're right." She understood his motivation. In fact, she even agreed with his logic. "But I'm still not happy about it. Vince, you can't just walk into my life uninvited and do whatever you want."

"Say the word, Teddy, and I'll leave."

His gray-eyed gaze held steady across the room, compelling her to look back at him, urging her to be truthful. If she wanted him gone, she should say so now. But she couldn't imagine what it would be like without him. In the midst of this tragedy and pain, he'd been her strength, her rescuer, her hero. She needed him. "Please stay." He nodded, as she had known he would. There was a connection forming between them—a rather disturbing bond—that made words unnecessary. Teddy took a quick breath. "Last night, I believe I outlined a plan."

"Something about rooting out suspects."

"I suggest we take these prints over to Russel's. I'm sure that all my family and half the town have gathered over there. To 'help.'"

He caught the bitterness in her voice, the barely veiled anger. After they were dressed and on their way in his little blue rental car, he asked her why she felt that way.

"'Helping' is what my family says instead of interfering. In any tragedy, they come in droves, offering casseroles and advice. When my mother passed away, they 'helped' until I was ready to scream. I wanted them to get out and leave us alone." As she spoke, she grew more and more flustered. Teddy flipped down the visor mirror on the passenger side and studied her reflection. "Does this scratch on my face look too awful?"

"It's hardly noticeable." The angry red line that ran from her forehead into the hairline above her ear was the most obvious of her injuries. The bandages covering her palms were large patches that the doctor had left behind and Teddy had applied herself after her shower. "I need some lipstick. My hands were too clumsy to put on makeup."

"I'll do it."

"Don't be silly, Vince. How can you put on my lipstick?"

He pulled onto the shoulder of the road and parked. "Give me the tube."

She flipped open the navy purse that matched the simple jersey dress she'd thrown on. When she fished out the gold lipstick case, she could barely hold it between her thumb and forefinger. "My hands don't hurt, but they're stiff. And the bandage is in the way."

He took the lipstick. "Look into my eyes and open your mouth."

"You sound like a perverted dentist."

"Better a dentist than a beautician." He rolled the lipstick up from the tube. As far as Vince could tell, the fresh pink color precisely matched the natural tone of her kissable mouth. Her eyes observed him warily as he leaned toward her.

Bracing his left hand behind her neck to hold her head steady, he fully intended to apply the glossy color. But when his gaze spread from her mouth to study the open loveliness of her face, desire struck. Vince could not stop himself. Still holding her neck steady, he lightly traced the satin curve of her lips with his tongue. Then he kissed her fully.

She murmured encouragement, and he kissed her again. Her mouth was hot. The scent of her perfume tantalized him. A kiss wasn't enough to sate the unbearable hunger he felt for her. If he didn't control himself, he'd push back the bucket seats and make love right here at the edge of the road.

Her hands groped helplessly at his shirtfront, and he caught hold of her fingers. He touched her fingertips to his mouth. They were both breathing hard. When he looked into her eyes, he knew they would make love again soon. But not now. He rolled down the lipstick and said, "You don't need makeup."

Teddy knew exactly what she did need. But she didn't dare make love to him again. The first time had been the result of an almost crazy passion, a hysterical need to affirm that life went on. The second time, if there was a second time, would mean something different. And she didn't want to make that commitment. She couldn't allow herself to become so attached to a man who would be leaving.

For the rest of the drive, she was silent. When they pulled up in front of Russel's house, her emotions had settled down enough for her to notice four different vehicles parked nearby. And three motorcycles. The family was here. They had descended. She hoped no one would take notice of her presence. Maybe she and Vince could slip in unannounced, ask a few questions about the whereabouts of people late last night and slip out.

She hadn't counted on Harriet, who was apparently coordinating the visitors. Aunt Harriet swooped down on Teddy and Vince with a loud cry. "Teddy, darling, thanks for coming. What did you bring?"

"Bring?"

"Casserole? Cold cuts?" She glanced at the briefcase Teddy had tucked beneath her arm. "What have you got in there?"

"Harriet, could I talk with you alone for a minute?" Teddy refused to parade the contact sheets for everyone's perusal. There were private decisions to be made about which photos should be enlarged. "Please, Harriet."

"Well, all right." She raised her voice. "Hey, everyone, look who's here. It's Teddy and her fiancé, Vince. Teddy and I need to talk. You all make yourselves comfy."

Harriet led her into Whitney and Russel's bedroom, which was, ironically, decorated in the same delicate peach color Teddy used in her bathroom. The lacy wallpaper was an almost identical pattern. On the bedside table was one of the first snapshots Teddy had ever taken—a glamour shot of seven-year-old Whitney, playing dress-up in their mother's clothing. A lot of Whitney was in that photo, Teddy thought. In many ways, Whitney had been the good little girl who never really grew up.

Harriet called her out of her reverie. "What did you need to talk privately about?"

"Elvis."

Teddy whipped around, trying to catch Harriet in an expression of nervousness and confusion. No such luck. Her aunt pursed her lips in surprise. "Elvis Presley?"

"The King of Rock and Roll. Big E. Priscilla's husband. Star of *Blue Hawaii*. Harriet, do you think he's still alive?"

"He'll never die. Every once in a while, I catch a glimpse of him in a magazine photo or hear one of his songs on the radio, and I think I've gone back in time. That I'm young again, young enough to be excited about a very sexy young man from Memphis." Very quickly she added, "But I'm not like *those* people, *your* people, the

ones who call the Elvis Sighting Hot Line that Merle's so
thrilled about."

"Merle's thrilled?"

"Indeed he is." She drew herself erect. "Is this all you
wanted to talk about? Because I have more important
things to worry about than that tabloid nonsense. Al-
though I must admit that Vince impresses me. I can't believe he edits one of *those* papers."

"I have the contact prints from the anniversary party,
and I wanted you to glance over them. I'd like your first
impression on which of these should be enlarged."

Harriet took the proof sheets, and the two women sat
side by side on the edge of the bed, slowly turning pages,
remembering Whitney as she had been at the party,
smiling and laughing, concocting devious little schemes—
one of which might have killed her.

Harriet paused at the same portrait that Teddy had
liked. "Here's a good one," she said. "She looks so
pretty and innocent. Not at all like real life, is it?"

"What do you mean, Harriet?"

"I adored your sister, and I would never speak poorly
of the dear departed. But, between you and me, our dear
little Whitney was a bit of a schemer. She was making a
play for Merle, you know."

"Yes," Teddy encouraged, "I know."

Teddy recognized a spark of the infamous Edwards
temper as Harriet continued, "Merle is my beau, and
Whitney knew that. Why, oh why, did she have to go after him?"

"Maybe it was the other way around. Maybe he was
going after her."

"Certainly not." Harriet was incensed. "Merle Chatworth might not be the prize catch of the century, but
he's an honest man. He would have told me if he in-

tended to end our relationship and go after Whitney. Anyway, she was married. Not available."

Teddy knew that wasn't the way Whitney had seen Merle. Though her sister hadn't wanted a "relationship," she would have used Merle to make her husband jealous. Whitney had liked to play the mating game, to tease and arouse. And it never occurred to her that someone like Harriet might be hurt in the process.

Though Harriet rattled on in her usual manner, her voice held a depth of unexpressed emotion. "I meant to have a talk with Whitney. A serious chat about men and marriage and what's proper and what's not. But it's too late, isn't it? Our poor Whitney is with the angels now."

"Harriet, are you all right?"

"I'm grieving," she explained.

The emotion was as familiar to Harriet as it was to Teddy. Her flighty aunt had lost her husband—just as Teddy had lost Jacques. And Harriet had been a stalwart support when Teddy's mother had died and her father had retreated into a shell of bitterness.

At that moment, Teddy wanted to hug her aunt, to tell her that she truly did understand her sorrow and her pain. But Harriet would have been seriously upset by a show of feelings. She was not a woman who encouraged tears.

Harriet pointed to the photograph of Whitney in her hand. "We should use this one. It's a little serious, but very attractive. Hides how skinny Whitney had gotten."

"She had lost weight," Teddy agreed.

"She wasn't happy," Harriet added in a low voice. "The dear girl was shopping too much and eating too little."

"Shopping too much?"

"That's what I always do when I'm depressed. Buy myself a trinket. And Whitney had started spending quite a lot on jewelry. You know the ring Russel bought for her?"

"The pink coral."

"Whitney picked it out for herself. And she bought things for Russel, too. Take a peek at his watch. It's not a Rolex, but it might as well be. And his rings. Heavy gold things."

The door swung open and Russel stepped inside. "Sorry, Harriet, I didn't realize you were—"

"Hi, Russel." Teddy stood. She hated all the insincere hugging that went on at family gatherings, but she accepted Russel's embrace. In a tired voice, he said, "Thanks for coming."

She looked into his weary, sorrow-filled eyes. There was so much to say, and no good way to say it. Teddy blurted, "Sorry, but I didn't bring a casserole."

"Doesn't matter." He bobbed his head on his skinny neck and turned away from her. With loping strides, he went into the bathroom off the master bedroom.

Teddy followed. Silently she watched as he took an amber prescription vial from the medicine cabinet and tapped out two small blue pills. Teddy almost commented that the doctor must have been here with his sedatives for Russel. Then she caught sight of the inside of the cabinet where other vials lined the shelves.

Apparently, she thought, while Whitney had coped with their marital problems by starving herself and shopping, Russel had resorted to prescription drugs. As he gulped down the pills, his gaze caught hers in the mirror, and she saw an instant of panic in his eyes. "We should talk," he said.

Teddy could feel Harriet's breath on her neck, and she turned to her aunt. "Would you excuse us, Harriet?"

"Are you sure you'll be all right?"

Teddy guided her toward the door. "I want to ask Russel about the photo, the one you liked. It might be difficult for him and I'd—"

"Then I should be here. If he needs a shoulder to cry on, I'm here."

"I'll take care of it," Teddy said firmly. She opened the bedroom door. "We'll be out in a minute, Harriet."

When she closed the door and turned toward Russel, he was watching her with a strange interest, as if he were appraising her, deciding what he could or couldn't say. Uncomfortably, Teddy said, "We don't know each other very well, Russel, but I want you to know that you can talk to me."

"We argued."

"You and Whitney?"

"Before she left the house, right before she was murdered, we had a fight. She told me I didn't pay enough attention to her. Same old thing we always fought about."

Teddy admitted, "Whitney and I argued a lot, too."

"But this just wasn't right, Teddy. I never denied her anything. We had a nice home. She had beautiful clothes and jewelry."

"Anything her heart desired." He sounded so much like her father. Neither one of these men refused any material want. Clothing. Cars. Presents. And a trust fund. Though Teddy had turned down family funds rather than be in debt to her father, she was certain that Whitney had collected a substantial amount. Quietly Teddy said, "Maybe Whitney wanted something money can't buy."

"Did she tell you that?"

Slowly Teddy shook her head. "We didn't often talk about serious things. We kind of grew apart."

"That's how I feel, too. And I worked hard to please her," he said. "Damn hard. Put in a lot of overtime."

"But you like your job."

"I do," he admitted.

"I can respect that." Even if he was working for her father. "There's nothing wrong with a hard day's work."

"Whitney never understood. She wanted me to spend every minute with her. That night, she told me..." Teddy waited while he took a couple of deep breaths. "She told me," he continued, "that she would take a lover. I didn't know if she meant Tom. I guess she did."

"You and Tom were always close friends, weren't you?" Teddy remembered something else. "You used to work on cars together. And cycles. What do you think of his Harley Pancake?"

"Panhead. Harley Panhead. Excellent bike," Russel said in the same awed tone Vince used in referring to the motorcycle. His expression darkened, and he looked like he might say something significant.

The bedroom door popped open. Harriet fluttered inside. "Are you all right, Russel?"

"He's fine," Teddy answered. "We're fine."

"Now, dear, there's no reason to be rude with me. I mean, I know you're preoccupied with these ridiculous Elvis sightings and all, but that's no excuse for—"

"Elvis sightings?" Russel asked. "What in blazes is an Elvis sighting?"

Though Teddy wished he'd spoken the dark thought that he'd been brooding about, his surprised amusement at the mention of Elvis told her that Russel was *not* her informant. She explained, "They run a hot-line number in Vince's paper, *Files,* and people call in with information about seeing Elvis. I go out and take pictures, too."

"You're joking."

"No, I'm not. I've driven halfway across the state in the middle of the night to follow up on tips I get."

"Waste of time," Russel said.

"My sentiments exactly," Harriet said.

Russel gestured toward the door. "Ladies, shall we? I should return to these people who are kind enough to pay their respects."

At the bedroom door, Teddy caught Harriet's arm and pulled her aside. "How is Russel holding up? Tell me the truth."

"Frankly, Teddy, I think all these people are beginning to bother him. He's been sneaking off by himself, and I've been encouraging him to do it. Yesterday he took off for a long ride on his bike."

"His bike?"

"His motorcycle, of course."

"Of course." Harriet started to leave, and Teddy stopped her again. "What about Dad?"

"I haven't seen much of him. He's been staying at his house, mostly. When people go over there, he opens the door and comes out on the veranda, but he won't invite guests inside."

Teddy gathered up the contact prints and followed Harriet into the living room where the ten or twelve people milling there seemed like a large crowd. Teddy had no interest in staying and sharing in the small talk. She'd decided on the course she would follow to help—find the killer.

After she rescued Vince from a small group of Edwards relatives who seemed more interested in the unending quest for Elvis than in remembrance of Whitney, they swung past the garage, where Teddy arranged for a mechanic to come out to her house and work on the van.

Back home, she shed her sedate navy blue outfit and dressed in a lightweight aqua sweat suit. It was time to get down to business. Let the rest of the family stand around with casseroles and cold cuts. Teddy had work to do. She aimed Vince toward the darkroom. "There's got to be some clue in those contact sheets."

"Let's hope so."

"Why else would the killer come after me? I don't know anything about anybody. All I do is take pictures."

She fanned out the plastic-encased sheets on the darkroom counters. There was Lilibet, dancing in an exotic red swirl. Merle Chatworth held a giggling Harriet. Groups of relatives and friends arranged and rearranged themselves in unextraordinary patterns. Faces laughed with no sound. Pink roses bloomed with no scent. Teddy wished she could relive the day, wished she could touch Whitney and warn her. But that time was gone forever. "Okay, let's put these in order from the beginning of the party to the end."

With contact sheets spread across all the counters in the darkroom, they walked through the sequence of events. From early afternoon through the buffet dinner—where, Teddy noted, Tom Burke was not seated at the head table—into the evening, when the lights on the country-club patio shone romantically on dancing couples.

Teddy noticed more than Vince because she knew these people. In her mind, it was significant when two ladies who hadn't spoken to each other in years were smiling congenially, when a divorced couple danced together, when close friends stood apart. She used a loupe to magnify the faces in group shots. Still, no one appeared suspicious. Nothing, absolutely nothing, seemed ominous. She sighed. "Looks like a perfectly normal gathering."

Vince stared down at a photograph of Tom and Lilibet. Her strapless dress had slipped precariously, and Tom was peeking at her cleavage. "Perfectly normal," Vince repeated.

"Here's one of you," she said. "With my father." The camera never lied. Though the two men were behaving in a proper civil manner, holding cocktail glasses and conversing, their expressions conveyed utter hostility. Teddy observed, "Not exactly a friendly twosome."

"Take a look at this," he said. It was Lilibet and Whitney. In this photo, Whitney's nose tilted skyward, smug and superior. Lilibet's dark eyes were murderous slits as she looked at the ring on Whitney's finger.

But apart from the obvious enmity, there was something odd about this picture, which had been taken after the dinner. Teddy remembered the moment when these two belles of the ball had stood face-to-face and bosom to bosom. Lilibet's curves, lusciously displayed in red, might have won more attention than Whitney's cream-colored poise, but at that moment Whitney had been the unquestioned princess. Why? Because of the coral ring?

"Wrong hand," Vince said.

"What do you mean?"

"Whitney's showing Lilibet the wrong hand." He moved down the row of contact sheets to a previous picture. "Here's Russel giving her the ring. He put it on her middle finger, next to her wedding band. And in this picture, Whitney is showing Lilibet her right hand." Teddy peered through the loupe. Unfortunately, Whitney's hand angled so the camera could not see the face of the ring. "We could enlarge that detail," Vince suggested.

Enlarging was a tedious and often unsuccessful process with color film, and Teddy would have been happier about finding a simple explanation. Perhaps Whitney had shifted the ring to her opposite hand because it rubbed against her wedding band. "You know, Vince, I don't think I have the patience to be a good detective."

Vince stared at the photo, lost in thought. What had these two women been saying to each other? What was the significance of the ring?

The telephone rang and Teddy answered on the extension in the darkroom. "Lilibet?"

"Sorry to bother you, Teddy, but Vince's assistant has a huge long message about Elvis sightings. Can I put her through to him?"

"Sure." She called to Vince. "Lilibet has Connie on the line. I'll be out front, talking to Anton."

"Anton?"

"The mechanic who's working on my van."

Vince took the phone. "Connie?"

"No, honey. This is still Lilibet. I'll connect you."

"Lilibet, wait!" Following a reporter's instinct, he said, "I know about the ring. In one of the photos from the party, Whitney was showing it to you."

"Then I guess you know why I think Tom Burke killed her."

Vince bluffed. "Yes, Lilibet. I believe I do. What exactly did Whitney say to you?"

"Well, she showed me Tom's class ring from high school, of course, and said she'd found it in a fancy little gift box beside her plate at dinner." Lilibet's genteel Southern accent held a definite sneer. "He gave her the ring, his motel-room key and a note that said nine o'clock. Ain't that a sweet little present for a married woman.''

"That's why you went to PJ's with Tom."

"You bet. I wanted to mess up that rendezvous. Not that I was all that crazy about Tom Burke, even before I knew he was a murderer." She paused. "You know, Vince, I still can't hardly believe it."

"That's why you didn't say anything to the sheriff." Vince understood her thinking completely. Police and sheriffs' departments were in the business of solving crimes. When they had sufficient evidence to convict, they stopped looking. In this case, he agreed with Lilibet. There were too many loose ends to know—without a shadow of a doubt—that Tom was the killer. "I'm with you, Lilibet. I won't be sharing this information with the sheriff. Not just yet."

"Your choice," she said. "I'll put you through to Connie."

As soon as the phone call was switched over, Vince felt a change in atmosphere from Westalian peaceful to the controlled frenzy of the *Files* offices. In the background, phones were ringing, computer printers were racheting away. He could hear the chatter of people's voices. "What have you got, Connie?"

"Get yourself a pencil and paper, boss."

"What for?"

"You've got some Elvis leads to follow up on."

Chapter Eleven

The name of the truck-stop diner, less than one hundred miles from Westalia, was the Big Muddy Café. It was one of those flat rectangular buildings with a huge sign that tourists zip past on Interstate 55 and say, "I'll bet the food there is great! Look at all the trucks parked out front."

Vince had never agreed with that kind of thinking. He never assumed that truck drivers had discriminating appetites. At Big Muddy, the best he and Teddy could hope for was ample portions and decent coffee. But they hadn't come for the food. They were responding to a hot-line call from a waitress named Marie, who said she'd served lemon meringue pie to Elvis Presley at ten o'clock last night.

At about four-thirty, Vince parked his rental car beside an ebony black semitrailer. Though the cloudy skies threatened storms, a sultry heat rose in waves from the blacktop surface of the parking lot.

"This feels good," he said, savoring the anticipation he felt. "I haven't been out on a story for a long time. I've been too busy sitting behind my managing editor's desk and counting the buttons on my double-breasted suit. I've missed this."

"I understand." Teddy unzipped her camera bag and checked her equipment. "Hold on a sec while I load a fresh roll of film."

"You understand? How? You've always been in the field. You don't know what it's like to be an editor."

"I understand that I wouldn't like it. I made that decision when I was seventeen. My father wanted me to work at his paper, but the only job he would offer at the end of the rainbow was desk work. Photo editor."

"Why?"

"He wanted me to be safe."

Vince figured there was more to this story, and he wanted to hear it. "Why wouldn't you be safe?" She shrugged. "Come on, Teddy, what happened?"

"I'd lucked out with a photographer's dream. I was in St. Louis with my high school debate team, and there was a fire at an apartment building. I got some amazing photos of firemen charging into the inferno, people running down the halls to escape, lowering children onto fire escapes."

"You went inside?"

"Pure instinct." She checked the lens of her Nikon. "I was lucky. Those pictures went national, and I got job offers from magazines."

He still couldn't believe it. "You walked inside a burning building?"

"I was on the street and saw the flames licking at the night sky. I went inside to warn people."

"But then you stayed and took pictures." Vince had a sudden flash of sympathy for Teddy's father. It must have been hell for him to realize that his daughter had the instincts of a world-class photographer and to know that her talent could lead her into danger. Ironically, Jordan Edwards had lost his wife and his stay-at-home daughter

while Teddy—who had no concept of personal safety—
had survived. "This was the break between you and your
father, wasn't it?"

She nodded. "I couldn't do what he wanted."

He didn't like her penchant for taking chances any
more than her father did. But Vince understood. Asking
Teddy to play it safe was like asking the Mississippi to still
its course. "Let's go find Elvis."

Inside the Big Muddy Café, the counter stools and
booths were covered in a brown plastic that was supposed to look like leather. Limp baseball pennants decorated the walls. Each Formica tabletop held a cut-glass
vase with a plastic daisy. Though the diner was clean, the
combined smell of grease, sweat and cigarette smoke
clung to the air.

He and Teddy took a booth near the cash register. The
tired-looking brunette who dropped menus on their table wore a white apron over a yellow uniform. "We're
looking for Marie," Vince said.

"You found her. What do you want?"

"I'm Vince Harding from *Files*. You called our Elvis
Hot Line."

"No! Really?" Her energy level soared. She yelled over
her shoulder to the cook. "I told you so! These people
are from that newspaper. About Elvis." She beamed at
Vince. "Do I get a reward?"

"If we use your story, we pay you a thousand bucks."

She wedged into the booth beside Teddy. "You'll use
it. This is hot stuff. Okay? So, it's last night. Almost ten
o'clock because I was waiting to go off my shift. And this
guy walks in. He's wearing tinted glasses. Not sun-
glasses, you know, but tinted."

"Right," Teddy said.

Marie frowned at her. "Who are you, honey?"

"Photographer."

"You're going to take my picture?" Excitement pinched her voice to a squeak. "I'm going to have my picture in the newspaper?"

"Tell me the story first," Vince said.

"Right, right. So, the first thing I notice is his hair. Really black, slicked back with sideburns like the young kids are wearing. But this guy was closer to my age. In his forties or fifties. Not bad-looking, but I couldn't really see him behind those big aviator-style glasses. In fact, it wasn't until he ordered that I thought it might be…him."

"What did he say?"

"'Are your tomatoes fresh?' And I said they were okay. And now I was really looking at him, and I asked if he'd been in here before. And he said that he reckoned not, because he surely would have remembered a handsome woman like me. That's what he said." The enormity of his statement hit her, and she fell back against the brown plastic of the booth. "Oh my stars and stripes, Elvis Presley called me a handsome woman."

The cook, a husky man in a yellow T-shirt and apron, came out from behind the grill and hovered beside their table. "Are you folks believing this?"

"Stranger things have happened," Vince said.

"It was Elvis," Marie said. "I'd guessed it by then, but I was playing it cool. I asked him if he'd like something special. And I offered to make him a fried peanut-butter-and-banana sandwich. Which is, as everybody knows, Elvis's favorite food. And he took off his glasses and looked at me with those blue Elvis eyes and said he'd really appreciate it. Peanut butter and banana. And a big slab of lemon meringue pie."

"The food sounds right," Vince encouraged. "Was he heavyset?"

"No, and that threw me. Because Elvis did get kind of hefty. This man was lean and hard. And sexy." She sighed. "He had on a black leather jacket. And I admired his gold pinkie ring with a lightning bolt that said TCB, Taking Care of Business."

"Big deal," the cook muttered angrily. "You can buy those rings all over Memphis."

"Shut up, Mike. You were back in the kitchen, telling me I'm crazy. This is my story."

Vince encouraged her. "Then what happened?"

"He ate. Then he thanked me very much and he left."

"Did you see his car?"

"A motorcycle. A big Harley."

"Did you write down the plates?"

"No." Marie shook her head.

"Dumb," said the cook. "If you really thought he was Elvis, why'd you let him get away?"

"Because I respect his privacy. If the man went to the trouble of staging his own death to get away from fans who want to crawl all over him, who am I to expose him?"

"You're doing it now," the cook observed.

"This is different. It's not like I'm turning him over to you on a silver platter or anything. Somebody else saw him in Branson. I'm just another wayside stop on his lonely road through life."

"Well, Marie," Vince said, "this is all very good, but I need something more."

"Proof? I got proof." She reached under her apron and took an envelope from her uniform pocket. "Here's what he left me for a tip." She tossed a one-hundred-dollar bill onto the table. "And here's the receipt." She smoothed out the small square of paper. It read: "Marie's the name of my latest flame." It was signed with a flourishing *E*.

Though the receipt was an excellent piece of evidence, Vince sensed she was still holding something back. He kept his enthusiasm carefully reined in. "Very nice, but..."

"You still don't believe me?" Her face crumpled. "I really need that cash. I could get my car fixed."

"If you had one more thing..."

"All right." Defiantly, she stood. "You've got to give it back."

"Of course."

She dug into her other pocket and pulled out a TCB ring, which she placed in the center of the table. She handled it as carefully as a crown jewel. "I took it to a jeweler today, and he said it's real gold. Those blue stones are sapphires. Blue as the King's eyes."

The cook exploded with fury, saying that Marie, his girlfriend, had not gotten that ring without giving something more than a peanut-butter-and-banana sandwich. And Marie battled back. The few other patrons of the Big Muddy gathered around to stare.

In a low voice, Teddy told Vince, "Elvis had dozens of these rings made up. He gave them to his staff."

Vince called to Marie. "Would you sell this ring?"

"Not for a million bucks. But I could use the reward."

"You got it."

When the crowd calmed down, Teddy took photos and Vince got quotes. It was a good story. Driving back toward Westalia, they were both content with a job well-done.

"Well, we haven't cured world hunger," Teddy said.

"And we won't get a Pulitzer," Vince added. "But this story will provide entertainment for thousands of people. Marie the waitress is about to become a legend."

Teddy settled back comfortably in the passenger seat. She felt better than she had in days. Tracking down a good story always left her with a feeling of contentment. And she especially enjoyed the fact that Vince was along to take quotes and do the interviewing part, leaving her free to concentrate on the pictures. "I can't believe how lucky we were. This was your first lead."

"Connie said they'd received over a hundred calls already. But it's not just luck, Teddy. Connie and my staff had screened out most of the worthless contacts."

"How can she tell?"

"We're asking for proof, and most of the callers say they've seen Elvis from a distance and then he was gone. Or he called them on the telephone. Or they were listening to the radio, and all of a sudden they got a mental message that he was fine, and living in Peoria with a wife, two kids and a hound dog named Blue."

She chuckled. "I ought to be upset, you know. My exclusive on the man who looks like Elvis is slipping away."

"It's hard for a free-lancer to compete with a big organization. Of course, there's no reason for you to remain free-lance."

"Why not?"

"Because I'm offering you a job, for the one hundred and fiftieth time, as the full-time *Files* correspondent in this area."

"Vince, I can't make that kind of decision right now. I need time to think. Maybe, when this is over, I'll want to move. To live in Paris. Or New York." The thought of staying here, in Westalia, suddenly seemed stifling to her. "Maybe I'll learn to fly an airplane."

"If you settle in Chicago, there's a job waiting for you at *Files*. And free flying lessons."

Over the years, she'd had other offers from more prestigious publications, but none of them sounded so good. "I'll think about it."

"I'd like to teach you to fly."

They were edging toward a commitment, she realized, soaring through dangerous skies. To the west, a breathtaking sunset in Technicolor hues streaked the clouds with gold-and-scarlet, and the light shone on Vince's strong profile as he drove. They made a good team, but could they fly together into that sunset?

He'd taken her there once already, Teddy thought, with the most inspired lovemaking she'd ever experienced. She'd felt like she *was* the sunset. And the moon. And the stars. Surely that wonder could not continue. In the long term, they might not live happily ever after. They might crash and burn.

She repeated, "I'll think about it."

BACK AT HER HOUSE, Teddy checked the note that the garage mechanic had left on her van. Though the body damage was such that the vehicle would have to go into intensive care for a week, he'd fixed the tires. Thankfully the gunshot into the engine had missed all the vital parts, except for one hose, which he'd replaced. Her van was drivable again.

Up in her bedroom, Teddy changed back into her sweat suit. She'd regained the use of her hands, she noted, if she ignored the slight twinges of pain. The palms still looked awful as she applied a fresh dose of healing salve. Her other muscle aches and bruises had healed enough that she was ready, even anxious, to get back to work.

She bounced down the stairs. "Come on, Vince. Let's hit the darkroom."

"I was thinking of another room." When he raised one eyebrow suggestively, his bemused gaze completed the thought lingering in the back of her mind.

"Don't even mention the bedroom. I will not consider going to bed for any purpose other than sleeping."

He spread his hands wide. "Did I say anything?"

"You were thinking about it."

He couldn't deny that assumption. Even in that baggy sweat suit, she aroused him. The idea of making love to her marched across his brain with increasing frequency. As he followed her to the darkroom, he took the opportunity to study the athletic swing of her hips from side to side. The only body parts left uncovered by her sweat suit were her slender wrists, her ankles and her bare feet. For the first time in his life, Vince considered the possibility that toes might be sexy.

On the dry side of her darkroom, Teddy unloaded the black-and-white film she'd shot at the Big Muddy Café. Then she paused and turned to him. "What happened to the black and white I took at the anniversary party?"

He went to a drawer, opened it, and took out three rolls of film. "I know how photographers are about developing their own black and white. I didn't dare touch it."

"Thank you," she said. "But maybe this film has the clue that the bad guy was looking for."

With an admirable economy of motion, she took all of her black-and-white film to the wet side of the room. Using a black bag to keep out the light, she loaded the film into a tall canister, then measured in the presoak to soften the emulsion, then the developer. She gave Vince the job of agitating the canister every thirty seconds. "Don't forget," she ordered.

"Isn't there a machine that can do this?"

"Of course there is. But I like the hands-on approach with black-and-white film. Machines can break down."

"So can humans."

"But you won't," she said confidently.

Teddy went to the counter where the proof sheets were arrayed, and carefully picked them up in order. There was such a proliferation of pink in these photos. All the pink roses. And now the flowers were gone, probably heaped in a Dumpster behind the country club. She imagined the stench of rotting velvet petals.

Remembered music from the dance band sounded discordant in her memory, though they had played very well during the party. Looking down at the contact sheets, she studied a picture of her sister in her husband's arms. Whitney's head was thrown back. Her long smooth hair swept out in a shimmering wave behind her. But she was so thin, so awfully thin. The tendons in her throat stood out. Her sharp chin jabbed the space between them.

In the picture, Russel seemed fond and indulgent, more like a big brother than a husband. But they'd argued. Before Whitney fled to the last rendezvous of her life, she and her husband had fought. What a terrible memory for him to live with! "Russel is taking pills," she said.

Vince studiously turned the film canister, lightly agitating the developer. "What kind of pills?"

"I saw him with those little blue ones, like the sedatives the doc gave me. And there were other prescriptions in his medicine cabinet."

"Working with your father might not be the perfect job."

"He says he loves it."

"Maybe so. You can love a job that drives you crazy."
Vince stood beside her. He pointed to a contact image of
two men standing together and laughing. "Tom Burke
and Russel. Hard to believe these two are friends."

"They were buds in high school. Of course Tom was
the big football star and got all the girls. Russel was more
like his sidekick, the guy they sent for beer."

"Now Russel is a proper businessman and Tom's a
mess."

"An alcoholic." Her brow wrinkled as she considered
Tom Burke. Was he a murderer or simply a mess? She
needed more information. "Did you believe Tom when
he said this was the first time in a year that he'd had a
drink?"

"Fits the addictive pattern. Even if he'd established
positive habits in his regular life, his return to Westalia
might have triggered his drinking. Being in his old
haunts. Seeing his old buddies."

"Russel should have stopped him."

"Easy to say, but hard to do. The only one who could
keep Tom from drinking was Tom himself."

"What about the blackouts? Would that be unusual?"

"I'm not an expert, Teddy. Tom's doctor is probably
the only one who could answer that question."

She eyed Vince carefully as he rotated the canister. Her
intuition told her that Vince wasn't being completely
honest with her. "Do you believe Tom?"

"I do."

"But he lied. He said he didn't ride his Harley from
PJ's, but I followed him. I saw him flying along back
roads like a madman. And then Tom said he didn't remember getting the duplicate key from Mrs. Klaus at the
Sleep Inn."

"He was drunk. He could have blacked out."

"Mighty convenient forgetting, if you ask me. Why are you defending him?"

"He's too obvious. The best possible alibi to give is 'I don't know' because the burden of proof is on someone else. And I don't believe Tom's smart enough to mislead us. Seems more likely he'd make up a complicated story."

She regarded him skeptically. "You seem to know a lot about the techniques of lying, Vince."

"It's an occupational hazard of being a reporter. People are always talking in half-truths."

"Lies." She went to the light switch beside the door. "And now it's time for a little blackout of our own." The red safelights on, she took the canister from Vince and went to the wet side of the room for the rest of the developing procedure. With the temperature-control unit on the tap set at sixty-eight degrees, she drained, dipped and washed. The process was second nature to her, and she talked while she worked. "Wish I knew more about blackouts. Is it like being unconscious or hypnotized?"

"A little of both." Vince was content to sit back and watch her work. "Once, we ran a story about a person who could speak five different languages under hypnosis."

"Was it true?"

"It's possible. Somebody believed it."

In the crimson glow, Teddy seemed different, unlike a mere mortal woman. A mysterious aura surrounded her. Her golden hair radiated a luminescence that fascinated Vince as she continued to speak softly in a mesmerizing cadence, discussing the possibilities of paranormal influences on subconscious states. "But what do you believe, Vince?"

"I like solid evidence. Facts."

"Facts are good. But sometimes I trust my feelings more." Setting the canister for the running-water wash, she said, "And I have a feeling that you're not telling me the whole truth. Am I right?"

"I can't lie to you." But he was withholding facts. He'd decided not to tell her what Lilibet had revealed about the ring. Nor had he mentioned Connie's call from "Elvis" asking directly about Mary Theodora Edwards. He didn't want to worry her or put more pressure on her.

"No lies?" she questioned.

"None." Deception was not possible, not with this woman, this red-tinted creature who created images from light and shadow. In the space of a few days, he'd become so close to her that they could almost read each other's mind. She bewitched him.

"But you're hiding something," she said. Teddy went to the light switch and turned on the overhead lights. The scarlet magic dispelled, and he saw the anger in her gaze. "I know what it is," she said. "When you printed the color negatives, you held back the photos I took when we went into the motel room and saw Whitney."

"You're right, Teddy. I forgot all about those pictures. But I did give copies to the sheriff."

"Hold it right there." Her eyes narrowed. "Are you telling me that you gave those pictures to Jake Graham, and you didn't give them to me?"

"I didn't want to leave them in with the others." He'd made prints, but he'd kept the two shots on a contact sheet all their own. They were too macabre to show to Teddy when she was in a fragile emotional state.

"I want to see them. Now."

"Why? There's nothing in those photos. Not a clue. Why torture yourself by looking at them?"

"Damn you, Vince." A horrifying thought occurred to her. "Oh my God, you're going to use those pictures."

"For what?"

"You'll publish them in *Files*. Actual photos of a murder scene. You couldn't pass up a scoop like that."

"I'd never do that." His own anger flared. How could she believe he would do such a thing? "I'm not a ghoul."

"But you are an editor who needs to pump up circulation. What could be better? Small-town murder and Elvis. Damn you, Vince. Just get out of here."

"Don't push me," he warned.

"Go on," she said. "You can leave. The bad guy isn't after me anymore. Your manly duty has been done."

"Fine." After all they'd been through together, she still didn't trust him. She accused him of lying and stealing when all he'd intended was to help. If that was what she really believed, then to hell with her. "The contacts and negs are filed by the door. Under *W* for Whitney."

Without another word, he left.

WHEN SHE FINISHED with the black-and-white negatives, Teddy went to bed. Too angry to cry herself to sleep, she groaned and tossed and turned until after midnight.

Then the telephone rang beside her bed. She lifted the receiver. From the corner of her eye, she saw the red light blink on, indicating that the recording machine had been activated. As of today, the phone trace was in effect. She prayed that her caller was the Elvis informant. "Hello, this is Edwards."

"Miss Mary Theodora Edwards?" The baritone voice sounded strangely familiar but she couldn't quite place it.

Teddy rubbed her eyes and glanced over to the other side of the bed. It was vacant. Vince wasn't there. But, of course, he wouldn't be. She had thrown him out. In her white-hot rage, she'd accused him of stealing her photos. She turned her attention back to the caller. "This is Miss Edwards."

"How are you doing? Are you lonesome tonight?"

Dark overtones colored the second question. Did he know she was alone and vulnerable? "Who is this?"

"Some people call me the King."

Elvis? For an impersonator, the voice was excellent. There was some phone distortion, but this man sounded enough like Elvis Presley to make her sit up straight and listen carefully. "What should I call you?"

"If you're lonesome, I could come over and tell you."

The recorder light flashed as regularly as a heartbeat. They could do voiceprints. "I'll meet you. Where are you?"

"I'm in Paulson right now. Know where that is?"

About twenty-five miles from Westalia. Even if Teddy drove above the speed limit, it would take half an hour to forty minutes to get there. "I can meet you there within an hour."

"I'll meet you in the gazebo in the town square. In one hour. Fair enough?"

"I'll be there." She glanced at the bedside clock. "At twenty minutes past one."

"And I got to ask you one more thing, ma'am. This is a get-acquainted meeting between you and me. No photos."

"But that's what I do." Though she held her voice to a reasonable level, a sense of excitement skyrocketed within her. His slight paranoia really did sound like Elvis. "I need photos. I'm not a journalist. I couldn't do justice to our meeting if I didn't take pictures."

"If y'all don't mind, I'd like to get to know you first. Just you and me, baby."

Baby? Elvis called her baby? She felt as giddy as Marie the waitress. "Whatever you want."

She waited for him to say the words she'd heard on almost every recording of a live Elvis performance: "Thank you, thank you very much." Instead he closed with a conventional "Looking forward to it, Miss Edwards."

Teddy hung up the telephone and swallowed hard. The voice couldn't have been Elvis's. This was some sort of con, a scam. Elvis was dead and buried in Graceland. Medical investigations and legal statements confirmed that fact. And yet she couldn't help dreaming....

"Dream on your feet," she told herself. Bolting from the bed, she hurried to the dresser. Only an hour. What should she wear? Running back to the window to check the weather, she saw the beginnings of a spring rainfall. Something warm, but not hot. A pair of Levi's. A long-sleeved hooded sweatshirt.

A glance in the bathroom mirror confirmed that she looked a mess. The scratch on her face was an ugly red line. How could she meet Elvis like this? A low groan escaped her lips but she dragged a brush through her hair, splashed water on her face, and did what she could.

Why had he insisted that she come alone?

For an instant, she recalled her stark terror in the van when the man in black had been hammering at the sides. And the subsequent fear as she ran and ran in a nightmarish attempt to escape. What if this was that same man? What if he'd come after her again?

She wished that Vince hadn't left. That she hadn't thrown him out. But she'd had to! He'd lied about the photos. He'd been doing things for her own good. How many times in her life had she heard that excuse, the world's worst rationalization for trying to manipulate her. She could take care of herself. "Looks like I'll have to," she muttered.

Surely this meeting with Elvis—coming on the heels of the attack on her van—was a coincidence. The two events bore no relationship to each other. Should she telephone the sheriff? No! She summoned up every ounce of determination. She had to go alone.

Beside the bathroom sink she saw her wristwatch, grabbed it and fastened it on. These doubts had consumed too much time. If she was late, she might never hear from this guy again. She might lose her chance at the story of the century—a story she would wrap up with a pink ribbon and throw in Vince's face.

As she ran out the front door and leapt into her van, the splatters of rain marked the windshield like crystalline tears. Halfway down the road leading to a main intersection, the rain became a downpour. Teddy had forgotten her slicker. Maybe it would let up.

But the rain continued to fall in a steady hiss, and heavy clouds blocked the moon. It was terribly dark. Few porch lights were lit, and she met no other cars. The backroad route she'd chosen had few street lamps. Teddy felt like she was driving into the impenetrable dark of an endless tunnel, with no light at the end, and no sure answers.

Teddy had never felt so alone. "Oh, Vince. Why did you have to go?"

By the glow of the dashboard illumination, she checked her watch. It was almost one o'clock. Only twenty minutes to go. There would be no extra time for making mistakes or taking the wrong road. At the outskirts of Paulson, she peered through the wet night, trying to read street signs. She cruised into a gas station to ask directions. It was closed. Her watch said one-fifteen.

Impatiently she tapped her fingers on the steering wheel. Which way? Following a wide street, she saw a stoplight in the distance. Green to amber to red. She turned and found the town square. Only five minutes late, she parked at a deserted curb, cut her lights and leapt from the van.

In the heart of Paulson, the square boasted a large block of grass, trees and gardens. Teddy had taken photos here before. By daylight, this idyllic spot, shaded by old oaks and slender maples, represented everything that was neighborly about the midwestern United States. Friendly people gathered on the park benches. On the sidewalks surrounding the square, new mothers strolled proudly with baby carriages. And the green center, about half the size of a football field, was crisscrossed with quaint cobblestone paths and tended by the Paulson Botanical Society.

But the pouring rain and the gloomy night distorted the innocence. Trees loomed above her, tall and sinister. The pathways beckoned with dark foreboding. Teddy pulled up the hood of her sweatshirt and hastened across the rain-slicked street. The wind keened through the greening boughs, and the rain pitter-pattered in dismal syncopation. The cobblestone paths were slick, and she stumbled once but caught herself before falling. Though street lamps illuminated the sidewalks, the center of the square was shadowed, hidden away like a secret garden.

In the middle stood the round gazebo, a fanciful white latticework structure whose only practical function was to provide minimal shelter on a night like this. Teddy darted inside. The gazebo was small, perhaps only six feet in diameter and surrounded by a railing all around, except for the entrance. Four arches surrounded her, obscuring her view of the gardens beyond.

As she stood there, her breathing sounded loud and rasping, and her pulse hammered. Would he be here? Had she arrived too late? Pulling off her hood, she paced across the gazebo. There was a crunching noise underfoot. Broken glass glittered across the wooden floor, and she realized there should have been a light in here. Looking up, she saw four empty sockets along the rim of the circular structure.

He had broken the bulbs, ensuring darkness. And the rain had trapped her here. Fear crept up her back as she circled the gazebo floor, pacing nervously like a caged mouse. Darkness made sense, she told herself. If the man on the phone really was Elvis, he wouldn't want to be seen. He'd be wary, cautious. Teddy clung to that explanation. The person who had called her, who had summoned her to this spot, was Elvis. Or *thought* he was Elvis.

But she felt trapped. Again. She was scared.

The Elvis voice couldn't be the same man who had terrorized her in the van. That black-clad attacker was after the film, not Teddy herself. When she'd fled from the van and thrown the camera bag at him, he had not pursued her. After Vince had turned over the contact sheets to the sheriff, there had been no more threats.

She heard rustling and turned toward the sound. "Hello? Is someone there?" Her voice sounded shaky, even to her own ears. Her heart pounded so loudly against her rib cage that she could hear nothing else but that rapid drumming within her. She stopped moving, stood at the railing and raised her voice above the sound of wind and rain. "Who's there?"

The voice she heard was that of her informant, shrieking into the wind. "You didn't listen to me!"

"My God, is that you?"

"Get the hell out of here, Teddy."

"Where are you? Please, don't leave. I've got to talk with you."

"You're in danger, Teddy. Don't you understand? You could be killed." The ghostly figure of a tall man separated from the shadows surrounding an ancient oak tree. He was already moving away from her.

From another direction, she heard the loud roar of a motorcycle engine starting up. She whipped around, turning toward the sound. Disoriented, she peered through the trees that seemed to be closing in upon her. "Who is it? Who's there?"

"Run, Teddy." Her informant's voice carried faintly on the wind. "Run while you can."

Chapter Twelve

Run.

But she didn't know which way to turn. The night and the rain shrouded her vision. Fear paralyzed her.

Run while you can.

The din of the motorcycle grew louder. He was approaching. From her left. Then from behind her. The noise was earsplitting, deafening. She could not move.

Then stay.

She forced herself to breathe, to think. She should stay right here, not run. Teddy visualized the rain-slicked garden paths, winding between trees and flower beds. A heavy motorcycle would hardly even fit. He must be trying to scare her out, to chase her into the street where he could run her down.

She was safer here, in the gazebo. In the secret garden. He couldn't possibly get to her in here. Not on his motorcycle.

Then the motorcycle noise faded. Soon, she knew, he would tire of this game. He would stalk her on foot. In the silence, he would come after her. His hand, his gloved hand, would shoot through the latticework of the gazebo. She would be caught.

Clutching the wet railing, Teddy peered into the night, hoping for a sign, an indication of where to go. A flash of lightning illuminated the street. Through a break in the trees, she clearly saw him, the person who had called her so many times—her Elvis informant. Limping, he headed toward an alley between two buildings. She recognized his lanky silhouette and his profile.

"Merle. Merle Chatworth."

Seeing him gave her strength. Merle was a gentleman. He wouldn't abandon her.

Teddy vaulted the low railing of the gazebo. Her feet hit solidly on moist earth, and she cautiously picked her way through the trees and flower beds where rows of daffodils nodded wetly. The motorcycle? The sound of it was gone. Was he coming on foot? She imagined his breath in the wind. The tree branches became dark fingers, snatching at her hair.

Through the rain, she saw another man charging down the street, running full out toward Merle. Teddy ducked down behind the yellow sprays of a forsythia bush and watched. Merle was caught, too easily. The second man held him. They shouted, but she couldn't make out the words. When Merle lifted his finger and pointed toward the square, she felt two sets of eyes, staring right at her. And she recognized Merle's captor. "Vince!"

A torrent of relief rushed through her. The knot of fear in her stomach unraveled, and she was free. Safe. Teddy fled from the trees and the garden. At the street, her feet didn't seem to touch the pavement as she ran toward him.

Without hesitation, without questioning how he got there, or why, she slipped under the shelter of his arm. He was holding firmly to Merle Chatworth with his other hand.

"Hey, Teddy." He squeezed her against him.

"There was someone on a motorcycle," she warned. "I didn't see him, but he was coming around the square."

"He's long gone," Merle intoned as they eased back a few steps to take shelter under a drugstore awning.

"Who was it?" Vince demanded.

"Can't say."

"Don't know? Or can't say?"

"You heard me right the first time, Vince."

"I don't know what the hell kind of game you're playing, Merle. Do you get a thrill out of scaring women?"

"No, Vince," Teddy interrupted. "Merle isn't the man who's been after me. He's my Elvis informant."

As always, Merle's weathered face remained passive and unemotional, but there was a hint of suffering in the deepening of creases around his eyes, and Teddy recalled his limp. "Are you hurt?"

"Twisted my ankle in the park."

"Why were you there?" she asked. She'd been summoned by a voice that sounded like Elvis's. Had that been another of Merle's disguised voices? "Was it you who called me and arranged this meeting?"

"Not tonight," he said. "I was following him, tracking him. He used the phone. Didn't know it was you he called."

"You watched him," she said. "He broke the light bulbs in the gazebo, didn't he? You knew he was setting an ambush." Merle gave a terse nod. "My God, Merle, who was it?"

"Can't say."

"Let's go." Vince gave a tug on Merle's arm. "Down at the end of this block there's a public telephone. I want you to call Sheriff Graham, Teddy."

They walked silently through the pouring rain. Teddy stepped gratefully into the enclosure of the phone booth while the two men stood in the recessed doorway of a hardware store. She dialed the Westalia police station and was transferred to Sheriff Graham, who promised to have a patrol car there within fifteen minutes. Before he hung up, he said, "Merle Chatworth, huh? Is he the killer?"

"He's the witness. He's the person who called me at the country club and told me to go to the Sleep Inn."

"I get it. He's the person who thinks he sees Elvis."

She didn't appreciate the sneering tone of his voice, but she didn't want to argue. "That's right."

"That figures. Old Merle isn't big on reality."

Sheriff Jake Graham was so nonchalant that he seemed half-asleep. He treated the attacks on Teddy like a jaywalking offense. Angrily she demanded, "Do you have any leads, Jake?"

"Not a damn thing. Can't see a single clue in those pictures you took."

"Me, neither." However, it seemed that the man in black was still after her. But why?

She hung up the phone and stepped into the doorway beside Vince and Merle. Teddy needed some answers. "Who was it, Merle? Who was the man on the motorcycle? I know he was coming after me."

"All you need to know is that you should be careful."

"What does he want from me?"

"Just don't go wandering off by yourself. You stick with Vince here, and you'll be okay." His eyes shifted between the two of them. "That's all I'm going to tell you."

A lump of pure frustration caught in Teddy's throat. There were dozens of questions she needed to ask. But she didn't know how to break down Merle's stone wall.

"Let's start from the beginning," Vince said. "Merle, you called Teddy at the country club, didn't you?"

He considered for a moment, then said, "Yeah, I did."

"You were at the Sleep Inn. Room 19."

"That's right."

"You saw the man who killed Whitney."

"Can't say that I did."

"He stabbed a buck knife into her heart, Merle. She was so beautiful in her white dress with her long blond hair. She was as pretty as a princess and she didn't deserve to die like that."

"No sir, she did not."

Vince was struck with a sudden realization. "She would have thanked you, Merle, for laying her out on the bed like that, so pretty and neat."

"I couldn't leave her crumpled on the floor."

"Of course not."

"I saw him leaving Room 19. Door was open. I went inside." His gentle Southern drawl cracked. "Broke my heart. I loved that girl. In a whole lot of ways."

"Why did you go there?" Vince took a harder tone. He wanted to keep Merle off-balance, to goad him into talking.

"I knew about the ring and the meeting she had set up for nine o'clock, and I was going to try to talk her out of it. Ain't right for a married woman to be messing around."

"Not unless it's with you," Vince said.

Merle stiffened. "Don't you go saying that. Whitney was a good girl."

"If you want this murderer caught, you've got to tell what you saw. You'll have to cooperate with the police."

"They won't take my word."

"You're a witness, man."

"Sheriff won't believe me. Nobody does. Nobody believes I played backup for Elvis. I could've been big, a country and western star. But nobody believes that, neither. People think I'm a little touched in the head. You tell him, Teddy."

"You're being too sensitive, Merle. Nobody thinks you're crazy. Except maybe Lilibet."

"That's right. Little old Lilibet talks to everybody and tells them I'm a crazy old coot."

Quietly she asked, "Is that why you used that fake voice to call me and tell me about Elvis?"

"Had to."

"Oh, Merle." She heard the distant wail of a police siren. The past had risen up again to muddy the present, to cause confusion. This time, the complications baffled her because Teddy knew very little of Merle's history. "I would have listened. I will listen. Tell me about Elvis."

He took a deep breath. "Sometimes, I hear him talking to me. I hear Elvis. But I know that can't be. And then, when I saw that fella, the guy who looks like the spitting image, I couldn't believe it. If that ain't Elvis himself, it's got to be his twin brother, risen up from the grave."

It was the longest speech she'd ever heard from this taciturn man, and she encouraged him to continue. "You followed him," she said.

"I'm good at following. When I was a kid, I could get on the trail of a coon and stay there for a whole day until I treed him. And that's what I'm fixing to do with the man who killed my Whitney. I'm going to get him up a tree. And I'm going to kill him."

The conviction of his statement, though spoken softly, resonated in the night. Merle wasn't bragging. He was making a promise, a pledge that he intended to keep.

When the Westalia Sheriff's Department car pulled up to the curb, Vince released his hold on Merle's arm and reluctantly turned him over to the deputy. Vince didn't expect that Sheriff Graham would find out anything from Merle. The old country and western singer who could've been a star was damn good at keeping his mouth shut.

Merle was crafty, too. The only reason he'd told them so much was because there was nothing Vince or Teddy could do about it.

After the deputy asked a few perfunctory questions and drove away with Merle in the back seat, Vince took Teddy's hand. "Let's get out of the rain."

She pointed. "My van is parked—"

"I know," he said. "I was riding in the back of it."

"You were?" Her blue eyes widened. "While I was driving . . . I wasn't talking to myself, was I?"

"A little," he teased. "I think you said something about missing me desperately."

"I did not. Why were you in my van?"

"Instinct. Come on, Teddy, let's go home."

After she'd thrown him out, Vince had been angry enough to jump into his rental car and drive a half mile down the road, cursing and fuming and wondering how he'd ever gotten mixed up with this stubborn woman who didn't have the good sense to know when he was trying to help her. Then he pulled onto a side road and sat there. He couldn't leave.

A strange feeling held him there, like some sort of magnetic force. Though he hesitated to call it a premonition—one of Connie's words—Vince knew there was a tie, an emotional bond, that drew him back to Teddy. He'd walked back to the house and watched over her. When it started raining, he took refuge in the back of her van.

Together, they crossed the town square. At the van, she tossed him the keys. "You drive." Her hands were shaking. She wanted to believe it was because of the cold, but it wasn't. The residual effects of her fear had chilled her to the bone. Huddled in the passenger seat, finally safe from the storm, she gazed at Vince. If he hadn't been here, she was afraid to think of what might have happened.

He touched her trembling shoulder and gave it a reassuring squeeze. "Hell of a night, huh?"

"Is that all you have to say for yourself?"

"If you're digging for an apology, Teddy, you're going to need a bigger shovel. I'm not sorry that I hid in your van, and I'm not sorry that whoever was on that motorcycle didn't get close enough to shove a knife between your ribs." He started the engine. "The motorcycle makes me think it was Tom Burke."

It didn't occur to her until he said the name. But Tom Burke did make an ugly sort of sense. He'd dressed up like Elvis in high school. He might be able to impersonate him on the phone. "But why? Why would Tom go to all the trouble of dragging me out here in the rain?"

"Because he's the murderer."

At one time, she would have agreed with him in a flash. Right now, she wasn't so sure. It seemed like the more information they uncovered, the more perplexing the crime became. "Do you really think it's Tom?"

He shrugged, eased the van into gear and pulled away from the curb. "Let's total up the facts. Whitney was killed in Tom's room. According to Merle, Tom set the meeting with her for nine o'clock."

"When Merle said he knew about the meeting and the ring, what was he talking about?"

They began to compare notes. Vince shared the conversation he'd had with Lilibet, and Teddy told him about Russel's admission that Whitney had picked a fight and then left. A clear picture began to emerge. Whitney had been making a play for Tom, and he'd responded by giving her the extra key to his room, his class ring and a note to meet him at nine o'clock.

"I saw the ring," she said. "In the motel room. I didn't know it was Tom's, but I noticed it because it looked out of place with Whitney's other jewelry."

After the party, they assumed, Whitney had picked a fight with Russel and had taken off for the Sleep Inn.

"Then she was murdered," Vince said. "The killer stabbed her and left. Then Merle went inside, arranged Whitney on the bed and called you."

"That makes sense," she said. "But it doesn't explain why the killer would be coming after me. I was one of the few people who didn't know about the ring and the meeting."

"You're right. So, let's take it from a different direction. What brought you here to Paulson?"

"Elvis, of course. You can listen to him on the recorder, maybe even run a comparative voice tape. But he sounded like Elvis, and he wanted me to come here and meet him. Alone."

"And you didn't think that was suspicious? Didn't you think you should call the sheriff?"

"Not really. After we'd talked with Marie, the waitress, I was thinking about a man with slick black hair who leaves hundred-dollar bills for a tip. Elvis seemed...real."

Vince understood. He was sympathetic to her curiosity, her need to chase after a story. And he hated that this bad guy, this murderer, had used the dedication and talent that made her so good at her job to lead her into danger.

Vince wanted to pull her close, to keep her safe, and guard her from anyone or anything that might harm her. But how could he restrain her? He couldn't ask her to be someone other than Mary Theodora Edwards, photographer extraordinaire. A bright, exciting, independent woman. And beautiful. Even now when she was as drenched as a drowned muskrat, she was lovely. Her eyes were luminous and hopeful, and an eager excitement radiated from her. He couldn't imagine being without her.

"The motorcycle doesn't prove it's Tom," she said. "Other people have motorcycles. Russel Stratton, for one."

"And your father?"

"I don't know if he has one anymore. At one time, he did. He used to take it to work." She grinned. "There he'd be in his three-piece suit and his starched white shirt, riding a Harley."

"I'm surprised you never got into motorcycles. Seems like your kind of risky thing."

"Who says I didn't?"

"You didn't recognize Tom's Panhead," he countered. "Anybody who's into Harley Davidson motorcycles would know about that fine and macho piece of machinery. So I figure you aren't an expert."

"You're right." She grinned. "I've ridden on the tail of a few Harleys in my time. But the urge to own one never hit me. I don't object to them, though. And they don't scare me like they do Lilibet."

"Lilibet's scared of something?"

"She'd never admit it. But when she and Merle were married, she hated when he would rev up his engine and go for a ride. She kept trying to ground him."

"Too bad," Vince said. "Lilibet looks like the type of woman who was made to ride bare-breasted on the back of a Harley."

"And I don't?"

He laughed. "You look like the kind of woman who needs a hot bath and a good night's sleep."

Back at her house, that was exactly what Vince encouraged. He hustled Teddy upstairs to get warm and to change while he made hot herbal tea and threw together a sandwich. Enough food had been salvaged from her van to create several full-course meals, but he didn't feel like cooking.

He felt like making love to her.

Even in his miserable wet clothes, he was warmed by a sexual heat. And when Teddy came down from her bedroom, dressed in a lacy blue peignoir, the flames soared higher. "You're beautiful," he said.

She trailed her hand, now sporting only a small bandage, along the silky folds. "In this old thing?"

Her eyes glimmered with a sapphire light. Was she teasing? Was she serious? She kept saying that they couldn't, shouldn't make love. But this lady was dressed for seduction.

She helped herself to tea. "I should have guessed that my Elvis informant was Merle. That's why he only called at night when Lilibet wouldn't answer the phone. She might have recognized his voice, even disguised."

"I should have guessed, too." Words were coming out of his mouth, but Vince wasn't sure what he was saying. "When I saw him lurking around Lilibet's backyard, I knew this was a person who liked to play at hide-and-seek. There aren't many men who'd go through such an elaborate charade to escape your aunt Harriet, even though she is intimidating."

"I think we'd better have a chat with Harriet."

"But not tonight."

"No, Vince. Not tonight." She gazed at him over the rim of her teacup. God, he was handsome. His gray eyes and the lines of his face were endlessly fascinating. She looked at his wet clothes. "You haven't changed."

"Left my suitcase in the rental car."

"Maybe you should get it." She tore her gaze away from him and looked out the window. "But it's still raining."

She felt him moving up behind her. His hand rested at her waist. "I'm glad you're all right," he said. "For a minute there, when I lost sight of you in the park and I heard that motorcycle circling, I was afraid for you."

"You didn't need to be. I can—"

"Take care of yourself," he finished her thought. Taking the teacup from her hand and setting it on the kitchen table, he turned her to face him. "For the rest of the night, let me take care of you."

His lips upon hers were warm and vibrant. Her body responded to his tender nibbling, and she arched into his embrace, not minding the dampness of his clothing against her body. Her arms twined around his neck. Their kiss deepened. His tongue thrust between her teeth, arousing the passion they had shared once before.

Weakly, she broke away from him. This might be the dumbest thing she'd ever done in her life, but she felt drugged, drowsy and complacent. "Would you like to take a shower? We can find something for you to wear."

"I don't need clothes." He lowered his head and kissed the smooth curve of her throat. "I want to make love to you, Teddy."

She placed her hands between them and pushed at his muscular chest. He was too near, altogether too wonderful. She was close to surrender. Too close.

"I'd like to go upstairs," he said. "To get out of these wet clothes."

"Of course."

With the rain pattering lightly on the rooftop, Teddy stretched out on her bed. By the glow of the lamp on her night table, she watched as Vince peeled away the layers of his damp clothing. He was magnificent. The sight of his naked body made her giddy. But she didn't laugh.

When he joined her in bed, she was anxious for his kisses. She flung her arms toward him, but he held her back. "Not yet," he whispered.

He slipped aside the lace that covered her breasts. His tongue traced slow, delicious patterns around her nipples. Gradually, with maddening slowness, he undressed her and gave the same attention to the other secret parts of her body. And every time she reached for him, he held her back. "Not yet," he said. A dozen times he spoke those words as he licked the lobe of her ear, fondled her breasts and stroked the length of her torso.

Exquisite pleasure shivered across the surface of her flesh, and Teddy moaned with anticipation. He positioned himself above her. His knees pushed aside her thighs. His hands grasped her wrists and pinned them above her head. Gazing into her eyes, he slowly entered. She bared her white teeth, thrashed against him. And he thrust hard.

Already at the brink of fulfillment, she gasped. The vision of his face swam above her, his expression reflecting her own frantic longing. He drove into her, harder and harder, and an incredible shudder quaked her entire body. Her inner flesh contracted around him, trembling. Teddy thought she'd reached the height of arousal. Utter lassitude overcame her.

But Vince maintained his hard strength. "Not yet."

He pushed her higher. She clung to the edge of a scream, unable to believe that such exquisite pleasure was possible. Then she abandoned conscious thought as her body rocked against his.

And when, finally, he allowed himself to complete their passion, she was limp. And more content than she'd ever been in her life. In that perfect moment, she curled up beside him. He had claimed her as no man had before, and she couldn't imagine living without him.

Though she hadn't intended to fall asleep, Teddy drifted into a deep unconscious state that lasted until well into the morning. When she awoke, her bedside clock indicated it was past ten o'clock. Vince no longer lay beside her. She reveled for a moment in the warmth of the sheets and the slight soreness between her thighs, unwilling to return to the mundane business of daily life. She would have been happy to make love to him for hours, days, weeks.

"Not yet," she said to herself. Not possible.

A sharp little pain went through her as she realized that Vince would soon leave her, but she dismissed it. She was glad for last night and would not spoil it by worrying about tomorrow.

Downstairs, after she dressed, she found him on the phone again. A yellow legal pad was filled with scribbled notes. He waved to her and said, "I'm talking to Connie. The Elvis Hot Line has taken over two hundred and fifty calls."

Teddy smiled weakly. How could he be so calm? Last night she'd experienced the most earthshaking passion of her entire life, and Vince was behaving as if today was just another day.

She thought the words she could never speak to him. *I love you.* Those words might bring her pain, but she could not stop her thoughts. She loved him. He had saved her life twice. Or three times, if she counted the break-in. But she owed him more than that. Last night, Vince Harding had made her life worth living again. No longer was she doomed to be a dried-up old maid, hiding away near the town where she was born.

He had given her the most precious excitement, and somehow she would learn how to live again, would teach herself that love did not mean sorrow. This time, Teddy decided, she would not accept a tragic ending.

Pouring herself a cup of coffee, she sat opposite him at the kitchen table. He hung up the phone and turned to her. "I've already arranged for another reporter to handle most of these calls, but I'm having Connie run them past me in case we find the guy who telephoned you last night."

"Did you listen to the tape?"

"Oh, yes. Excellent impersonation. I made a couple of copies and expressed the original to Connie so she can do some voice comparisons. And I've also checked with Lilibet on tracing the call."

"And?"

"Whoever called you last night used the public phone in Paulson. The same one you used to call the sheriff."

She lazily sipped her coffee. "You've done all that? It's not even noon."

"That's not all."

He took her hand and raised it to his lips. Teddy thought he might be preparing to make a declaration of love. Or at least to mention last night. "Yes, Vince?"

"The sheriff is set to make an arrest."

Though this was indeed momentous news, she felt disappointed. "Merle talked?"

"No. It was Lilibet. When she heard what happened to you last night, she came forward with her own information. After she left Tom Burke at PJ's, she returned to the Sleep Inn, thinking she might break up the meeting between Tom and Whitney. But Lilibet was too late. She saw Whitney's car parked some distance away. And she saw Tom's motorcycle outside his room."

"And that's enough for the sheriff?"

"You sound disappointed," he said.

"Of course not. I'm glad," she hedged. The solution didn't seem quite right to her. "All along, I've been sure it was Tom. Now . . . it doesn't feel right."

"I understand. It's hard to believe when somebody you know commits murder."

But her discontent with this obvious solution went deeper than that. Some of the little bits and pieces didn't fit. Her mind sifted out the most obvious one. "Why? Why did he kill her?"

"His motive? Who knows? The sheriff won't find out until he can find Tom and arrest him. He's taken off."

"Another admission of guilt," Teddy said.

"They've put out an all-points bulletin, but if he's left the area, it'll be harder to catch him." He lightly stroked her hair. "That's why I arranged for another reporter to handle the Elvis calls. I'm staying here with you, Teddy. And you're not going anywhere until they've arrested Tom Burke."

"Do I need protection?"

"You don't need to worry."

She looked directly at him. Teddy had never been good at playing games. She preferred the truth, no matter how painful. "Is that the only reason you're staying, Vince?"

"No."

Did he love her? She wanted to ask him, but her usual candor deserted her. Perhaps she was afraid to hear the answer. "Why else are you staying?"

"You still haven't given me a commitment."

A fragile bubble of hope grew within her. What was he asking? What did he mean? A commitment? "About what?"

"The job. For *Files*. Will you work for me?"

The bubble burst. He was talking about work. About the tabloid. Apparently last night had been nothing special for him. An uncharacteristic urge to sob caught in her throat, but she fought it. She would not fling herself pathetically into his arms. She could not demand that he love her.

"What do you say, Teddy?"

Her self-control took over. Her voice was calm. "We can talk about it later."

After forcing herself to eat, she went into her dark-room while Vince stayed on the phone. Teddy turned off the lights and sat in the dark. "Oh, God, Vince," she whispered, "why don't you love me?"

Nothing seemed more important than Vince and the overwhelming love she knew she could not allow herself to feel for him. All the other facts seemed only details in a tapestry. Whitney's murder. Tom's guilt. Merle's secrets. So many missed chances. So many wrongs.

Her fingers flicked on the safelights. Life went on. Of that fact, Teddy was sure. And there was work to be accomplished.

Taking the color film she'd also shot at their meeting with Marie, she loaded her color processor. There might be a good cover shot in there. Her other negatives, the black and white she'd made yesterday, were ready, and she went to the dry side of her darkroom and turned on the enlarger light.

After blowing up several of the pictures of Marie and the TCB ring, she made a contact sheet of the few black-and-white anniversary party shots. She would also need to blow up color pictures of Whitney for the funeral. It had been scheduled for the day after tomorrow, and now that Sheriff Graham had decided Tom was the murderer, there would be no reason to postpone Whitney's final ceremony. But right now, Teddy didn't want to confront those pictures again.

Somehow she felt deflated by the finality of the conclusion. Tom was guilty. She'd known it all along, but hadn't wanted to believe it.

Into the enlarger she put the negatives of the film she'd taken on the night before Whitney was killed, the night she'd first laid eyes on Vince Harding. The mood photos she'd snapped at PJ's had some merit, and she played with the exposure times and composition. Her artistic sense rose to the fore, eclipsing her pain and other problems. Always, Teddy could find solace in her work.

As she processed the three prints of the TCB-1 license plate on the wet side of the room, she noticed light and dark shadows in the clouds above the motorcycle. They seemed to take on a solid palpable form. Sometimes that happened with double exposures, but Teddy was far too experienced and her equipment was too sophisticated for that sort of beginner's mistake.

She enlarged the images to 8 × 10. "Incredible."

In the foreground was a distinct picture of a motorcycle, lit by the neon of PJ's many signs. Light reflected from the driver's black helmet. The letters TCB were clear. Part of the rider's profile was visible. His left hand, gloved, clenched the handlebar grip, and his black leather jacket stretched across wide shoulders.

Above him, in the misted sky, she saw a face. Shadowed eyes. Dark sideburns. It was, without much imagination, the visage of Elvis.

The phone in her darkroom shrilled.

Chapter Thirteen

"You must be an important person, Miss Edwards."

Teddy clutched the telephone receiver tightly. The voice was similar to the Elvis drawl from last night. But was it the same? She needed to hear more. "Why do you say that?"

"You're harder to reach than the president of the United States. I had to go through an answering service and some other guy who calls himself Harding to talk to you."

"And have you spoken to the president?"

"Not lately." He chuckled. "Maybe I should. I believe he is a fan."

He sounded the way she imagined Elvis would sound. But if this was the same man who called her last night, he was dangerous. According to Merle Chatworth, he was a murderer.

"Last night," she said, "I answered my own phone."

"And that's a good thing. You can get too protected. Know what I mean? You can get so's all that's real important about life is left behind. You never hear the meadowlark singing in the morning. Never see the sun."

She still wasn't sure. There was a light tapping on the darkroom door, and she stretched the phone cord to reach the doorknob and open it for Vince. "Last night," she persisted. "Did you have your motorcycle?"

"I'm on my Harley all the time, baby."

Was this Tom Burke? "Why didn't you stay and talk?"

"I want to talk. I'm ready."

Vince was watching her closely. When he gently took her hand, offering support, she felt a calm within. Handling this call might be one of the most important things she would do in her life. If she set up a meeting properly, the police could take her sister's murderer into custody. But Teddy's mind was blank. She didn't know what to say next?

"Are you okay?" the Elvis voice questioned. "Should I come to your place? Teddy, are you lonesome?"

It was the same man. She might have panicked, but Teddy held herself in check.

"I'd like to meet you," he said.

"All right," she said. But not in a dark gazebo. Not in some enclosed hidden locale. She would never allow herself to be trapped again. "On the Westalia High School football field."

"What's that?"

"You heard me. On the fifty-yard line of the Westalia High School football field."

He chuckled. "Okay by me. As long as you don't bring along a marching band."

"But not after dark," Teddy said. "At dusk. At seven o'clock."

"You got it."

The phone went dead. When she replaced the receiver, a tremor raced up and down her spine. Her skin felt clammy.

Vince regarded her with a puzzled expression. "On the football field?"

"The man trapped me in my van. He trapped me inside that gazebo. On the football field, I'll see him coming. He won't have anywhere to hide."

Vince pulled her into his embrace. "Neither will you."

That aspect had not occurred to her. She had a sudden startling vision of herself standing in the middle of a field while a man on a motorcycle rode down on her. He might even have a gun. He could stand back fifty yards and shoot her. "What have I done?"

"It's okay," he murmured into her hair. "You're not going within ten miles of that place. We'll notify the sheriff, and he can use a policewoman double to stand in for you at the meeting. They can apprehend Tom Burke. And then this will all be over, Teddy."

"What if he really is Elvis? You heard him on the phone, Vince. Don't you think there's a chance?"

"It's a chance I won't let you take." He held her a little closer. "Don't argue with me about this, Teddy. It's too damn dangerous."

"But, what if—"

"He did sound like Elvis. And the guy on the tape last night sounded like Elvis, too. Could you tell if they were the same person?"

"It was the same man." *Are you lonesome tonight?* Last night, he'd taunted her. It was almost as if he'd known she was alone. "But we ought to do the voice-tape comparisons.

"Absolutely. And we'll check the phone trace with Lilibet. It's six hours until the meeting time you've set up. That's enough to do some planning."

As they headed back toward the kitchen, she closed her darkroom door and asked, "Why didn't you walk right in here, Vince? The lock on the door is broken."

"I didn't want to take the chance that I'd let in light and mess up your prints." He gave her a fleeting kiss on the forehead and reached for the telephone. "I respect your work."

Though she knew that Vince appreciated her skill and talent, the question that stood uppermost in Teddy's mind was how he felt about her as a woman. *Do you love me?* But there was no way to phrase that query that didn't sound whiny and pathetic.

He spoke first to Lilibet in a businesslike voice, then he rang through to Sheriff Graham. Plans and arrangements began to take shape under Vince Harding's capable leadership. Though he wore Levi's and a casual knit shirt, Teddy could easily imagine him as a high-powered Chicago executive whose office for the moment was her humble kitchen table covered with a clutter of yellow legal pads, maps and scheduling sheet. Trying not to disturb him, Teddy puttered around the kitchen, put together a sandwich she wasn't hungry enough to eat, tidied up the dishes, and watered the houseplants.

Every few moments, he would turn to her and dispense an informational bulletin. Her phone call had been traced to a public phone booth in nearby Murphysboro. The sheriff had released Merle Chatworth. No progress was being made in the search for Tom Burke. A deputy would be stopping by shortly to pick up the tape of the last Elvis phone call.

"Teddy," he said, "get the tape from upstairs and bring it down here for him."

"No," she responded.

He looked up at her, actually seeing her, and a slow grin spread across his face. Not only was he a powerful man who was good at making executive decisions, but he possessed enough sensitivity to know when he'd gone too far. "Sorry."

"I don't take orders well," she said.

"And I give a lot of them."

"Yes, you do. You're acting like the boss. And I want to make one thing very clear. I am not your secretary, your assistant or your...wife."

"I would never give orders to my wife."

"Then you don't believe in the 'obey' part of 'love, honor and obey.' Is that right?"

"I believe in sharing. With a woman who is strong enough to think for herself."

He reached for her, but she moved beyond his grasp. "Tell me what you're setting up here, Vince."

"I've kept you abreast of what's going on."

"What about the calls to Connie at your office? This schedule?"

"After the ambush at the football field, which Sheriff Graham is setting up, the killer will be apprehended." He paused. "I have a reporter in this area who's following up on most of the Elvis-sighting calls, but the response has been overwhelming. As soon as I know you're safe, Teddy, I'll take off."

Take off? Ouch! "I appreciate your honesty." Though she wanted him to stay with her, Teddy had no reason to hope that he would. Vince Harding was a logical man. He'd come here to offer her a position on his paper. And that was all. He'd made love to her as no man ever had before, but passion didn't equal love or commitment. And he wasn't leading her on with promises.

"As soon as we have this Elvis story wrapped up," he said, "I'll be back."

She'd heard that line before. Teddy felt certain that when Vince took off in his single-engine Cessna, she would never see him again. Except, possibly, in a professional capacity. And she couldn't stand that. She couldn't work with him without remembering the magical way she'd felt in his arms. But Teddy didn't cry or plead with him to stay. She exercised her talent for controlling her feelings. When the doorbell rang, she was glad to have a reason to leave the kitchen and answer it.

Her father stood in the doorway. Though he shuffled from one foot to the other, he appeared to be more himself. She was relieved to see that his shirt was starched and fresh. He had shaved. The first words out of his mouth were "I'm sorry, Teddy. I behaved badly and I'm sorry."

"It's okay, Dad." She held the door open. "Come on in."

"Negative. I have a lot to do." He gave her a sly glance. "But I was right about Tom Burke, wasn't I?"

"I guess so. What else have you heard, Dad?"

"Everything. When you're the editor of a newspaper, you know everything about everybody. I knew Tom Burke was an alcoholic before he came back to town. That's why I refused to have him in my house. And I knew about Merle and his Elvis fantasies. By the way, the police didn't hold him."

"Did he tell them what he saw at the Sleep Inn?"

"No, but it doesn't matter. Why hang on to Merle Chatworth? He's a lousy witness, anyway. Too crazy."

Teddy stated the obvious reason. "They should hold him because he's threatened to kill Tom Burke."

"So did I," her father added. "But I'm over that. You were correct, and I will allow the law to take its course."

"It's the best way," she concurred.

"Right. But that's not why I came over." He took a deep breath. "I want you to sit with me at the funeral. Day after tomorrow. Ten o'clock."

The funeral. Though she'd already known about it, the word hurt with a pain that was almost physical. She felt like she'd been punched in the gut. The breath went out of her lungs. Her sister's funeral. Whitney would be gone forever.

Instead of offering comfort or sharing his grief, her father turned and went down the two porch steps without looking back. Self-control, she thought. She'd learned from a master.

In the kitchen, she could hear Vince talking on the phone, planning the time in the near future when he could leave her. Soon, she thought, life would return to a normal pace. After the funeral, Teddy would adjust to her sister's death, just as she had learned to live without her mother and without Jacques.

Teddy watched her father's car pull away. But she didn't go back inside. The sun was shining. The skies were unusually clear, washed clean by last night's storm. She strolled onto the porch, toward the light, toward the musical whisper of the nearby stream that fed into the Big Muddy River. The scene was idyllic, pastoral. The sun warmed her. Tree leaves sparkled, catching the light, and tall grasses rustled in the breeze.

But the sense of well-being she usually felt when she was outdoors was missing. In Teddy's ears, the breeze made an endless moan while birds twittered warnings. She stood by the stream, full to the very edges of its banks. The rushing water shimmered like a cascade of diamonds.

She walked a little farther into the forest. In the absence of well-formed plans, she hoped for a sign, for answers to the nebulous question circling in her mind. Where was she going? In the next few minutes, where would she be? Next year? At the end of her life?

She enjoyed being alone. Solitude embraced and comforted her. Yet she hated being lonely.

On the far side of the stream, she saw the remnants of an extinguished fire, charred branches in a circle of rocks. A small lean-to, a simple tarp strung in the lee of two trees, was close by. Someone had camped here. Teddy went to investigate.

On the other side of the clearing, she glimpsed a flash of silver, a gleaming reflection in the sun. She saw the Harley. The big bike lay on its side. The TCB-1 license plate was visible.

She turned to run but heard a voice. "Help." It was weak. Pathetic. "Please, help." Dodging around the rocks, she went to the opposite side of the Harley where a human form lay huddled on the ground. In his black leather jacket, Tom Burke clutched his arms across his chest. His knees were drawn up. He looked at her with eyes that spoke of unbearable pain. When he reached toward her, his hand was covered with blood. "Help me, Teddy."

She went to him and knelt beside him. His eyes closed. His shirt was soaked in blood. "Can you hear me, Tom?" She didn't know what to do, how to help him. "I'll call an ambulance." His eyes wavered open. Weakly, his fingers closed around hers. "You're going to be all right," she said. His face was white and waxy. He looked like a man who was dying. "Hang on, Tom."

"Teddy?"

"Yes, Tom."

"Nobody...nobody rides...my...Harley." His eyes closed and she felt the strength fade from his fingers.

Even as she ran back to her house, Teddy knew it was too late. Tom was so near death that it would take a miracle to revive him. She burst into the kitchen where Vince was still on the telephone. Gasping, Teddy pressed down the plunger and disconnected his call. "Need an ambulance," she said. "Tom Burke. He's been shot. He's dying."

Efficiently, Vince started the wheels in motion. He summoned aid, then returned to the forest with Teddy where they found Tom, still unconscious. His breath came in shallow puffs. While Teddy raced back to the house to lead the paramedics into the woods, Vince started rudimentary first-aid procedures. When Teddy returned with the paramedics, Tom's pulse was barely discernible. He was in a coma.

After the ambulance team had left, Vince picked up the Harley and maneuvered the bike back to the house. Though he gazed longingly at the motorcycle as if he meant to clean off the forest debris, Vince followed Teddy inside.

Quietly she said, "I didn't think it would end this way."

"At least it's over now."

"This isn't the way I wanted Whitney's murder to be avenged. I wanted all the doubts resolved. I wanted to know the truth, and now I never will."

"Tom might survive."

"Then what? Another investigation? Merle wanted to kill him. My father wanted to kill him. And, I suppose, if someone put a gun in Russel's hand, he would have killed Tom, too."

Vince sat silently on the sofa beside her, knowing he could never console her on this matter. It would have been conclusive if Tom had made a full confession . . . if he'd admitted to riding back to PJ's on the night before the murder and getting an extra key . . . if he'd said he had used the key and his class ring to make a nine o'clock appointment with Whitney.

A confession would have left things neat and tidy, but life seldom cleaned itself up so conveniently. With Tom dead, there were complications that would never be explained. If Tom stabbed Whitney, how did he avoid getting blood on his hands and clothes? Why did he kill her in his own room? And why? Why did he commit murder?

"His last words," Teddy said. "The last words Tom Burke ever said were 'Nobody rides my Harley.'"

"I don't know what that means."

"Something to do with keys?" she wondered. "Maybe he was saying something like . . . he never let the keys to his Harley out of his possession, and therefore he would never have given his motel-room key to Whitney?"

Vince shook his head. "If he comes out of the coma, we might get some answers."

"Otherwise, it's over. Assuming that Tom was the person who called me and set up the meeting at the football field."

"Who else?"

"Maybe Elvis himself." She sighed. "I might just go down there tonight and hang around. Just in case."

"Teddy, I wish you wouldn't. I'd like to take off and get some of these other things taken care of, and I don't like the idea of you wandering around alone."

"Hey, Vince, you're forgetting something. You don't have to worry about me. I've always worked alone."

She sat up straight on the sofa. The look she gave him was pure independence. Clear blue eyes. A thrust to her chin. He didn't doubt for a moment that she would be all right without him. Without anyone. She truly was one of the strongest women he had ever known. "I'll come back for you, Teddy. We need to talk. When all this craziness dies down, we need to—"

"Thank you for being here with me, Vince. We'll stay in touch." Quite clearly, he was being dismissed. She rose to her feet and extended her hand for a businesslike farewell. "Go ahead. Take care of business. TCB. You don't need to stay here and protect me anymore."

Instead of a handshake, he gripped her wrist and pulled her back onto the sofa. Startled, she fell against him. He firmly held her slender back and kissed her, full and hard, on the lips. Her resistance lasted only a microsecond. Then she responded, offering him a taste of the passion that sparked so beautifully when she was in his arms.

He was already hard when she forced herself away from him. "You need to leave," she said.

"But I want to stay. Teddy, I—"

"It's okay, Vince. I'm okay. Like you said, you'll see me later, after this Elvis frenzy calms down." She walked away from him, heading toward her darkroom.

After he'd gathered up his things and made the final plans for his departure, she was still in the darkroom. Vince tapped on the door. "Teddy?"

She whipped open the door. In her hand she held a brown letter-size envelope. "This is a parting gift."

"I'm not leaving forever."

Tersely she said, "Then I'll see you when you get back."

Teddy went back into her darkroom and listened to the sounds of his departure. The door closing. The sound of the rental car starting. He was leaving. It was over. Everything was over.

Teddy lifted her chin and looked at her watch. It was just after four o'clock. Maybe in three hours she would meet Elvis at the football field. The hope gave her something to cling to as she worked on enlarging the photos of Marie from the Big Muddy Café.

AT THE AIRPORT in Carbondale, Vince gassed up the Cessna and prepared for takeoff. His first stop would be Branson, Missouri, where he would meet the field reporter and bring him up-to-date. At the very least they ought to get a couple of interviews from local celebrities. Or a hint of gossip.

He should have been feeling positive. This flurry of Elvis-sighting activity would certainly bolster the sagging fortunes of *Files*. But he felt empty, bereft. He wanted to be with Teddy. If she'd been with him, he would have been excited about this trip. And he was worried about her. Though there was no logical reason, he sensed that she was still in danger.

"Damn." He eased the throttle forward and taxied to the runway. Never before had he been so reluctant to take off. His feelings for Teddy were keeping him here, grounding him. Worse than that, not only did he feel as if he should stay, he wanted to stay.

She'd made no demands, hadn't wept or clung to him. He kind of wished she had, kind of wanted her to be the one who came to him instead of vice versa. He glanced at the clock on the instrument panel. Already it was five-fifteen. She'd be getting ready to go meet Elvis.

No one would be there, he thought. The Elvis voice on the phone must have been Tom, trying to lure her out of the house. Tom was the murderer. Lilibet had identified his motorcycle outside Room 19. Tom had made the appointment. He was the one who had killed Whitney.

Vince announced his departure over the radio for any traffic in the vicinity. "Carbondale traffic. This is Cessna 4762 Tango. Departing runway one-zero."

He accelerated down the runway, pulled back on the control yoke, and became airborne. His usual exhilaration was missing, but Vince kept his course steady, aiming for Branson.

TEDDY LOADED HER NIKON and film into her bag and went to the van. The sun had begun to slant across the horizon, and she looked up. Somewhere in that vast sky,

Vince was flying to his next destination. She wished him well and hoped he would have better luck on his Elvis sightings than she expected to have this evening.

The Elvis voice was probably Tom Burke's. He'd ridden to Murphysboro, telephoned, then come to the forest near her house to make sure she went to the meeting alone. But what about the campfire and the lean-to? If Tom had spent the night there, he couldn't have been the man on the motorcycle who'd terrorized her in the Paulson town square.

But it had to have been Tom.

VINCE SETTLED BACK behind the controls. He had almost reached Branson when the premonition that Teddy was in danger had become intense. It seemed that every mile he put between them increased his sense of danger. As he stared into the fading blue before sundown, Vince reminded himself that he was a logical man, one who did not succumb to intuitions and premonitions. No one had ever accused him of being a sensitive, nineties kind of guy. And he was proud not to be.

So why was he experiencing this unnamed dread? He cared for Teddy, admired her talent, enjoyed her personality. And she was a vivacious lover, a wonderful, erotic creature. He hadn't expected his separation from her to be so difficult, almost painful.

Was she the one? Was she the woman he was fated to love? When he looked into the distant skies, he could not imagine a future that did not include Teddy. Without her, life would be bleak. After Branson, he thought, he would return to Westalia. He would convince Teddy to return to Chicago with him.

Vince couldn't say what subliminal urge prompted him to reach for his briefcase. Usually when he piloted his plane, he kept other thoughts at bay. But he did take out the envelope she'd given him—her parting gift. A photograph. The 8 × 10 black-and-white glossy print showed a foggy night surrounding a motorcycle. An artistic picture.

"Amazing," Vince muttered when he saw the image in the clouds. Elvis seemed to be hovering overhead. The foreground showed a motorcycle and a rider with a helmet. The license plate said TCB-1. This must be one of the photos she'd taken on that first night when she went to PJ's in response to a call from Merle. The night Vince had first laid eyes on Teddy.

He took a closer look at the bike. Immediately he knew something was wrong. It was a Harley, all right. But not a Harley Panhead with seat shocks.

Nobody rides my Harley.

Those were Tom Burke's last words. And this is what he meant.

In his mind, Vince reconstructed what he knew of that night. Tom and Russel Stratton had been drinking. Tom claimed to have blacked out. But Teddy had taken this photo in the parking lot and someone had gone to the Sleep Inn and demanded a second key. What was it that Mrs. Klaus had said? In his helmet, the man had looked like an alien.

What if Mrs. Klaus had seen the plates on the bike, and the helmet, and assumed it was Tom? It could have been someone else. While Tom sat in PJ's in a drunken stupor, maybe even a *drugged* stupor using those little blue pills the local doctor was so happy to pass around, someone else could have gone to the Sleep Inn, posing as Tom to obtain a second key to the room, a key that was used to lure Whitney.

But Tom wouldn't part with the keys to his Harley. Nobody rode his bike, his most prized possession. The murderer must have pulled the plates off Tom's bike and switched them to his own.

Vince tried to stay calm to think this through. Who could have impersonated Tom? Who in Westalia had a motorcycle? Merle did. And Russel. And Harriet had mentioned Jordan Edwards's bike.

It would have been simple, once the murderer had the room key. He could have found Tom's class ring in his room and prepared a note for Whitney. He could have arranged for her arrival at her own murder.

Tom said he'd been framed.

And Teddy was on her way to a meeting. Alone. Vulnerable.

Vince reversed his direction 180 degrees. He spoke into the radio. "Carbondale Unicom, this is Cessna 4762 Tango. I need to get a message to Sheriff Graham in Westalia."

IT WAS GOING TO BE a beautiful sunset, Teddy thought. She stopped on her way to the football field and ordered a fast-food dinner of hamburger and fries. Even if Elvis didn't show up, she could have herself a pleasant picnic on the fifty-yard line.

As she parked behind the stands, a cold nostalgia swept through her. This field had been the site of Tom Burke's greatest triumphs when he was a star football player in high school. And now, these many years later, he lay in a coma, fighting for his life, accused of murder.

Practically convicted. No one seemed to have the slightest doubt of his guilt. But no one, Teddy thought, had suggested a motive strong enough for murder. Why had Tom killed her sister? And why had he come after Teddy? There had to be some clue she hadn't figured out—something she'd seen, something she'd overheard.

Teddy strolled across the track and plunked herself down in the middle of the field, surrounded by the sweet scent of new grass. The sky was still fully lit, but dusk was coming on soon.

She'd arrived a bit early, but not enough that she was worried about it. Elvis had been notoriously unpunctual, and had never worn a watch. Neither had Tom. She never remembered seeing him wear any jewelry at all. But his pockets had always bulged with keys. And he'd worn the buck knife in a leather case on his belt.

Was it a crime of passion? She bit into her hamburger. Before she'd finished it, she heard the distant drone of a motorcycle.

VINCE WAS WITHIN twenty minutes of arriving at the airport in Carbondale. But it was too late. Nine minutes until seven o'clock. There was no way he could land his plane, grab a rental car and get to Westalia High School in time.

He talked to the Unicom at the field. "Did you figure out how to patch me through to Sheriff Graham?"

"Hey, man, it's not like we've got state-of-the-art equipment here. I'm doing what I can."

"Did you call the sheriff?"

"I did."

"Good." The sheriff would get there in time. "Then he's on his way to the Westalia High School football field."

"I passed on your message. I don't know what the sheriff is going to do."

"Why wouldn't he go to the field? What did you say?"

"I told him that the guy who sounded like Elvis wasn't Tom. Then I said that Teddy was in danger and he should go to the field. And then he laughed and said something about beating a dead horse."

"Call him again. Repeat the message until it gets through his thick stupid skull."

Vince hung up the handset and unleashed a stream of furious profanity. Didn't these guys understand? This was a matter of life and death. And the life that hung in the balance was Teddy's.

Though he was a cautious, safety-conscious pilot, Vince lowered his altitude and set a visual course. In the distance, through the treetops, he could see the rising hill where Teddy's father lived. Beyond that was the bell tower.

THE HARLEY BUMPED over the curb surrounding the field and came straight toward her.

Teddy stood. Was this him? Was it really Elvis?

He came closer, so close that she bent her knees and prepared to leap out of his path when he stopped and turned off the engine. The resulting silence was deafening.

He climbed off the bike and removed his helmet. In a deep Elvis voice, he asked, "Are you lonesome tonight, Teddy?"

"Russel?"

"Poor little Teddy is all alone. Her boyfriend took off."

"If this is a joke..." But there was nothing humorous about the revolver he took from the inner pocket of his black leather jacket.

"Don't be a fool, Russel. The police can trace the bullets. They'll know it was your gun."

"This isn't mine. I took it from Merle's house. I used it to kill Tom. I'll use it on you. And I'll return it to the same place I found it."

"Tom's not dead," she said.

"Doesn't matter. He didn't see who shot him."

Did you kill Whitney? Your own wife? As soon as the thought formed, it made perfect sense. Russel had a motive. He was, perhaps, the only person with a motive strong enough to commit murder. With his wife dead, he would inherit her trust fund, get her life insurance and all their shared assets.

He checked the clip, cocked the revolver. At this range he couldn't miss. And Teddy knew she would die. The dice had been thrown. It was her turn.

He gestured to her with black gloved hands. "Toss me your camera bag. Slowly."

She did as she was told. "What are you looking for?"

"Any pictures you might have. I already got the negatives and contact sheets from your darkroom. I'm just making sure that you don't have any other prints."

"The sheriff has copies of everything."

"No, Teddy." He pulled out a manila envelope and took out an 8 × 10 black and white, the duplicate of the photo she'd given Vince. "He doesn't have this."

She stared at the picture. From the angle of the motorcycle, she saw the rider's arm and wrist. He was wearing a wristwatch. A shining gold band that matched the one Russel was wearing, the wristwatch Whitney had given him. *Russel was the rider she chased.* "How could you frame Tom? He was your best friend."

"Because it was so damn easy. I knew about his drinking before he got here, and I got him drinking again. Dropped a couple of sedatives in his beer. Nothing to it. I also knew Whitney had the hots for him, so I just let human nature take its course."

"But Lilibet saw Tom's motorcycle outside the room."

"Lilibet is as dumb as you are when it comes to a Harley. She saw a bike and assumed it was Tom's. But it was my bike."

Teddy remembered how Lilibet had hated Merle's riding and refused to go along with him. To her, one motorcycle looked like another. "You killed my sister. Why, Russel? Didn't you love her?"

"Hell, yes. Whitney was more to me than a wife. She was the rich girl on the hill."

"She only wanted your attention."

"But she was talking about divorce, and I couldn't let that happen, Teddy. For the first time in my life, I had a good job. I had enough money to do whatever I wanted." He aimed the barrel of the gun. "I'm not going to give anything up."

Teddy prepared to die. She closed her eyes and tried to imagine the faces of her loved ones who had gone before her. Her mother. Jacques. Whitney. But their features would not focus clearly.

Her eyes snapped open. It wasn't her time. "There's another copy of that photo," she said. "I gave it to Vince as a parting gift because of the Elvis image in the clouds."

His eyes assessed her, but his gun hand did not waver. "Ironic, isn't it?"

"What are you talking about, Teddy?"

"You used the Elvis sightings to trick me into coming out here alone. But the Elvis image in that photo is why you won't get away with this. You're caught, Russel. Vince will figure it out."

The single-engine Cessna dropped through the sky. The wings barely cleared the goalposts. The whirring propeller came directly at them.

Teddy dived to the ground.

Russel raised his gun. He fired at the belly of the plane, getting off four shots before he also ducked. The wheels of the plane touched down on the football field, and the plane dragged to such a sudden stop that the nose pitched forward, almost striking the propeller on the ground. The engine went dead. And the sound of police sirens shattered the air.

"Vince!" Teddy was on her feet, running toward the plane.

Russel raised his arm, but did not fire. Two police cars had rocketed onto the field. The deputies leapt from their vehicles, guns drawn. Teddy heard their shouts. "Freeze!"

She glanced over her shoulder and saw Russel lifting his hands above his head, surrendering his gun. Finally, her sister's murderer had been apprehended.

But Teddy had only one thing on her mind. Vince. Why wasn't he getting out of his plane? Had one of Russel's wild shots struck him? Was he bleeding? Was he dying?

The cockpit door was flung open. Vince was holding his forehead. But he was all right. He was alive. As soon as his feet touched the ground, she embraced him. His arms, loosely holding her, felt like heaven.

"You're a hard woman to leave, Teddy."

"Then I guess you better not try that again."

"I don't believe that I just landed my plane on a football field." He looked down at her. "Don't you want to take a picture?"

"I'm finished with standing and watching life go by." She reached up and traced the line of his jaw. "I love you, Vince."

"I love you, Teddy." The premonition of dread inside him was replaced by a warm sense of fulfillment. "We were meant to be together. And I'm never going to leave you again."

ON THE STREET that ran beside the Westalia High School football field, another man on a Harley pulled to the side of the road and stopped. He had just come from the hospital, where he'd heard that a man who owned a restored Harley Panhead had been injured and might be looking to sell his bike. The guy, Tom Burke, had recovered enough to say he wouldn't sell to anybody.

The rider slipped off his helmet and ran his hand through his coal black hair. He didn't know what was going down there on the field. One guy was being taken off in handcuffs. And there was a little Cessna almost up against the south goalposts.

And there was a couple. A woman with wild blond hair and a tall man who was holding her like he meant it. Even from this distance, he could tell that they were in love.

"Love me tender," he hummed. Silently he wished them happiness.

He mounted his Harley and rode off into the sunset.

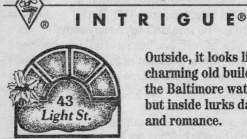

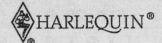

HARLEQUIN®

Weddings, Inc.

Harlequin Books requests the pleasure of your company this June in Eternity, Massachusetts, for WEDDINGS, INC.

For generations, couples have been coming to Eternity, Massachusetts, to exchange wedding vows. Legend has it that those married in Eternity's chapel are destined for a lifetime of happiness. And the residents are more than willing to give the legend a hand.

Beginning in June, you can experience the legend of Eternity. Watch for one title per month, across all of the Harlequin series.

HARLEQUIN BOOKS... NOT THE SAME OLD STORY!

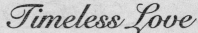

INDULGE A LITTLE 6947 SWEEPSTAKES
NO PURCHASE NECESSARY

HERE'S HOW THE SWEEPSTAKES WORKS:
The Harlequin Reader Service shipments for January, February and March 1994 will contain, respectively, coupons for entry into three prize drawings: a trip for two to San Francisco, an Alaskan cruise for two and a trip for two to Hawaii. To be eligible for any drawing using an Entry Coupon, simply complete and mail according to directions.

There is no obligation to continue as a Reader Service subscriber to enter and be eligible for any prize drawing. You may also enter any drawing by hand printing your name and address on a 3" x 5" card and the destination of the prize you wish that entry to be considered for (i.e., San Francisco trip, Alaskan cruise or Hawaiian trip). Send your 3" x 5" entries to: Indulge a Little 6947 Sweepstakes, c/o Prize Destination you wish that entry to be considered for, P.O. Box 1315, Buffalo, NY 14269-1315, U.S.A. or Indulge a Little 6947 Sweepstakes, P.O. Box 610, Fort Erie, Ontario L2A 5X3, Canada.

To be eligible for the San Francisco trip, entries must be received by 4/30/94; for the Alaskan cruise, 5/31/94; and the Hawaiian trip, 6/30/94. No responsibility is assumed for lost, late or misdirected mail. Sweepstakes open to residents of the U.S. (except Puerto Rico) and Canada, 18 years of age or older. All applicable laws and regulations apply. Sweepstakes void wherever prohibited.

For a copy of the Official Rules, send a self-addressed, stamped envelope (WA residents need not affix return postage) to: Indulge a Little 6947 Rules, P.O. Box 4631, Blair, NE 68009, U.S.A.

INDR93

INDULGE A LITTLE 6947 SWEEPSTAKES
NO PURCHASE NECESSARY

HERE'S HOW THE SWEEPSTAKES WORKS:
The Harlequin Reader Service shipments for January, February and March 1994 will contain, respectively, coupons for entry into three prize drawings: a trip for two to San Francisco, an Alaskan cruise for two and a trip for two to Hawaii. To be eligible for any drawing using an Entry Coupon, simply complete and mail according to directions.

There is no obligation to continue as a Reader Service subscriber to enter and be eligible for any prize drawing. You may also enter any drawing by hand printing your name and address on a 3" x 5" card and the destination of the prize you wish that entry to be considered for (i.e., San Francisco trip, Alaskan cruise or Hawaiian trip). Send your 3" x 5" entries to: Indulge a Little 6947 Sweepstakes, c/o Prize Destination you wish that entry to be considered for, P.O. Box 1315, Buffalo, NY 14269-1315, U.S.A. or Indulge a Little 6947 Sweepstakes, P.O. Box 610, Fort Erie, Ontario L2A 5X3, Canada.

To be eligible for the San Francisco trip, entries must be received by 4/30/94; for the Alaskan cruise, 5/31/94; and the Hawaiian trip, 6/30/94. No responsibility is assumed for lost, late or misdirected mail. Sweepstakes open to residents of the U.S. (except Puerto Rico) and Canada, 18 years of age or older. All applicable laws and regulations apply. Sweepstakes void wherever prohibited.

For a copy of the Official Rules, send a self-addressed, stamped envelope (WA residents need not affix return postage) to: Indulge a Little 6947 Rules, P.O. Box 4631, Blair, NE 68009, U.S.A.

INDR93

INDULGE A LITTLE
SWEEPSTAKES

OFFICIAL ENTRY COUPON

This entry must be received by: MAY 31, 1994
This month's winner will be notified by: JUNE 15, 1994
Trip must be taken between: JULY 31, 1994-JULY 31, 1995

YES, I want to win the Alaskan Cruise vacation for two. I understand that the prize includes round-trip airfare, one-week cruise including private cabin, all meals and pocket money as revealed on the "wallet" scratch-off card.

Name_____

Address _____ Apt. _____

City_____

State/Prov._____ Zip/Postal Code_____

Daytime phone number_____
                          (Area Code)
Account #_____

Return entries with invoice in envelope provided. Each book in this shipment has two entry coupons—and the more coupons you enter, the better your chances of winning!
© 1993 HARLEQUIN ENTERPRISES LTD.   MONTH2

INDULGE A LITTLE
SWEEPSTAKES

OFFICIAL ENTRY COUPON

This entry must be received by: MAY 31, 1994
This month's winner will be notified by: JUNE 15, 1994
Trip must be taken between: JULY 31, 1994-JULY 31, 1995

YES, I want to win the Alaskan Cruise vacation for two. I understand that the prize includes round-trip airfare, one-week cruise including private cabin, aii meals and pocket money as revealed on the "wallet" scratch-off card.

Name_____

Address _____ Apt. _____

City_____

State/Prov._____ Zip/Postal Code_____

Daytime phone number_____
                          (Area Code)
Account #_____

Return entries with invoice in envelope provided. Each book in this shipment has two entry coupons—and the more coupons you enter, the better your chances of winning!
© 1993 HARLEQUIN ENTERPRISES LTD.   MONTH2